F
S

Sommer, Scott.

Still lives

STILL
LIVES

Books by Scott Sommer

Nearing's Grace
Lifetime
Last Resort
Hazzard's Head

SCOTT SOMMER

STILL LIVES

VIKING

VIKING
Published by the Penguin Group
Viking Penguin, a division of Penguin Books USA Inc.,
40 West 23rd Street, New York, New York 10010, U.S.A.
Penguin Books Ltd, 27 Wrights Lane,
London W8 5TZ, England
Penguin Books Australia Ltd, Ringwood,
Victoria, Australia
Penguin Books Canada Ltd, 2801 John Street,
Markham, Ontario, Canada L3R 1B4
Penguin Books (N.Z.) Ltd, 182–190 Wairau Road,
Auckland 10, New Zealand

Penguin Books Ltd, Registered Offices:
Harmondsworth, Middlesex, England

First published in 1989 by Viking Penguin,
a division of Penguin Books USA Inc.
Published simultaneously in Canada

10 9 8 7 6 5 4 3 2 1

A portion of this book first appeared in *Interview*.

Grateful acknowledgment is made for permission to
reprint an excerpt from "The Dry Salvages" from *Four
Quartets* by T.S. Eliot. Copyright 1943 by T. S. Eliot,
renewed 1971 by Esme Valerie Eliot. Reprinted by
permission of Harcourt Brace Jovanovich, Inc. and Faber
and Faber Ltd.

LIBRARY OF CONGRESS CATALOGING IN PUBLICATION DATA
Sommer, Scott.
  Still lives.
  I. Title.
PS3569.O6533S75 1989   813'.54   88-40404
ISBN 0-670-82581-6

Printed in the United States of America
Set in Garamond No. 3
Designed by Francesca Belanger

For my brother, Dean

Then touched he their eyes, saying, According to your faith be it unto you.
And their eyes were opened . . .

—Matthew 9:29

We have to think of them as forever bailing.

—T. S. Eliot

STILL
LIVES

Frankle had seen enough. He closed the studio door behind him and lugged his tangle of shoulder-strapped cameras down the corridor past the empty cubicles of the *Concupiscence* centerfold staff.

His assistant, Vogel, was being dismissed by Bernheim with the same obnoxious stridency Frankle himself had endured in silence two hours earlier. Ironically, Vogel had been the one to help Bernheim procure the photographic evidence that foreclosed any defense on the part of Frankle, who could only imagine, from the one-sidedness of the shouting, his disloyal assistant's expression of astonishment. Of course, as Vogel hadn't been around long enough, he knew next to nothing of Bernheim's talent for orchestrating disquiet and revulsion, such as the bald man's malicious manner of rejecting for centerfold inclusion any number of Concubine of the Month manquées due to their "inexpressive pussy."

Frankle pushed the crimson nipple, and the elevator doors parted to reveal Laurie Larsen, standing alone, centered perfectly in the walnut-paneled cavity. Her black dress and hair shimmered bewitchingly as Frankle stood mesmerized.

"I've been fired."

"I know," she said. "I'll go down with you."

Frankle stepped beside her, inferring at once from the glare of her gray eyes that her comportment would remain strictly professional.

Well, she was Bernheim's mistress, and he—though surely not the only or the last—had been the one to get caught.

"How'd he find out?"

"He had the apartment bugged."

"Did he show you Vogel's photographs?"

She nodded. Frankle was relieved by her honesty but surprised that her hauteur seemed directed at him.

The doors opened to the lobby, and Laurie Larsen stepped out first into the crowd forging toward the revolving doors. Frankle followed her to a marbled corner.

"What," he asked, "did we hope to accomplish?"

She took his hand in a way that felt condescending.

"Lust isn't something you accomplish, Thom. It's a head-on collision you just hope you can walk away from. Walking away's going to be our accomplishment."

With annihilating clarity, it occurred to Frankle that Laurie Larsen had accompanied him to the lobby not to commiserate but rather to see him out.

"Is that all it was?" he said. "Lust?"

She hooked a slant of black hair behind an ear. "Did we want to take responsibility for anything more?"

Reflected upside down in her eyes, Frankle answered, "I would have."

"Woulda, shoulda, coulda, Thom. What will you do now?"

Frankle's sigh surprised him. "Patch things up with Monica, I suppose."

Laurie Larsen smirked no less skeptically than the others who knew about Thomas Frankle's five-year relationship with Monica Webb. At least, Frankle called it a relationship.

"For the record," he said, "it was more than lust."

Laurie Larsen referred conspicuously to her wristwatch before replying—in what Frankle knew would serve as the ep-

itaph for whatever it was that had occurred between them—
"Gentleman to the last," and scooting away girlishly to an
open elevator.

Outside, Frankle looked up for the late-October sun and
found it glinting in a skyscraper's upper windows. Where he
stood, the avenue was deeply shadowed and cold, and he
turned up the collar of his jacket.

The four lanes of traffic inched uptown in a rush-hour
standstill. There was neither any point in nor any chance of
catching a cab, and the thought of transporting four grand's
worth of camera equipment via subway resigned Frankle to
walking. He maneuvered cautiously among the pedestrian
herd, his penchant for ungovernable alarm manifesting itself
as a sudden hypersensitivity to the city's sounds.

The panic didn't register formally until he reached the
phone booth proximate to the clock of the Sherry Netherland
Hotel. He had trouble clearing his throat, and it took him
three pokes to choreograph his trembling finger to the correct
punch keys.

With the first ring he palmed his ear to abate the blare of
horns and whistles. When the answering machine triggered,
he hit the playback button on his portable remote controller
and listened as the machine reviewed the day's messages: a
warning from the dogwalker that a raise in rates would begin
the following week; a rebuke from the landlord that the rent
was late again this month; a reminder from Stanley Stark
about the weekly handball game, and then the rankle of a
man's unfamiliar voice intoning, with an urgency verging on
distemper, "If you're there, Monica, pick up the phone!
Hello? You're *not* there. All right, then. I'm sending the
limousine to the set."

Two beeps followed, indicating the conclusion of calls, and
Frankle left an apologetic message about being later than
usual and wanting to take Monica to dinner and *talk*. Ad-

mittedly, the latter request might well set them off their meal. Neither one was inclined toward examination, especially Frankle, whose introspection began and ended with the photographic interface of surfaces.

Traversing Central Park, Frankle rested in the twilight near Tavern on the Green, where he watched the six o'clock circus of joggers, roller skaters, and cyclists dodge horse-drawn carriages carrying tourists snapshooting everything in sight. It came back to Frankle in a flash of regret that he'd gone into photography in the first place because he couldn't believe his eyes. More than likely, had he known ten years earlier what he knew now, he would not have allowed his aesthetic wonder to calcify into a career. Then again, this general mid-life lament might be a cover for a more specific fear that his firing would be the excuse he sensed Monica had been seeking for the better part of two years to end her own kind of wrong move. Or was it, to the contrary, the excuse Frankle had been seeking and one he had unconsciously employed Laurie Larsen to help him play out?

He supposed he'd find out soon enough.

Cabs were backed up on Columbus Avenue from Lincoln Center. Frankle didn't need the horn-blowing and cursing. He bought a bottle of whiskey and a bouquet of flowers before escaping into the quiet of the brownstone.

He disengaged the alarm and three locks and entered the darkened duplex. When Jack failed to greet him, he peeked into the bedroom, thinking that the Airedale and Monica might be napping. But the bed was empty, and he closed his eyes to picture the two of them in the park.

He set out whiskey and snacks on the kitchenette counter and carefully arranged the flowers in a vase. Then he stood for a moment, smoking a cigarette, at the base of the spiral staircase in the high-ceilinged living room. He stared at the monochromatic shimmer of the white pots of plants hanging before the long windows that opened onto the avenue below. Somehow the crimson of taillights, catapulted mysteriously upward, splashed against the darkened panes.

Upstairs, in the roof-level room, what Frankle took to be a figure staring in from the terrace through the glass of the sliding door revealed itself, when lights automatically clicked on, to be his own reflection.

For years the upstairs space had been used as an audiovisual den—a media room, Monica called it. Frankle, however, imagined he could convert a section of it into a studio for head-shot work and still allow sufficient space for Monica to review her videotaped performances in *Still Lives*. Shooting heads now seemed Frankle's most expedient strategy for covering his "apartner's" share of the duplex's exorbitant rent.

He unstrapped the cameras and hung them on hooks protruding from the exterior wall of the closet-size darkroom. Though he had no objective reason to panic, the room's mortuarial silence sent Frankle dashing downstairs for a drink of that whiskey.

The clock above the refrigerator indicated several minutes past seven. Reaching for ice, Frankle tried to recollect if Monica had mentioned she would be using Jack in yet another segment of the soap opera that had brought her celebrity and wealth through her role as Clara Ravens. The answer wasn't within the freezer compartment's swirling vapor, although, as Frankle closed the door, a sheet of paper loosed itself from the shiny exterior and floated back and forth in its descent to the floor.

Frankle found himself in full genuflection as he read:

Thom, I can't tell whether I'm bored with you or with myself or if I'm actually in love with Victor. In any event, we're going, Victor and I, to London for a break from the hellish taping schedule. After that, I just don't know. I'll be in touch. Monica.

He reread the note enough times to memorize it, but for some perplexing reason he couldn't remember a word of it; and when he rose from his knees he felt a great disorienting distance between himself and objects in the apartment. Grabbing the throat of the whiskey bottle, he wandered down the hallway to the bedroom. The traverse seemed to take forever, and leaning to rest against the jamb of the doorway, Frankle noted the wooden hangers both hanging empty in the closet and scattered on the floor in a trail to the open drawers of Monica's antique bureau. Undoubtedly, she'd been in a hurry.

The bottle raised itself to Frankle's lips, and he turned away. He started next door to speak with Harry Chambers, then remembered that his neighbor wouldn't be released from the V.A. detox clinic for another week. Turning in a circle to the closed bathroom door, he shouldered the warped thing open.

The glare from the bulbs surrounding Monica's beauty mirror forced his eyes to the floor. Shredded tampons lay all over the tiles. Then Jack pulled his head from the toilet, from which he had been drinking to wash down the flecks of his cigar-shaped snacks, and leaped at Frankle in a frenzy of relief while drooling the blue dye of Ty-D-bol. Frankle backed away to avoid the stained tongue and cracked his head on the hot-water pipe vertically bordering the bathtub. He went down directly, relinquishing his grip on the whiskey as the lights momentarily imploded. The shattering glass sent the Airedale scrabbling madly into the hallway.

When the pain at the back of his head cleared sufficiently, Frankle opened his eyes, touched his hand to the back of his head, and checked his palm. But the only bloodlike color to reach his eyes adhered to the mirrored medicine cabinet.

The lipsticked message read: U CAN KEEP THE DOG!

2

The phone rang twice before the machine intercepted the call. A bag of ice pressed to his head, Frankle wobbled down the hallway and picked up.

"Thomas Frankle?"

"Speaking."

"Stanley Stark here. I don't know if you remember me. I've played handball with you every Wednesday night at this time for the past ten years?"

Frankle employed "sorry" twice before Stark interrupted him.

"I'm sorry myself, Thomas. I just relinquished the court and am standing in the locker room adjacent to the pool. I'm suited up in filthy jock and shorts, after a very bad day at the office. Needless to say, your absence gives umbrage."

"I can explain, Stan."

"Please."

Frankle shouldered the wall and closed his eyes.

"Jack's sick. His tongue's blue. I was forced—"

"Blue, you say?"

"Ceruleanly so, Stan."

"Curious. You didn't happen to read the latest EPA study on lead in our drinking water?"

Frankle sat down on Monica's side of the bed and conceded he'd been busy.

"Study came across my desk this very morning. Thirty-eight million are suffering. Lead solder on the pipe joints and so forth. You'll be interested to learn that symptoms include anxiety, learning disability, and—pay attention—blue tongue. Jack continues, I presume, to drink from the toilet?"

Frankle opened his eyes. "Excuse me, Stan, but Monica and I are in the middle—"

"Again!"

"Would you mind letting me off the hook here?"

"Absolutely not. In fact, I'm going to insist we meet on East Sixth for our scheduled Indian fare. When can you be there?"

Frankle insisted on an hour, but Stark wheedled him down to forty-five minutes.

"Don't get me wrong," Stark put in. "I myself am perplexed at the degree of my obduracy. Might it be Susan's pregnancy problems?"

"What pregnancy problems?"

"And don't let me forget to tell you about a rather curious call I received from Harry Chambers."

Crammed on a platform before dirty windows, the Indian ensemble consisted of sitar, tabla, and tanpura. Frankle sat at the bar in a sweltering, low-ceilinged room draped in sheets of ballooning madras. He was considering whether the ragas or the three bottles of Bombay beer should be credited with soothing his nerves, when Stanley Stark appeared, wearing a gas mask. In the process of removing the contraption, Stark pushed his mohair toupee into misalignment.

Stark was a lanky man with a disproportionately large head and lugubrious brown eyes. Frankle believed it was the beard and long nose that imparted to his friend's face a benign, old-fashioned homeliness.

"What's with the mask?"

"That time of year. And technically, it's a respirator."

"That time of year?"

Stark assumed a stool beside Frankle. "Boiler start-ups, Thomas. Autumn. The burning of waste oil laced with such contaminants as arsenic, cadmium, chromium, and halogens —all of which issue relentlessly from thousands upon thousands of chimneys. The resultant health disorders stagger—"

"Please," Frankle said, "cease with the disorders."

Stark called out for a mineral water. "Heart and renal disease is skyrocketing, and women in their forties are dropping from cancer like flies. Statistically speaking, it's the leading cause of these untimely mortalities. Mrs. Stark herself is approaching this target group."

Stark poured his imported water over ice. His suit, Frankle noted, was an ill-fitting polyester thing, and he wore galoshes to protect his shoes.

"There's no end to it, Thomas: the devastation. My environmental work's strictly rear guard. Ecosystemically speaking, these are the latter days."

Frankle stared into his beer and thought about the good earth; vague memories of once feeling part of it came to mind.

"How's yourself?" Stark inquired.

Frankle gave this a moment's thought, then shrugged.

Stanley nodded solemnly, his lips pressed together. "History, Thomas. It's gone off the track for good, I'm afraid. It's driving us all mad."

Frankle cleared his throat and told Stark about the firing and Monica's running off.

Stark pulled at his nose. "Are you hopeless?"

"With your help, I'm getting there."

They stared at the bar's varnished gleaming, hands folded piously.

"I can see you're a lot more upset than you're letting on," Stark said. "Which reminds me. Harry Chambers called this morning from Pennsylvania. State troopers found him in his car in a ditch off the road."

Frankle set down his beer and wiped his chin with the back of his hand. "What are you talking about?"

"Our one-day warrior skipped detox and hit the road with a quart of Heaven Hill bourbon. Troopers found him—and the empty bottle—off the road, with the windows of the car taped and a vacuum cleaner hose inserted into the backseat through a hole in the trunk. He was revived and charged with attempted suicide. As you know from his last try, suicide's illegal."

"Harry tried to asphyxiate himself again?"

"For which he's been incarcerated in a state hospital outside Harrisburg."

"Are you telling the truth?"

"I always tell the truth, Thomas. It's why I've never earned more than thirty-two thousand dollars in any one year. I've been on the phone with his parents half the day. They've hired a shrink, who will have him transferred to the custody of a private facility here in the city. For financial reasons, I advised they return him to the V.A., but Mr. Chambers wants to give a private-sector shrink a shot. Big waste of money, if you ask me. Not likely they can do any better with Harry than the government quacks."

Frankle shook his head. "I can't believe he didn't call me."

"I'm sure he was too embarrassed to call. He only phoned me for free legal advice."

Frankle ordered another beer. "What will they do with him?"

"The usual, I presume. Enough ECT and antidepressants to animate a stone. When's the last time you saw him?"

"Before he went into detox last week." Then Frankle added defensively, "Why would you ask me that?"

"Suicides usually give clues, Thomas."

"Chambers has been giving clues for the last twenty years!"

"Which further reminds me. He wants you to collect his mail."

"That's all?"

"Considering he just attempted suicide, that seems a lot."

Frankle lit a cigarette and snapped smoke rings toward the ceiling. "I can't believe he tried it again."

"To be blunt, Thomas, you have a tendency to displace and project. I'm confident you're the one in deep shit. Feel free to talk about it."

"With all due respect," Frankle answered, "you've been living with your psychotherapist too long."

"Unarguably correct. In my defense, however, I've tried everything in my power to get Susan to file for divorce. Alas, nothing seems to work. Neither indifference nor months of lack of cooperation. Now she's five months pregnant and submitting to one test after another. I'm trapped, Thomas. Utterly so, I'm afraid."

Frankle waved his hand dismissively and moved from the bar to a white-clothed table.

Stark joined him, fidgeting in the room's heat until he finally pulled the toupee from his head and pocketed it. Frankle leaned forward and removed a piece of tape from the crown of Stark's head.

"Don't they have paste for these things, Stan?"

"Myriad pastes. But the ingredients are dangerously absorbent. Melanomas, brain tumors, embolisms . . . Tape's safer. Without exception, the old-fashioned is always safer than the new and improved. For example, choose horse to automobile, foot scooter to dirt bike, life to lifestyle."

Frankle consulted the menu. "Split the regular fare?"

In answer, Stark removed an apple from his jacket and began buffing it with a handkerchief.

"As of yesterday, I've renounced consuming all nonorganically grown foods. The studies on the toxins inherent in cyanide-based pesticide and insecticide applications stagger the imagination. We're being systematically poisoned, Thomas. Cancer rates are projected as high as fifty percent by the turn of the century."

Frankle kept his eyes closed an extra moment to underscore his exasperation, before signaling the waiter and ordering half a dozen dishes.

Stark requested another mineral water.

When the waiter withdrew, Frankle said, "I believe you wanted to discuss Susan's pregnancy?"

"Frankly, Thomas, I'd rather hear about Monica's latest infidelity. Who's it this time? Another Eurotrash type?"

Frankle tilted his head and squinted charily.

"Very well, then," Stark said. "If you insist upon interrogating me, I'll mention that a major test result came back last night. Apparently, Thomas—and this is confidential—there's some genetic problem. Some mutogenic business."

Frankle frowned as Stark nervously buffed the apple on his lapel.

"Apparently, the fetus is all fucked up."

"Don't talk like that, Stan."

"We're old friends. Old male friends. We can take it."

The food arrived in little silver cups, crusty and overcooked, as if prepared earlier in the week.

"Fetus is male." Stark stared at his hands, enfolded around the apple. "This incipient son of mine, however, is going to be either a blathering Mongolian idiot—to employ the old-fashioned rubric, which I prefer to Special Person—a boy with breasts and no balls, a psychopath with hair growing from his forehead, or, possibly, a midget with a penis for a head and legs where his ears should be."

"Keep your voice down, please," Frankle whispered.

"Susan can't decide what to do. For myself, it's rather clear. Either abort the fetus day after tomorrow or open a traveling circus by summer."

Frankle gazed into the *saag paneer*—chunks of cheese floating in spinach—and slowly pushed the plate away.

"Confidentially, Thomas, I'm not as shocked as Susan. The gruesome environmental studies on the mutogenic and teratogenic chemicals saturating the environment cannot be fathomed. For the record, Susan and I—and the fetus, for that matter—are merely downside statistics."

Frankle raised his eyes furtively and was shocked at how radically Stark's comportment had changed. He seemed to have sunk sadly into himself, and his skin appeared pallid and waxen.

Frankle cleared his throat. "Why don't we take a walk?"

Stark drummed a spoon nervously against the back of his hand and stared imploringly at Frankle. "What would you do?"

Frankle looked heavenward. Had Monica and he not chosen the abortionist, they'd have two children, five and three. "What I thought best, I guess."

"Naturally, Thomas. But for whom? Yourself, the wife, the fetus?"

"I don't know," Frankle said finally.

Stark bit into the apple, picked a splinter of red skin from his teeth, then pushed his chair from the table.

"That walk," he said. "I've an early court date."

After escorting Jack around the block for the terrier's nightly, Frankle showered and climbed into bed. His mind was jumping, and he sipped a cup of whiskey. The Airedale lay beside him, munching a Milk-Bone. The Bible didn't work, and Frankle extinguished the lamp and lay quietly in the dark, listening to the racket of traffic.

He had known Stanley Stark and Harry Chambers from his adolescent days in Park Slope, Brooklyn. The Chamberses lived across the street and the Starks next door. By a complex process of insecurity, inertia, and affection, Frankle had remained friends with both men for the better part of twenty-five years, even though the passage of such time had taught him that the three held little in common, beyond a shared sense of the past, which Frankle found comforting, despite its frequent inconveniences in the present. Deep down, he had never understood either of his friends, particularly their fervid idealism, though Frankle knew instinctively that without the anchor of their intensity he would have felt abandoned to the inconsequential surfaces of his life with Monica Webb and *Concupiscence*.

Stark and Chambers, as litigator and writer, respectively, were drawn to investigation. Frankle admired them, even though their dedication seemed to drive them both decidedly crazy, as well as deeper and deeper into trouble, as if the world were just waiting to ambush them for their relentless scrutiny.

When Harry Chambers, for example, as the high school's valedictorian, had decided against college and allowed himself to be drafted in 1968, it had impressed Frankle as merely one more grandiose gesture that he imagined he would never understand. Without a word of warning, in the autumn of 1969, while Stark and Frankle dodged safely into college deferments, Chambers had gone off valiantly to Vietnam. Walking point on his first patrol for a volunteer S and D platoon, he tripped a toe popper. Three months later, he hobbled home on a prosthetic foot, with a marble for a right eye. Ever since then, he had waged a war with words, as if language could somehow redeem his lost past or restore the missing parts of himself.

As for Stark, he had graduated from Harvard in three years, during which time he lost all his hair as the result of a nervous condition. After one semester of law school at New York University, he married Susan Friedman, matriculated toward a doctorate in psychology at the same school. Before the war's end, they had bought a brownstone in Brooklyn, not far from where Stark was raised. Notwithstanding Stark's weekly handball game and dinner, Frankle suspected the man didn't take any time away from his desk at the state Environmental Protection Bureau in the World Trade Center.

If, as Stanley Stark surmised, Chambers had indeed gone to war to prove something to his father (just as Stark had driven himself through Harvard and New York University at record-breaking speed to impress his father), neither Nick Chambers nor Irv Stark seemed, to Frankle's way of thinking, impressed with their sons. In fact, Irving Stark had died before Stanley won his first case (against a Queens dry cleaner who was illegally disposing of trichloroethylene), and Chambers's father hadn't even greeted his son at the San Francisco airport when Harry was shipped back from the war.

For that matter, neither Stark nor Frankle had met Chambers at the airport. Frankle's excuse had been that he hadn't known of Harry's wounding until Chambers gimped into Frankle's Lower East Side loft in the summer of 1970. Stark himself didn't have any excuse beyond considering all Vietnam veterans war criminals, guilty of both genocide and the rape of Asian flora and fauna. Stark was probably the only lawyer alive who had filed a class action suit with the World Court on behalf of tigers and monkeys. On the other hand, Chambers had never said a word about Vietnam, though he'd written a trilogy of little-read autobiographical novels about the life of a man before, during, and after the war, which Hollywood had paid him handsomely to adapt for the screen. Though none of the scripts had been produced, Chambers had saved enough to live fashionably in Manhattan for the five years he had lived next door to Frankle.

Frankle figured he had remained friends with the two for the same reason he had cohabited with Monica Webb without asking many serious questions: life frightened him and he admired combative people, recognizing that he participated vicariously in their extroversion. If the truth be known, Frankle had suspected all along that Monica resented him for not being aggressive enough to keep her interested in him. Certainly Frankle could have been more demonstrative in his devotion. Nevertheless, the tawdry and fickle infidelities in which she had engaged before dumping him was another matter, one that intimidated him far more than he was comfortable acknowledging, especially since trying to match her tryst for tryst over the years only further weakened his precarious sense of self-esteem.

Naturally, as Frankle was familiar with the fashionable "psychology of blame," he knew that lurking behind his troubles with Monica Webb were far more inveterate conflicts with his progenitors. But he didn't have the fortitude to review those twin catastrophes and preferred leaving that part of his past out of his present. A stroke had buried his seventy-year-old father, and Frankle's mother, beyond asking what he was looking for in the refrigerator, had always been manifestly uninterested in her son's personal life. For years Monica had pushed therapy on him, but Frankle didn't believe in the "talking cure." What he wished for secretly was something called Humility, and from his understanding of the concept, there was simply no talking your way through or around its fiery initiation.

Down on the avenue, a garbage truck's compactor droned thunderously. Frankle employed the remaining puddle of whiskey to knock back the last of Monica's prescription of Valium. In the room's ambient light, the black-and-white blowups of her, which Frankle once vaingloriously considered Avedonesque, stared back at him with a grotesqueness reminiscent of the malicious Arbus.

There was no point in denying it: What begins with a screwing ends with a screwing. Love had nothing to do with Thom Frankle and Monica Webb.

3

Frankle spent the first dawn of his unemployment in an obsessive frenzy of assigning Monica's belongings to boxes and then hiding the boxes in closets. Then he lost control and scrubbed walls, vacuumed and mopped the floors, dusted and oiled furniture, and, finally, moved the bed into a different corner of the mirrored room. When he recovered a dusty pair of Monica's panties behind the headboard, it all came crashing down, and he knocked back two shots of whiskey to corral a regret that he feared might start a stampede.

Because his voice sounded slurred when he telephoned the cleaning woman to explain that he and Monica were moving and, therefore, would no longer need her services, he slurped two cups of coffee before phoning Kikki Epstein.

"Studio."

"Kikki, please."

"Who's calling?"

"Blair?" Frankle guessed.

"Blair's gone for the day."

"Tell Kikki it's Thom Frankle."

"I'm afraid Kikki's busy busting some A.D.'s balls. Can she get back to you?"

Frankle gave the guy his number.

The phone rang half an hour later.

"Thom Frankle speaking."

Kikki Epstein said breathlessly, "Thom! How utterly bizarre you should call."

Frankle revealed that he'd finally summoned the courage to quit the *Concupiscence* job and was preparing to resume more serious work.

"But in the meantime," Kikki said, "do I infer percipiently that you need money?"

Frankle confirmed her intuition and asked if she knew of any available work.

"Serendipitously enough," she told him, "our boy Blair botched up in a major new way this morning."

"He's been a botcher since our Visual Arts days," Frankle said, and proceeded to listen to Kikki Epstein describe Blair's fall down an elevator shaft while rigging strobes.

"Can you be in at noon?" she said.

"Today?"

"Yup."

Frankle felt a professional obligation to ask about the shoot before assenting.

"Action stuff," Kikki said. "Your basic gymwear histrionics. Stretching and jumping. There's a mat sequence involving running and tumbling. It's seventy-five a day, Thom."

He told her he'd be there at noon.

"You gotta admire a guy," Kikki said, "too proud to mooch off his rich girlfriend."

Frankle left a message with Laurie Larsen's secretary before flicking on the television to watch *Still Lives*. The woman with whom he'd been parasitically overmatched for five years came immediately into focus. As the monstrous Clara Ravens, Monica was revealing to her mother-in-law that she was running off for two weeks with her husband's brother; Clara wanted to learn if her sister-in-law suspected anything. The camera commenced an extreme over-the-shoulder close-up of Clara's reaction to the mother-in-law's response. Frankle figured he knew the answer, and he clicked off the set.

A church tower's bells tolled twelve times as Frankle locked his bicycle before Kikki Epstein's Twenty-ninth Street studio. He stared at the church before signaling on the studio's intercom button. Eyes raised, Frankle beheld a young man lean out the studio's window, eclipsing the bells and waving keys.

"Lock's on the fritz," he called. "Catch!"

Frankle watched the keys tumble and glisten as they sailed out and down, and then beyond his lunging effort, only to strike and smash the windshield of an illegally parked Triumph.

The bell's resonance ceased as Frankle reached nimbly through the shattered glass onto the dash for the keys.

The young man came charging into the street. "You were supposed to catch the fucking things!"

"Missed."

"Missed? You didn't even try!"

The young man stared disconsolately at the smashed glass and Frankle took in that postmodern look: Hawaiian shirt, arcane earring, crew cut, eyes without depth or ostensible recognition of a world beyond the properties of one's mind, running shoes designed for a lunar terrain.

"Hi," the young man said finally. "I'm Terri. Terri Max. Either one's okay."

Frankle recommended that Terri Max leave a note on the remnants of the windshield.

"Thing is," Terri Max explained, "one more fuckup and Kikki'll can my ass. Guess how I fucked up yesterday."

They went in, Frankle holding open the elevator door.

"You pushed Blair down the elevator shaft."

"Elevator shaft! Blair fell off the fire escape, rigging lights."

"Kikki said elevator shaft."

Terri Max shrugged. "What I did was fuck up the strobe settings. The exposures came back way off. Last week I synced the camera wrong, and the shots came back black. Kikki's giving me one more chance."

The elevator opened to the studio.

The western wall was a series of windows against which the sun reflected in a splash off the glass skyscraper across the street, then washed away with cloud coverage, only to emerge a moment later. Closer in, dressed in tight and faded denim, Kikki was standing with her hands on her hips, observing as an art director choreographed a model's leap from the parallel bars. Kikki's bleached-blond hair was piled haphazardly on top of her head, and she fussed with it nervously after requesting that the model swing and leap one more time. The model complied, only to overshoot her landing and become entangled in a turmoil of wires.

"Terri!" Kikki called, wheeling. "We're tripping over sync cords and cables. We emphatically do not want to be."

Terri started over, only to stumble on an extension cord.

"Exactly, Terri!" Kikki acknowledged Frankle with a wink.

Kikki's husband, Johnny Smoke, with whom Frankle boxed occasionally at the Y and attended various sporting events, gestured histrionically while shouting into a cordless phone in a corner.

"Wait a minute!" Smoke was saying, the phone tucked in his chin as his hands rose into a position of surrender. "Hold it right there, Milton. You're not listening to me. Your people never listen to me either. They must get it from you!" Smoke lit a joint and paused, frowning. "What are you, Milton, dense? Didn't I just finish saying that I can't use the Vivitar 285?"

Kikki approached and kissed Frankle with the exaggerated caution of the once promiscuous.

Terri Max handed them each a Styrofoam cup of coffee.

"Did you ask Thom if he takes cream or sugar?"

"Black's fine," Frankle said.

Kikki pulled off a false eyelash. "Sun's going to drive us bonkers, Thommie. Be a good guy and rig a strobe on the fire escape so we can get the illusion of outdoor light." She glanced at her watch. "Terri, shutter the other windows. And why isn't Dakota ready?"

Kneeling among the cables, Terri said, "She wasn't getting along with the makeup gal. She's in the ladies', doing it herself."

"Doing *what* herself?"

"That's really great," Terri said petulantly. "Really first-rate humor. May I stop laughing now?"

"You may wash the lenses now, Terri."

"Do you want the cables out of your hair or not?"

"Help Thom Frankle with the strobe rigging."

An hour later, Dakota was somersaulting and leaping as Kikki fired away. The account executive wanted movement in the hairdo, so Frankle rigged two Mole fans. Then the art director wanted more expression in Dakota's eyes when she was swinging on the gym rings.

"Not sexy enough," he complained, and Frankle was assigned, to his genuine chagrin, to stealthily goose the model with a yardstick whenever she got complacent. This left her looking more sour and defiant than dreamily sated, but the art director was all smiles and nodded Frankle's way whenever he wanted her prodded.

Darkness had fallen by the time the bodywear shoot was finished and Johnny Smoke had returned with a portable Sunpak 411. Smoke had an uncanny way of showing up fifteen minutes before a bar was assaulted.

"Somebody smashed my windshield," he told them incredulously, setting down the compact contraption in the path of Terri Max's vacuuming. Terri couldn't hear a word and amiably detoured around the equipment.

Smoke toked on a joint and offered it to Frankle, who declined. "Just as I'm coming out of 47th Street Photo," Smoke resumed, "I spot this little dude smashing the windshield of my car with a pipe."

"In broad daylight?" Kikki's skepticism gave her voice an exhausted quality.

Smoke nodded, exhaling white rings.

"Black?"

"What do you think?"

"Did you do anything?" Kikki took the joint from him.

"What I did," he answered, coughing, "was chase the fucker for two blocks and beat the piss out of him."

"You're lying!" Kikki turned to Frankle. "He lies all the time. Like a rug. Always sneaking off with some chippy and covering it up with stories."

"Cross my heart and hope to die." Smoke insisted that Kikki see for herself.

Frankle went down with them, Terri Max remaining behind to empty the garbage and lock up.

Outside, Johnny Smoke pointed smugly to the windshield.

"Well, well," Kikki said, arms folded against the raw night. "Johnny tells the truth for once in his life."

"Maybe you'll believe me from now on."

"Fuck around and deny it," Kikki said. "See if I care."

"Tonight I'm covering a Jets game at Shea."

"That's a good one," Kikki said, winking at Frankle as she leaned against the Triumph.

"Hey," Smoke said defensively. "*Sports Illustrated* wants some stills."

"Fine," Kikki told him. "I've got paperwork."

Terri Max emerged, froze a moment on the sidewalk, then waved and started away.

"Hey!" Smoke called. "Look at this, Max. Some kid smashed my windshield and I beat him up. Drew a crowd of several hundred. Outboxed him."

"Sorry I missed it," Terri Max said, backing away.

"Wait a second!" Kikki said to Smoke. "Did you say the Jets?"

"That's right."

"The Jets haven't played at Shea Stadium in years."

Smoke flushed. "What a bunch of space rangers those *Sports Illustrated* people are."

Kikki snorted her skepticism. "That's right, darling. Call and tell her you can't make it tonight."

Frankle unlocked his bicycle and straddled it. Kikki appealed to him with doleful eyes. "Tell Monica I tape her soap and watch it every night. I'm betting she's going to run off with the gynecologist instead of the brother-in-law."

He had the lens cap popped before they could blink and caught them faced off, glaring. He didn't know why their physical resemblance should be so eerily familial, though the transformation seemed endemic to the relationships of nearly everyone Frankle knew who had spent any number of years carnally involved.

Ten blocks north of the studio, Frankle sought sanctuary from the sudden downpour in a Hell's Kitchen church. It was beautifully cavernous and simple, and Frankle sat alone, staring at the stained-glass windows before bowing his head to the prayer book and opening it at random.

For we are saved by hope: but hope that is seen is not hope: For what a man seeth, why doth he yet hope for?

But if we hope for what we see not, then do we with patience wait for it.

This was not for Frankle; it frightened him to forsake the phenomenological order his eyes created of the surface of things. He closed the book and studied the stained glass. In a myriad of color, Jesus was nailed to a cross.

Frankle got the hell out of there.

4

The dogwalker had left his football helmet and shoulder pads on the kitchenette table, along with a brief note reemphasizing that each walk would be raised, hereafter, to three dollars, which worked out to sixty-three dollars per week; and this new policy required cash payment *in full* on the Sunday evening preceding the new week. Frankle envied the ten-year-old his entrepreneurial candor and made a mental note to fire the kid's incipiently Republican ass before year's end.

The telephone rang.

"You busy?"

Frankle heard music playing loudly and had trouble discerning the voice.

"Harry?"

"Let me buy you a drink? I'm down the block."

"Down what block?"

"You know the bar."

"They released you?"

"Who?"

"Skip it," Frankle said, and told him to sit tight.

"Step on it," Chambers said.

———

A bronze plaque announced the year of The Inn's founding, and from the smell of cigarette smoke and beer, Frankle would have bet his two-thousand-dollar bank account that the place hadn't been aired out since opening night.

Chambers stood in the dark watching television at the far end of the varnished bar. He wore his combat jacket and a beige fisherman's cap with a long black bill. By the way he was standing, slightly canted to the left, Frankle inferred he'd been walking a lot and was favoring the right leg, with the prosthetic foot. Even in the interior darkness, Chambers hadn't removed his mirror-fronted sunglasses.

Two mugs of beer waited on the bar. Frankle lit a cigarette and drained one of the mugs.

"What's going on, Harry?"

Chambers kept his attention on the television and spoke furtively. "In a word, it was most uncool of me to go into the boonies alone. Wiggy, to say the least. Let's leave it at that."

Frankle cleared his throat. "I thought you were downtown in detox."

"I *was* downtown in detox. Left to go hunting. Humped around west of Harrisburg. Very freaky place, Harrisburg. Has that Hiroshima reverb to it." Chambers picked up his beer and drank slowly. "They're calling it a psychotic episode." He kept both hands on the beer mug.

"Then it's true," Frankle said, "about the state troopers?"

"True for *then*."

"You've been released, you mean?"

Chambers nodded. "Affirmative."

Frankle started to extinguish his cigarette, then allowed Chambers to finish it.

"What happened in detox, Harry?"

Chambers finally faced Frankle, who couldn't find any of the old menace in his friend's expression; he seemed frightened and vanquished.

"They got me scheduled for electroshock plug-in tomorrow. I skipped out an hour ago."

"Back up a second," Frankle said. "What happened in detox?"

Chambers raised the empty beer mug and stared through it at Frankle. "For a shallow guy, you're very intuitive."

"What happened?" Frankle persisted.

"Day I was scheduled to leave, I heard from McGaren. Squid didn't like the new manuscript."

"Meaning what?"

"Meaning," Chambers said impatiently, "I find another publisher for the novel."

Frankle couldn't suppress his incredulity. "McGaren visited you in detox to say he wasn't publishing the novel?"

"He telephoned."

"At the clinic!"

"Said better in there than out here."

Experience had taught Frankle not to compete with Chambers on issues of personal misfortune. Still, Frankle suspected mentioning his firing might provide comfort. The commiseration, however, seemed not to register.

"So much for friendship and business," Chambers resumed. "Of course, I'm old enough to recognize that all friendship is based on a bargain, and that the renewal of all bargains is a matter of mutual expediency."

Frankle folded his arms protectively. "You're saying your editor's rejection of a manuscript required you to suck on a gas pipe?"

Chambers stared at the bar top. "I'm afraid it's true, my friend. Between people, there exist only bargains. The only commitment men seem interested in making is to the devil."

Frankle had long ago inured himself to Chambers's grand pronouncements; he ordered a shot of Paddy's, then chased it with the last swallow of his beer.

"What is it I can do for you, Harry?"

Beyond Chambers, a graphic of the Commander in Chief's cancerous intestinal tract was being diagnosed on the television screen.

"I need a place to crash for the night."

Frankle told Chambers he was heading downtown to shoot the Christopher Street Halloween parade.

"Like I said," Chambers repeated, "I need a place to crash."

"Are they looking for you or something?" Frankle touched Chambers's shoulder, but his friend didn't turn to him.

"No doubt."

"Does it make any sense, then, to stay next door? Won't they check it out?"

Chambers removed his sunglasses and fingered his glass eye as if it were hurting him. "Do me a favor, Frankle. Don't interrogate me. I've been interrogated all week."

"I'm just saying if they come looking . . ."

"Let'm look. Next door is the last place they'd expect me. And if they suspect something, you'll say you don't know anything. It's all very simple: you either trust me or you don't."

Frankle held up his hands in capitulation. "Calm down. You tell me to trust you, I'll trust you."

"I'm calm. I'm calm and keeping my head down. When they bust caps, always stay calm, always keep your head down. You got keys for me?"

They paid up and went outside. A raw wind had blown up from the river, and Seventy-second Street flashed with the crimson of storefront neon. Frankle handed Chambers keys to the roof-level burglar gate and glass door and told him to use the foldout next to the darkroom.

The aperture and shutter speed on the Nikon were preadjusted for purposes of immediate shooting, and Frankle roamed the graffitied downtown local, searching for a target. The photo book on which he had been working for a decade was entitled, tentatively, "Where They Lived and What They Lived For," but he couldn't find a subject to shoot that he hadn't shot before. Indeed, even the parade's gay grotesques impressed Frankle as too clichéd for inclusion, though he messed around with a 200-millimeter wide-angle zoom in the hope of exaggerating into a new realm of burlesque the morbid gawking upon the morbid. But he hadn't shot more than two frames when it occurred to him that he had best call it a night.

Back on the subway platform, he came upon a homeless drunk, hopelessly unconscious and spread-eagled on a bed of newspapers, wearing a silver-foil helmet and pot-holder mittens. Obviously, it wasn't much of a photograph, just another exercise in the exhausted genre of journalistic realism, but for the moment almost any subject impressed Frankle as worthier of his modest efforts than pussy shots, "expressive" or otherwise.

He stuffed a fiver in the poor fucker's jacket pocket and boarded the uptown local.

5

A note lay on the kitchenette counter. Harry Chambers had panicked and returned to Payne Whitney after a psychiatrist had agreed to forgo electroshock.

Frankle stared out the window as a bottle of Irish whiskey raised itself to his lips. Down on the street, a lion, a scarecrow, and a tin man were cued to board a bus.

The phone rang.

"Mr. Frankle?"

"Speaking."

"Fooled you again!" Stanley Stark dropped the Karloff imitation. "You ever receive a death threat?"

"Monica once. We'd been drinking." Frankle lit a cigarette and splayed himself on the floor like that homeless soul.

"I received one myself today. Caller didn't sound like a Halloween prankster either. Instructed me and my department to knock off an investigation of Kenway's illicit toxic waste disposal in the Suffolk County sewer system. 'Knock it off or else' is how he put it."

"Or else what?"

"What the hell else do you think 'or else' means?"

"No need to shout!"

"That's what the FBI operator told me. Then an assistant to an assistant of the regional assistant was kind enough to inform me that the mob's behind most hazardous-waste violations. I assured him I was familiar with this fact. Incidentally, Susan had the abortion. Hello?"

"I'm listening," Frankle said disconsolately.

"Do you believe it? Day after the gynecologist hacks and vacuums the fetus, *I* get a death threat."

"How's Susan doing?"

"Susan's gone away. California, apparently, to visit family. In all honesty, Thomas, I find Susan's going fishy. Patient of hers called and wanted to know what Susan meant by canceling all appointments until further notice. I didn't know what to say. I called Susan to inquire, and she told me to mind my own business. I fear she's blaming me for the fetus."

"Obviously, she's in mourning," Frankle said mournfully. "Let her mourn."

"You'd think she'd want to be near me."

"Stan, I know you're—"

"Listen, Thomas. Be a loyal friend and bring me one of Chambers's pistols. I'd ask him myself, but our rapport has been somewhat strained for the better part of the decade. A thirty-eight snub-nose, I'm told, will do the trick. Incidentally, this is strictly confidential."

Frankle sat up to swill some whiskey. Outside, firecrackers exploded.

"I can't get you a gun, Stan. Besides, Chambers's guns are all facsimiles."

"*I need a gun!*"

A car alarm went off, and Frankle bowed his head. "Let's both of us calm down."

"How the hell can I calm down when someone from the mob with a ten-syllable last name from Queens has got me on his hit list?"

"Stan," Frankle whispered emphatically, "Chambers's handguns are all facsimiles. If you don't believe me, ask him yourself. Call him at Payne Whitney and ask him."

"Try to understand something," Stark rejoined with comparable condescension. "Put your thinking cap on. The chemical people and their haulers know that if my department is awarded a summary judgment against them, it's going to have national repercussions. We're talking millions of dollars in claims."

"Either way," Frankle answered equably, "we both understand that a toy gun will not protect you."

"These hoodlums have tried for months to have me dismissed by the A.G.'s office. They've failed. Murder's always their final solution."

Frankle reclined and covered his eyes with his arm. He could feel his Airedale's hot breath against his neck.

"Stan, this business with Susan is driving you around the bend. Why not take a brief vacation?"

"Thomas, when I suggested to Susan that we go together to the Coast and make it a vacation, she nixed the idea immediately. Of course, I told her I haven't decent time for a vacation. Tuesday next, we've got the possibility of a momentous summary judgment. A vacation's absolutely out of the question. As for Susan, I can't decide whether she's planning on leaving me or whether I'm hoping she's planning on leaving me."

"Why would Susan leave you?"

"I can only speculate on why I might be *hoping* she will. For one, I don't like her. Between me and you, I'm glad we didn't have a baby."

"Don't say things you don't mean."

"The truth, I'm afraid. Because I don't like being intimate with her. Something's gone wrong with her breath. I suspect it's the impacted wisdom tooth she's fearful of having extracted, Or perhaps it's stomach acidity from all that coffee she drinks."

"Stan, I think you're more upset about the baby than you're able to admit."

"*Fetus,* Thomas. And it's the chemical people who are responsible for that mutogenic fetus. I've seen the studies. Twenty thousand chemical accidents in the last five years. That's almost ten a day. We're talking spills and emissions totaling *twenty million pounds*. But okay, forget the known stuff they're dumping. Because the chemical people aren't satisfied with known stuff. They're manufacturing one thousand new and deadlier concoctions every year. And what do they do with this stuff they introduce into the food chain to systematically poison us? They sell it and spread it before its toxic properties are ever adequately researched. Because the burden isn't to prove it's safe, but to prove it isn't deadly!"

"The point here, Stan?"

"My wife's dead fetus!"

Frankle cleared his throat as Stanley Stark began to sob.

"I'm with you," Frankle whispered.

Stark blew his nose.

"Why do you think we've got a third of the population contracting cancer? The food chain's contaminated. Our fatty tissues overflow with toxins. Biocide accumulations, Thomas! We're seeing carcinomas never before reported in history. They're cutting out things from people's digestive and reproductive tracts that have an extraterrestrial look to them."

Frankle struggled to sit up, then wiped his mouth with the back of his hand.

"Stan, would you like to spend time at my apartment? I'd certainly enjoy your company."

Stark said he didn't have time to hold Frankle's hand.

"If they hunt me down and kill me, Thomas, don't forget to blame yourself. Goodbye!"

Frankle was assured by someone who identified herself as "Reception" that Harry Chambers was indeed listed as a patient at Payne Whitney but that she wasn't permitted to allow phone calls after 10 P.M. He might try the next day, after nine in the morning. Frankle thanked her, then collapsed on the bed downstairs. The sheets still smelled of Monica, but even after he changed them he couldn't sleep.

Taking two cameras and Jack, Frankle descended to the street. On upper Broadway, a prostitute offered her services for twenty-five bucks. Frankle paid her ten bucks to pose in the doorway of the SRO hotel. She wasn't unpleasant to look at until she smiled, which she did a lot, thinking Frankle a very funny man to pay her to take her picture.

When Frankle finally sat down on a bench to share a slice of pizza with a young Airedale struggling to stay awake, the digital clock crowning the prewar building north of Needle Park indicated 2:33. And when Frankle finally climbed between the sheets, he did so upstairs, sprawled on a foldout mattress free of memories.

Outside the studio's window, in a herald of first light, sparrows stirred at the bird feeder in the roof garden, which, with October finished, had turned brown and flowerless.

6

Sunday, after clipping to dry six prints of "Passengers," taken the previous day in a Grand Central Terminal waiting area, Frankle scooted downstairs to torment his eyes with the televised showdown from New Jersey's Cancer Alley, between the football Giants and the hated Dallas Cowboys.

At halftime, Frankle ordered in Chinese food to celebrate his team's ten-point lead; but less than four minutes into the third quarter, the Giants had blown their lead by way of unimaginable turnovers, and Frankle contemplated heaving the tin of cold noodles and sesame sauce at a close-up of the apoplectic head coach.

The phone rang.

"Thom?"

His breath caught at the slamming of his heart. "Hold on a second."

He turned off the sound of booing and lit a cigarette.

"Am I interrupting something?" Monica said.

"No, no," Frankle said. "I'm great. And you?"

"I've been having a smashing time. I phoned because I figured you'd be watching your football team."

Frankle cleared his throat. "I've got people in for brunch. You sound closer than London."

"I'm ringing you from Kennedy Airport."

He lit a second cigarette off the first, then frantically extinguished both.

"I'd be happy to pick you up."

"That's awfully good of you. But no, thanks."

"I didn't expect you back so soon." His capitulation signaled as plaintiveness. "It's good to hear your voice."

"Thom, I miss Jack."

"He misses you, too. Really, Monica, I don't mind picking you up."

"Listen, Thom, I don't want to fight about this, but I want Jack back."

Frankle stared at the TV. The Cowboys kicked a field goal.

"What did you say?"

The operator demanded twenty-five cents for the next three minutes and Frankle listened to depositing coins. Then a computer voice said, "Thank you!"

"Victor and I are flying to L.A. tonight," Monica resumed. "We were all set to spend two weeks in Paris, but Victor's picture got a go. I'm going to be in a movie, Thom."

"Hold it, Monica. You're calling me because you want the dog?"

He heard her speaking to someone. Then she said to Frankle, "Victor and I have reserved Jack one of those kennel cages. We've got a three-hour layover. We thought we'd zip in directly and get him. Is four o'clock a good time?"

Frankle told her as pleasantly as possible that he wasn't about to lose custody of Jack.

Monica's tone changed abruptly, becoming pernicious.

"He's my dog, Thom. You bought him for me."

"As you suggest," Frankle replied, "let's not fight about this."

"Victor and I are coming in for Jack. I'd prefer if you left him in the apartment and went out. I have my keys. We'll drop in at four, as planned."

"I won't be here at four."

"That's fine. This way there shan't be a scene."

"*Shan't!*"

"Stop it, Thom!"

"Don't come here, Monica." Frankle's tone began to gather stridency. "For everyone's sake—mine, yours, Jack's, Vicky's."

"Don't call him Vicky."

"Don't come in, Monica."

"Jack's mine. And don't forget that the flat's mine as well. It's in my name, in case you've forgotten."

"It's in both our names."

"*Wrong.* I've already checked with my lawyer. So don't push me. I'll be there at four."

She hung up. It was nearly three.

Frankle phoned a locksmith. By three-thirty, the locks had been changed and Frankle was out fifty bucks.

He had no sooner hidden with Jack in a doorway across the street from the brownstone when a black limousine pulled up. In Frankle's eyes they looked like extraterrestrials alighting. The sheen of their androgynous outfits, silvery and puffy, glinted even in the overcast twilight. They went into the building and Frankle waited.

When they reemerged, Monica threw her keys into the gutter and went to the corner phone booth. He watched her look up to their apartment windows. At first she appeared angry, but when she put the phone down, Frankle could see she was crying. Victor had disappeared into the limousine, and for a moment Monica looked a little lost.

What Frankle hoped for then, sequestered in the doorway, was that Monica would send Victor off to L.A. and reconcile things with her two "apartners"—Thom and Jack. That he needed Monica for the wrong reasons, and that the need might, technically speaking, have nothing to do with love, didn't make it any easier for him to remain hidden as Monica returned to the limousine.

The elongated windows were coated with a mirrorlike substance, and Frankle beheld only a streak of reflections when he tried to catch a last glimpse of her as the automobile passed. He stepped out to the sidewalk and walked the other way, to a corner phone booth.

It surprised him to hear Laurie Larsen's real voice rather than the recorded version.

"You're supposed to be in California."

"Never went," Laurie Larsen said. "Dell Jordan's people canceled the interview just as I was about to board. Thank God I had my *Concupiscence* beeper."

"Didn't your secretary give you my message?"

"Where was I supposed to call you? Your place?"

"Monica's gone. We broke up."

"Again!"

"I'd prefer to talk about this in person."

"Can't."

"I'm on the street, about to hop a cab."

"Someone's here."

"Couldn't you go out for cigarettes?"

"I don't smoke."

"Something else, then. This is important."

"Thom," Laurie Larsen whispered, "success requires more than talent. It requires calculation. It's something you never learned."

"Don't talk like that. That isn't you, Laurie."

"Success requires calculation," she repeated emphatically.

"What about us?"

"Us was a miscalculation. Us got you fired."

In the background, Frankle heard a man call out something.

"Listen," Laurie Larsen whispered, "don't ruin my memories of you," and hung up.

An internal voice recited, *Ye ask and receive not, because ye ask amiss, that ye may consume it upon your lusts.*

Frankle fed the terrier, then played fetch with him using the blind stuffed rabbit, before seeking sanctuary from Sunday in a nearby revival house, where two Marx Brothers films offered salvation through secular laughter. Sure enough, this trinity's mitigating antics brought back Frankle's appetite for the world; he hurried home, hungry enough to give those sesame noodles and string beans a second chance.

Stanley Stark telephoned as Frankle was raising the chopsticks to his mouth.

"Just listen, Thomas. I'm in Saint Louis, awaiting a connecting flight to L.A. Susan has filed for divorce."

"Filed? Shouldn't she have at least first threatened to file?"

"When I had the audacity to ask that very question, she told me to consult her lawyer. I'm on my way out to go toe to toe with her."

"If you'll permit me, Stan, calm down."

"Wrong, Thomas. My male instincts tell me if I get aggressive with her early, I've got a chance of prevailing. But if it goes more than fifteen minutes, she'll wear me down with uncountable accusations."

Frankle chewed the noodles contemplatively.

"You've both been through hell, Stan. Patience and compassion are required here."

"Thomas, how many times must I repeat to you that Judeo-Christian concepts do not work in the postmodern arena. Repentance and Humility have been excised from the discourse. Interface and Impact are the new and improved Lords. Control, Thomas. Speaking of which, the court denied me that summary judgment. I've been so upset I hopped the wrong plane out of Kennedy."

"Stan, I spoke with Harry Chambers yesterday."

"Forget Chambers. Focus on me. Focus on Stan. Are you focused?"

"Yeah," Frankle said. "Shoot."

"Over the years, you've demonstrated—no offense now—a remarkably shameless talent for winning back Monica in not dissimilar circumstances I now face with Susan. Is there any particular advice you can offer?"

"Only the obvious."

"Namely?"

"Leave your self-respect in Saint Louis."

"I left it in Brooklyn."

Frankle heard a flight announcement for Los Angeles in the background.

"Farewell, Thomas! Farewell!"

"Don't you ever weary of this flippancy, Stan?"

"The bedrock of our friendship, I'm afraid."

7

Since Terri Max had accompanied Johnny Smoke to Las Vegas to cover Irish Teddy Mann's middleweight comeback bout for *Ring* magazine, Kikki Epstein and Frankle worked alone that week in the studio.

Their first assignment featured still lives for a special cooking insert in one of the fashion magazines. Monday morning, Frankle shopped specialty stores for fresh fruits and vegetables, which he later sprayed with some mysterious toxin that lent a varnished sheen to their colorful surfaces. After that, the work bogged down in the typical requirements of composition, lighting strategies, and fetishization. Aesthetics could get pedestrian. For example, heat from the strobes created technical problems.

"Hold up!" Frankle called, stepping into the frame. "My dill's drooped."

As he applied ice and awaited the return of turgidity, a fly alighted on a spangled banana. Frankle was ordered to step in with a swatter, then was forced to sponge away smashed wings and eyes and legs.

Midweek, shooting cookies seemed simple but wasn't. When the cream-filling between the chocolate-crusted outer layers appeared unappetizingly dried up in the test prints,

Frankle and Kikki resorted to scraping away the sugary filling and replacing it with caulking compound. This brazen manipulation of images left Frankle disquieted. If he participated in misrepresenting cream-filled cookies to children, to what extremes of prevarication might, say, government officials be indulging in matters more significant than snacks?

Ice cream was no picnic either. Shooting a mountain of twenty-seven scoops of a designer dessert upon big blocks of ice seemed as if it required a clean-up crew commensurate to a metropolitan sanitation staff. Specifically, the ice cream's opacity created shadows through the ice's transparency, and it took Kikki and Frankle three hours to correct the lighting, by which time they had gallons of melted ice cream and water all over the studio floor. The dessert company's kindly creative consultant hired an office-cleaning service to lend a hand, but Frankle was required to scoop twenty-seven dollops of the chocolate dairy treat fourteen times before the advertising representative approved the shoot.

Toward the end of the week, the art director orchestrating a beer shoot envisioned the still life in Jungian terms. He insisted that the prone bottle's brown hole, juxtaposed to the mug of amber beer with its white soufflé head, must resonate with the industrial world's archetypal fantasy of Eros as Refreshment. But beyond this subtextual issue of coital recreation, there existed the surface problem of "fish eyes," those oversize bubbles that appear in a beer's head when the glass hasn't been fastidiously cleaned. Consequently, once the backlight's towering flash was integrated with the fiberglass diffuser's smoky ambience, Frankle had to concentrate on pouring *the* perfectly clean glass of beer. This required forty-three bottles of beer and eight hours of chemically rinsing glasses with distilled water.

Finally, after the Friday shoot, with the beer and the agency people gone and the studio empty, Kikki informed Frankle that she and Johnny Smoke would be leaving the following week for a two-month travel shoot in the Caribbean. The assignment had just been confirmed by *Trend*, and Kikki apologized for closing the studio on such short notice until after the first of the year.

Frankle was alarmed but knew better than to let on.

"Drink?" Kikki offered.

"Anything but beer."

"Jack Daniel's?"

Frankle nodded his approval, then inquired about Johnny's prolonged absence.

"*Ring* sent him to Reno after the Las Vegas bout to cover some fighter named Benny Paret."

"Benny 'Kid' Paret?" Frankle asked.

"I think so. Why?"

"Benny 'Kid' Paret died in the ring twenty-five years ago."

Kikki kept her eyes closed for dramatic effect.

"Ice?" she whispered finally.

"Neat."

They knocked glasses and drank.

"What will you do now?" Kikki asked.

Frankle savored the swallow.

"Shoot heads till summer. Maybe then I'll travel around."

"Run away, you mean?"

"I'm told running away doesn't work."

"What does, Thommie!"

Frankle helped himself to another shot.

They were leaning against a wall, facing each other. Kikki posed forlorn.

"What's with you?" he asked.

"My looks are totally gone. I'm middle-aged and my ass is sinking. More horrible than that, I don't feel anything for Johnny anymore. I don't feel anything, period. I honestly don't know what to do—stay married and bored or split up and become desperate." Kikki finished her drink. "What ever happened to us after that bunch of weekends in college?"

Frankle frowned dismissively. "What happened was we were kids."

Wistfulness glistened in her eyes. "Remember how so many marvelous possibilities seemed just *inevitable?*" She smiled ruefully. "How is it you wake up one day in your thirties and all those possibilities seem little more than fantasies inspired by stills of exotic sunsets?"

Frankle smiled. "Some exotic sunsets would do you good."

Kikki sighed. "All our teachers thought you were such an extraordinary photographer. You really were, you know."

"I was a completely ordinary photographer."

"You were original. All eyes."

"I was all thumbs in the darkroom."

"You were impatient. You should have persisted."

"We all should have persisted!"

"Why didn't we?"

"We wanted money."

Kikki studied him. "What is it we wanted before we wanted money? I can't even remember."

He lit her cigarette, then his own.

"All week," Kikki said, "you've looked so detached. Like right now. You're looking at me like I'm a ghost." She took his hand. "And you feel like a corpse, Thom. There's no life in these fingers."

"We're both tired and overworked."

She searched his eyes. "I can keep a secret if you can."

Frankle feigned a laugh and averted his eyes.

"Listen to me, Thom. If you can keep a secret, so can I."

Frankle stepped away to set down the glass of whiskey, then disengaged his hand and pretended to search for an ashtray. "Monica's expecting me by seven."

Kikki snorted. "You cheat on her like crazy."

"Never."

"You're lying."

"I swear."

"I know you're lying, Thom. Johnny tells me what you talk about when you guys run."

"I lie to Johnny to impress him."

"Liar!"

"Honestly, I've got to be going."

Frankle left the room for his coat, then stood by the door and blew her a goodbye kiss.

"Chicken!" she said.

An envelope with Frankle's name on it was taped to the door of the foyer. He read the note as he began the long walk up.

Thom, I don't want you to be any more surprised than you have to be. I took Jack from the dogwalker this afternoon. It wasn't the boy's fault. Meanwhile, don't worry. Jack will be fine, even if you won't. Cheerio. Monica.

Frankle sat for a long time in the empty living room, staring at the place where Jack normally lay and listening to his own breathing, raspy from years of chain-smoking. He wondered what it indicated about himself, psychologically and morally, that even as a man of thirty-seven, he couldn't imagine anything worse in the world than having your dog kidnapped.

8

On the first Saturday of November, as rain drummed on the roof and lashed the glass sliding door, Frankle composed an eight-by-eleven promotional sheet, *Head Shots* at the top and *By Frankle* at the bottom; in between, he pasted a glamour photo of Monica, taken years earlier, just after they'd met, and a year before his girlfriend had become the notorious Clara Ravens.

By Monday, the promo had been reproduced two hundred times. Frankle placed a two-inch-square reduction of the sheet in *Backstage*, then bicycled around town for the next several days in the rain, distributing the promo sheets to ad and modeling agencies, placing them on restaurant and laundromat bulletin boards and, finally, in bus stop shelters and apartment house foyers. By Thursday, though he had caught cold, he had completed his equipment purchases from a Canal Street wholesaler of the stands, clamps, floodlights, umbrellas, and reflector cards required for head-shot work. But before bicycling uptown to conclude his ambitious week of work, Frankle submitted another kind of advertisement to the *Village Voice* Shares column. It described the two-bedroom apartment and asked for a woman roommate. Smoking was okay.

Though Frankle spent the next week on the studio's foldout to inure himself to the confinement a roommate's presence would demand, the phone did not ring with a single response to his ads or bulletins. Indeed, it wasn't until the week of Thanksgiving that he received a call. Returning in a hailstorm from an afternoon shoot of the deserted boardwalk in Coney Island, he played back a telephone message from one Constance Frame, who simply said she'd try again, "sooner than later." From the raspy languor of her voice, Frankle hoped it would be sooner and that she would inquire about a roof over her head rather than an eight-by-ten glossy.

He had just poured a heated can of tomato sauce over steaming spaghetti and sat down to read the sports section, when the telephone rang.

"Thom Frankle?"

"No," Frankle said. "But I can take a message for him."

"I'm calling about the share he advertised. Is it still available?"

"Is this Constance Frame?"

"Yes, it is."

"Let me get him for you." Frankle covered the phone and counted silently to ten. "Hello, this is Thom Frankle."

Constance Frame said, "Mr. Frankle, your ad didn't mention the rental fee. That's sort of centrally important, don't you think?"

Frankle explained that her share would be seven hundred, for which she would have her own bedroom and could share everything else, including a roof garden and terrace.

Frankle listened to static crackle on the line.

"I'm afraid that is going to be way too steep."

"It's very fair," Frankle said. "And it's less than the share I'll be paying."

"I'm sure it is very fair," she said raspily. "I just can't afford it."

Swooning slightly, Frankle said, "I can't afford it myself. My girlfriend and I used to split it."

Immediately, he wished he'd kept that bit of melodrama to himself, but it was November, with the shortest days of the year impending, and Frankle felt the pressure of winter's imminence.

"Have you seen anything you can afford?" He spoke now merely to hear once again the sound of her voice.

"Just junk." She thanked him in what sounded like a farewell.

"Listen," he said impetuously. "Maybe we could work something out. Rapport is important in this kind of arrangement."

"I'm not too rapport-minded at the moment, thank you."

"I didn't mean to imply—" Frankle stopped at what sounded like a receiver being picked up.

A man shouted, "Didn't I just say you could stay here? What is it with you? You get your kicks blabbing about your dead husband or something!"

"Hang up, Duke!"

"You can't accept a favor from me?"

"*Hang up*, please."

When he did, Constance Frame apologized for disturbing Frankle and thanked him for taking the time to talk to her.

"I don't mean to get personal," Frankle put in, "but what that guy just said . . . Do you mind if I ask how old you are?"

"Why should I mind? I'm thirty-two. Why do you ask?"

"What that guy just said about your husband dying confused me."

"My husband was killed in a motorcycle accident."

The man shouted in the background, "He doesn't care, Constance! No one does!"

"Listen," Frankle said. "Why don't we have dinner or something and see if we can work out something about the apartment?"

In the silence that ensued, Frankle rebuked himself for his desperate presumption.

"When?" Constance Frame said.

He cleared his throat. "Are you busy tonight?"

"I wouldn't mind getting out of here for a while."

"Where are you?"

"Downtown."

Frankle offered to take the subway.

"Where would you like to meet?" she asked.

Frankle suggested a place at Spring and Lafayette. Constance Frame knew the place but wanted to know how she'd know him.

Frankle told her he'd be wearing a collarless white shirt but that she probably wouldn't see the collar anyway, as his brown hair was quite long.

Before hanging up, they set a time.

Frankle worked on a shot of Paddy's and a chaser of draft while waiting at the bar. In the next ten minutes, two women entered the restaurant and sat at the bar. To Frankle's relief, neither one responded to his shirt. This parsimony of spirit augured an attitude that Frankle knew better than to fuel; he switched to club soda.

Sometime later, however, with the entrance of a trench-coated woman with cascading roan-colored hair, Frankle could feel a change register in his heartbeat. Since the woman wore sunglasses, her only revealed features were a sculpted nose and a full mouth, slightly downturned and lipstickless. She unbuttoned her coat and stood directly across the bar's corner from Frankle, who watched her order a beer. She appeared to notice him, but even after he made something of a show of stretching his arms as if tired, she failed to respond.

Frankle was searching for a line that might insinuate him into her life, when she lowered her sunglasses and squinted.

Suddenly demure, Frankle pretended to be lost in a meditation of the racked bottles before the bar's mirrored wall.

It was in the mirror that he noticed her reflection coming toward him.

"You're not Thom Frankle, by any chance?"

He knew at once from her voice that it was Constance Frame. He nodded, and they shook hands.

"Your shirt looked beige from my glasses." She sat beside him. Smiling, she revealed very white, crooked teeth.

Smitten, Frankle felt his mind go blank.

"Can I get you a drink?" he managed finally.

She held up her beer, then removed her sunglasses.

Frankle noticed that her eyes were brown, like Jack's, and that the left one wandered. He asked where she was from, and she told him she used to live in Venice, California.

"That's at the ocean," Frankle heard himself say, as he watched her eye float.

"It's an astigmatism that makes it do that," Constance Frame told him, appearing momentarily cross-eyed.

Frankle looked into his soda. "It's nice." He felt foolish.

"Now that I've got that out of the way," she said, "I'm going to put the sunglasses back on."

"No need to."

"They're prescription. I'm blind as a bat."

Frankle asked why she'd left the ocean for a city of . . . well, a city.

"To see this old boyfriend."

"The guy in the background?"

"Literally and figuratively," she said.

Frankle ordered a double shot and a chaser.

"Do you drink a lot?" she asked.

"Lately."

He grabbed the drink the second it was poured. "Here's to meeting you." He knocked her beer mug with the little glass, then looked heavenward.

"Jack was drunk when he wiped out," Constance said.

"Your husband?"

"He was with a teenager. She died too."

Frankle didn't want to get into that and looked into his puddle of Paddy's.

"I'm a photographer," he said. "My ex-girlfriend ran off with the assistant director of her soap opera series."

"What kind of photographer?"

He told her as best he could, keeping the self-disparagement to a minimum. Then he listened to her explain that she was grooming dogs uptown but used to design sweaters and run a boutique in Santa Monica.

Frankle couldn't conjure any more questions; he'd pretty much given her his life story, which added up to fearfully little.

"Are you hungry?" he asked.

"Starving, actually."

Eating for the first time with an unknown woman left Frankle nearly as apprehensive as breaking the ice with her in bed.

"You want to eat here or go someplace else?"

"I wouldn't mind walking," she said.

"Mexican food?"

"I know a nice place near Sixth Avenue."

They went out together, to discover flurries littering a raw wind. They walked west, then north. Frankle experienced the anxiety of a first date and had to concentrate to complete the simplest sentence. But Constance chatted easily. At one point, she even hooked her arm in Frankle's and divulged that she was having a good time, just strolling the city like a normal person, holding the arm of another normal person.

Frankle let it pass.

At the restaurant, they took a table in a quiet corner. Constance talked about her husband and the store she lost to Main Street's gentrification. Frankle was proud of himself for not once, despite two margaritas, bemoaning his unhappy childhood or the emptiness that weighed in his chest where his heart once ruled. He stuck to photography and his Airedale, and since he had demonstrated such restraint, he determined he could now invite Constance Frame to share his apartment (without worrying about the rent for the time being) and still appear only normally desperate in his desire for her presence.

He waited to make the proposal until he had paid the check and they were again walking on Sixth Avenue, though it occurred to him that he didn't know where the hell he was going.

"You heading for the subway?" he asked.

"You?"

"I asked first."

"I guess." She took his arm.

He moved in as close as was physically possible without tripping over her, and remained with his shoulder and hip touching hers until they neared the subway. Since Frankle wanted to be outdoors, steadied by the chilly air, when he broached the apartment issue, he halted with the pretext of tying a shoelace. Then he lit a cigarette.

"How come you smoke so much?"

"Anxiety."

"Always?"

"Pretty much." He inhaled deeply.

"I hate anxiety," Constance said. "How do you handle it?"

"Badly." Then he said, "Listen. About the apartment thing. If you wanted, I could let you stay in the extra bedroom and we could negotiate something financial down the road. My free-lance business is really picking up, and I placed that share ad before it had picked up."

"That's very kind of you," she told him, "but I wouldn't be comfortable with that kind of arrangement."

"I'm serious," Frankle said.

"So am I."

They descended into the subway and purchased tokens.

"Aren't you going uptown?" she asked.

He was about to follow her through the turnstile to the downtown side.

Frankle laughed to cover his chagrin. "What the heck am I doing!"

He stepped aside to let someone pass, and the next thing he knew, he was facing Constance Frame with a gate between them.

"Maybe we could do this again or something." All articulateness was gone.

"You bet." But she answered with an exaggerated enthusiasm that left Frankle feeling rebuffed.

He wanted to ask when exactly but realized he had been invasive enough. "If you wouldn't mind, I'll call next week sometime."

"Or I'll call you," she told him.

After he'd written down her phone number, the downtown local pulled in.

"Well, okay, then. Great meeting you." His hand was raised in a wave.

"Bye, Thom."

He waited for her to board the car. To his relief, she waved back through the window as the train pulled away.

Back at the apartment, Chambers's melancholic message, reminiscent in tone and pace of Frankenstein's early verbal efforts, requested that next day Frankle bring whatever mail had accumulated and take a walk with him to the river.

9

Snow flurries gave way to scattered sunshine as Frankle walked crosstown to Payne Whitney. Before a picture window, Harry Chambers sat in the silent reception room, his hands folded in his lap as he twiddled his thumbs. His shorn hair and the gray pallor of his face bestowed a vulnerability and an exhaustion that moved Frankle. He fired his Leica four times without Chambers suspecting a thing.

"Good to see you, Harry."

Chambers stood and listlessly shook Frankle's hand. Frankle could see the sedation in his friend's eyes as he browsed slowly through the manila folder of mail, which he dumped, without opening a single letter, into a trash receptacle adjacent to the reception desk at which he signed out.

"I've got an hour," he told Frankle, who followed him through the revolving door into the crisp November afternoon. Chambers lit a thin cigar and zipped up his combat jacket before leading Frankle toward the East River.

At the boardwalk that bounded the river south of the mayor's mansion, they selected a bench and sat facing Queens. The wind was up, and Chambers put on a blue knit cap.

"I'd be scared to do this alone." He spoke softly, his eyes directed into the distance.

Frankle put his arm around Chambers and patted his shoulder. "You look good, Harry."

Chambers snorted. "We go too far back for that bullshit."

"We do go way back," Frankle agreed.

Chambers bent forward, resting his hands on his knees. Then he stood restively and limped through the wind to the boardwalk's railing. It was a long fall to the freezing water, and Frankle knew the pace of his own traversal betrayed his distrust.

Chambers stared down at the rushing river. "My agent phoned this morning. Found a publisher for the book."

Frankle raised his voice to be heard above the wind as he congratulated his friend with a hug. "How many times I tell you it'd work out!"

Chambers smiled, then stared into the distance, his expression suddenly grave.

"I wouldn't exactly say it worked out. My dick's bigger than the advance."

They turned their backs to the wind and Frankle lit a cigarette. It was quieter turned from the river.

"Tell me about the publisher," Frankle said.

They began strolling south.

"New editor's name is Busch. Gordon Busch. Young guy. To his credit, he didn't resort to the usual bullshit about being honored to publish the book while regretting he couldn't pay me more than dishwasher's wages. It's probably only a line, but he thinks he can help me find some supplemental bucks. Something about a screenplay deal through a friend."

Frankle stood on Chambers's blind side. The flesh around the glass eye still showed scars from the shrapnel wound.

"This morning," Chambers resumed, "I was telling the new shrink about my father. How the guy didn't hug me when I came back to the States, me standing there in uniform with a patch where my eye had once been and a robot's foot. You know what the shrink said to me? 'Who cares about twenty years ago!' " Chambers smirked. "I think I'm going to get along with this guy."

Across the river, brick chimneys emitted black plumes of smoke above the industrial landscape. Frankle turned back to his friend.

"God made you tough, Harry. If he'd made you less tough, I'd probably like you a lot more, but he made you tough so you'd last."

"If I'm so tough," Chambers said spiritedly, "how come there hasn't been a day in ten years I haven't been terrified?"

"Like you told me yourself," Frankle said, "you can't write unless you feel terrified."

"Did I say that?"

"Many times."

"Well, I say a lot of dumb shit. I'm a writer."

Frankle pushed his friend affectionately and studied the movement across the river of the chimneys' black smoke fading into the movement of the rushing water and clouds. If he had the proper lens, the trick would be to capture movement in the stillness of the composition.

"I'm cold," Chambers said.

They headed back to the hospital. At the entrance, Frankle asked Chambers's permission for a couple of shots.

"For your biographer."

Chambers shifted into a posture of solemn anguish, and Frankle quickly focused and fired.

"Thank you, Mr. Chambers."

Pretending his hand was a pistol, Chambers pulled the trigger before turning and hobbling indoors.

10

Notwithstanding rapport, shooting heads required firing a Nikon F-3 with a 180-millimeter lens, loaded with Plus X black-and-white film. For one hundred dollars, the client received the contact sheet and two prints.

By November's end, Frankle had arranged his days around one or two morning and afternoon clients. After the morning sessions, he'd run five miles in the park, lunch on oranges and club soda (laced with a little whiskey to assuage his anxiety), and greet the first afternoon client with his hair still wet from a shower.

For weeks, whenever the phone rang, Frankle hoped the caller would be Constance Frame, returning one of the messages he had left on her "boyfriend"'s answering machine; and even though he had not heard from her, he had informed others inquiring about the apartment that it had already been sublet.

No one would ever accuse Frankle of being practical.

In the raw twilight of early winter, Frankle hiked crosstown with the day's film to a Sixth Avenue lab, where he used Kikki Epstein's account number to receive a discounted printing fee. But being back in business didn't make the seven o'clock emptiness of the apartment any easier to abide, and

Frankle worked at navigating a new path back home. Before long he was stopping in a different church each evening, to sit alone in its chapel. Sometimes he sat for as long as an hour, either reading the prayer book or simply reflecting.

One evening, after wandering way south in the snow to photograph the lighted latticework surrounding the landmark police station under reconstruction on Lafayette Place, Frankle realized he was across the street from the bar in which he and Constance Frame had first met. Impulsively, he dropped a quarter into the corner phone booth and punched out her number.

"Yeah?"

"Constance Frame, please."

"Gus?"

"Duke?"

"She said she's going to be a little late and will call to tell you where you should meet her. That's all I know."

It was more than Frankle wanted to know. He walked west on Spring Street, leaning into the gusting snow as he trudged past gated stores.

He rode the K train uptown. The rage implicit in the graffitied interior depressed him, and he closed his eyes. For an instant he thought he heard an internal voice whisper, *Be strong, I am with thee.* But when he listened again, all he could hear was the racket of the train's metal wheels racing along metal rails.

The note was affixed with chewing gum to the glass of the brownstone's foyer door.

Eating what they used to call spaghetti across the street. Join me.

The communication was unsigned. Frankle crossed the street and entered a meretricious joint notorious for the late-night presence of actors who spent a lot of time playing insouciant. A bridge and tunnel set crowded the tables. Frankle settled at the bar. Ordering, he noted Stanley Stark's mirrored image emerging from the men's room.

Stark sat concurrent to the arrival of the whiskey and downed the shot, gasping after the swallow. "My ulcer."

"Serves you right. Where's the toupee?"

Stark breathed into his fist as if trying to warm himself. Frankle ordered another whiskey.

"Toupee has run away, Thomas. I chased it as far north as Columbus Circle before giving up and dropping by your place to ask for help."

The whiskey arrived, and Frankle gulped it.

"Let it go," Frankle said. "Toupees are happier in the wild."

Stark cocked his head slightly, reminding Frankle of Jack, about whom Frankle worried nightly in his dreams.

"Truth is," Stark said somberly, "after work I took the express the wrong way. Didn't discover the mistake until Seventy-second Street."

Frankle signaled for another shot before inquiring about Stanley's visit with Susan.

Stark reached for a bowl of salted peanuts, then thought better of it.

"In a word, the visit was unproductive. We met at her mother's place. Condominium by the sea. Waves, sunlight, the soughing of freeway traffic in the back—"

"I can picture it," Frankle interrupted.

Stark cleared his throat. "Susan started with a medical update according to her West Coast specialist. Apparently, her uterus is a mess of cysts, polyps, and so forth. In short, she's a reproductive catastrophe. *Issue*, as it were, are out of the question. She could have an operation, but the doctors don't advise it. Gynecologically speaking, it's no race—a five-hundred-to-one shot at best."

Stark leaned in for conspiratorial emphasis.

"When I told Susan that children didn't matter to me, that

I loved her regardless, for some reason this inspired her to turn on me. To begin with, I know nothing about who she really is—you know, *essentially*. Seven years together, she says, and she feels like a perfect stranger."

"What was your response?"

"I said, 'Of course we're perfect strangers; we're adults, aren't we?' At which point she tells me I'm a cheapskate, a lousy conversationalist, self-centered, unconscious, spiritually impoverished, tyrannical—"

"She called you tyrannical?"

Stark appeared to count to ten before resuming.

"All I care about is hazardous waste, and all I talk about is litigation strategy. 'Boring' came up a lot." Stark now munched a peanut. "Worse than that, Thomas, I fall asleep at night when she's telling me how much her patients try her patience. Also, I have no interest in the finer things displayed in museums, galleries, Bloomingdale's."

Frankle sighed. "Didn't you defend yourself?"

"In a manner of speaking, yes. I begged her to give me a second chance."

"How'd she respond?"

Stark raised his eyes to the ceiling, squinting with the effort of memory. "She began throwing things. Then her mother interceded and threw me out of her seaside condominium. For the plane ride home, I purchased Fenichel's *Psychoanalytic Theory of Neurosis* but found nothing on the subject of abortions or abortion hysteria. However, I did learn that Susan's fixation on straightening her nose betrays an unconscious desire for a perfectly functioning penis. With Susan, therefore, we might be looking at a permutation on penis envy, as it seems the woman regards the baby as her substitute penis. What follows then, or so I infer, is that due to the abortion, Susan's furious with me for not making a man of her!"

"Was there anything on mania, Stan?"

"I should never have supported her decision to abort the

fetus. In Susan's deeply disturbed mind, the pregnancy was a test of my devotion to her. Never mind that four doctors warned us that severe physical and psychological disfigurement was probable. And what did Susan imagine we'd do with such a baby?"

Frankle raised a hand for Stark to stop.

"Thomas, look at the favor Chambers's parents would have done him by way of an abortion. Kid was a head case from the get go. Harry Chambers is the greatest living argument for safe and inexpensive abortions. Family planning ought to put him on TV."

Frankle placed a hand on Stanley's shoulder. "Is Susan returning to Brooklyn?"

"Susan and I are finished, as far as she's concerned. And as far as I'm concerned, I'm finished. Incidentally, the woman from whom I'm separated at present has been engaged in an affair with a patient of hers for about a year now. Or so she insinuated."

Frankle moved his eyes sideways, concentrating. "Are you suggesting the baby might not have even been . . ."

"Insinuation indicated the patient's a woman."

Frankle's consternation signaled as a frown. Stark nodded slowly, lips puckered in disgust.

"I can't tell you, Thomas, how lucky you are that Monica consistently dumped you for other men."

Frankle observed Stark's reflection observing Frankle's reflection.

"You really think I would be more upset if Monica had run off with a woman?"

"Of course. Think about it."

Frankle did. "Let's get the hell out of here."

Outside, rain was falling. Stark opened an umbrella. "Walk me home, Thomas?"

"To Brooklyn!"

"Didn't I mention I've moved?"

Stark cried out for a battered Checker, which abruptly traversed three lanes and skidded to a halt, eliciting horns.

"Forget I mentioned it." Stark hopped into the cab and was gone before Frankle could get a phone number or an address.

11

Sunday morning, a client phoned desperate for prints, which she needed in hand by six that evening. Frankle agreed to shoot her, but explained that the charge for a one-hundred-percent rush on development and printing would require, logically enough, a one-hundred-percent increase in price.

"Oh, really?" the woman said. "How stupid do you think I am?"

Since Frankle needed the money, he scheduled a noon appointment.

The woman arrived an hour later in a black leather getup redolent of the hundred-dollar-an-hour Dominatrix Frankle had once shot for *Concupiscence*.

"Dakota," she said.

Frankle shook her hand and introduced himself.

Something about her black hair kindled his memory.

"Haven't we met before?"

"Don't you remember goosing me with a yardstick during a shoot last month?"

Frankle mouthed "Ah" and offered a belated apology.

"For what? Making a living?"

After the shoot, when Frankle was required to collect the two hundred bucks, Dakota claimed she was seriously low in cash but was willing to barter her "professional talents" for a reasonable discount. Frankle glanced from her blue eyes to behold her hand unzipping a flap of leather encasing her crotch. The next thing he knew, Dakota, with the mellifluousness of a magic act, had unencumbered his dong and unfurled a prophylactic. Upon entry, Frankle experienced a hypnotizing increase in heat. Tight and lubricious, she moved, standing, with evocative economy.

Frankle's lashing release rendered him sated for the better part of a minute, at which point he realized that for the price of a minute of pleasure he had indeed been screwed.

Withdrawn, Frankle lowered his attention, to discover the condom gathered peculiarly. He pulled off the defective device and passed his finger in and out of its rupture.

"Broke," he whispered incredulously.

Dakota zipped up her leather flap. "Happens all the time."

"It does?"

"It's only for your protection."

Frankle frowned. "What about you?"

She put her hands on his cheek. "I'd appreciate if you'd messenger the prints to my building and leave them with my doorman."

Frankle nodded, accepting her card: *Dakota. Modeling. Surrogacy. In and Out.* Three phone numbers were listed.

"Tell your friends about me." She slung a leather bag over her shoulder. "I depend on word of mouth."

"Ditto."

Frankle showed her out.

The woman who answered on Sunday evening told Frankle that Constance Frame had moved—to Hoboken or Jersey City—but she hadn't left a forwarding number. ("Don't answer any questions, Melanie!" a familiar voice called out in the background.) About the only thing Melanie could tell

Frankle was that she thought Constance was grooming dogs in a pet store, or was it working for a hairdresser?

Frankle left his name and number in the event that Constance phoned in. Melanie agreed to take the number but said that according to Duke, the thing about Constance Frame was that she could disappear for a year and then show up suddenly as if only a day had passed.

12

Owing, perhaps, to word of mouth, Frankle's head-shot schedule had fallen off by the middle of December to one client every other day. He called Kikki Epstein for some ideas, but Terri Max, who'd come in just to water the plants, reminded Frankle that she and Smoke wouldn't return until the beginning of the year. When Frankle confided that business was way off, Terri Max assured him that business was always slow before Christmas and suggested that he wait until the New Year to panic.

Frankle spent days outdoors in snow flurries, wandering the Upper West Side with a tripod and an equipment bag, photographing churches. For him they were taking on the status of home, and more and more he was calm only during his sessions inside them.

Midweek, at dusk, he ended up reading in the cavernous chapel of St. John the Divine.

The light of the body is the eye: if therefore thine eye be single, thy whole body shall be full of light. But if thine eye be evil, thy whole body shall be full of darkness. If therefore the light that is in thee be darkness, how great is that darkness.

Because Frankle was in no hurry to return to his apartment, he positioned his tripod where the bus stopped to discharge and admit passengers at Ninety-sixth and Broadway. He then spent an hour waiting for the best side shot of the bus's center aisle, where passengers stood packed like cattle. Something about the overhead fluorescence lent a purgatorial pallor to people's empty expressions; at least, Frankle hoped it was attributable to the fluorescence.

Warming himself in a coffee shop at the corner, Frankle glanced up from the advertisement column for Dogs And Other Pets and thought he caught a glimpse of Constance Frame descending into the subway across the street. He threw down money for the Greek salad and lugged his burdensome equipment underground.

There was a long line at the token booth, but Constance Frame wasn't standing in it. Frankle considered jumping the turnstile but was reluctant to try pole vaulting with his tripod. By the time he reached the tracks, the rear lights of the southbound express were disappearing into the tunnel.

Back on the street, he stood working at a thought. Jack came to mind, and Frankle remembered a quiet spring morning when Monica and he had walked up Amsterdam Avenue with their Airedale puppy to buy a pet shop bone.

The Pet Bowl's door opened onto stacked bags of organic dog food. Beyond the bags, a young woman was hanging up a line of dog and cat apparel. Frankle asked if Constance Frame happened to work in the store.

"Are you Gus?"

"Will Constance be in tomorrow?"

"I don't know her schedule."

Frankle nodded, then turned away to browse at organic biscuits, king and bite size.

"How about a number where I can reach her?"

"You'll have to speak with the manager about that. She'll be in tomorrow."

"Isn't there an appointment book?"

"My job's fashion, not grooming."

Frankle took one of the shop's cards and telephoned immediately from the corner, requesting a grooming appointment for his poodle. The woman instructed him to bring in the dog the following morning at ten.

Poodleless, Frankle reached the pet store just after ten. Bells tinkled at his entrance, and he immediately beheld Constance Frame, standing in a trench coat on the far side of a pile of kitty litter. Since she was wiping her glasses clean, it took her some time to recognize Frankle. When she did, her voice sounded different than Frankle remembered it.

"Thom. How weird."

Frankle cultivated his own persona for the occasion. "I can't believe this! Can I buy you a coffee?"

Constance referred to her wristwatch. "I have a ten o'clock appointment."

Frankle puffed his cheeks in chagrin and confessed that he had made the appointment.

"You did?" She looked for a leash. "Where's your dog?"

"He was stolen, actually. If you'll have a coffee with me, I can explain."

Her compliance seemed grudging, and as they walked up the gentrified avenue to an eatery featuring imported coffee and sandwiches, she didn't take his arm, as on their first meeting. Seated, Frankle explained events, beginning with sighting Constance on Broadway and ending with scheduling a grooming appointment for a fictitious poodle.

"I didn't know how else to get in touch with you," he concluded.

Constance Frame popped a piece of cranberry muffin into her mouth.

"I wasn't even uptown yesterday." She washed down the muffin with coffee. "I didn't call you because of an unexpected involvement with someone else."

Frankle reached in a nervous reflex for his coffee cup and spilled the first sip down his chin.

Constance handed him a napkin. "Rough week?"

Her eyes seemed kinder now, and Frankle's embarrassment abated.

"One demanding actress after the next. I'm just taking a short break here." He cleared his throat and fell silent.

Constance's eye floated toward her nose as she studied the muffin. "These don't look like cranberries."

"I thought they were raisins."

"Did you rent your apartment?" she asked.

"Not yet. Where are you living these days?"

"This actor's place in Jersey City. Hundred a month." She frowned. "You look sadder than a basset hound, Thom."

Frankle waved his hand dismissively. "I just need some sun. Fortunately, I've got a Caribbean assignment." He pretended to notice the time on the wall clock above her. "Jesus, I've got to get back for a shoot."

Constance reached for money, but Frankle insisted it was the least he could do and popped up to pay the check.

Outside, Constance said, "Surely you understand my not calling was nothing personal."

"Don't mind me," Frankle said. "Recent studies indicate this sort of thing is seasonal. Too little sunlight."

They walked south on Amsterdam in silence. Traffic sped north, the movement weirdly synchronized to the carnivalesque music issuing from a grocery store doorway.

"I don't know why I should feel as if I did something to harm you," Constance said. "Especially since you were the one who had me come all the way into town for a phony grooming appointment."

They stood in front of the pet store. Frankle apologized lamely and offered to pay for the appointment.

"Please," she said. "Don't add insult to injury."

Frankle didn't say anything more; he figured it was written all over his face. Beyond that, he was feeling the shame of his characteristic talent for imposing his will and then feeling victimized by the other's refusal to comply.

"What you were asking rentwise," Constance said, "was simply too much for me."

"I told you you could stay for free."

"I didn't want to stay for free!"

"Why not?"

"I didn't trust you. And you wouldn't have trusted me if I had agreed." She shook his hand goodbye. "Have fun in the Caribbean."

He apologized for his, well, for everything, and turned away with a feigned sense of purpose.

Outside the lobby door of his brownstone, Frankle uncapped the just purchased pint of Irish whiskey, breathed in the chilly air, and swilled a shot to snap out of it. It was on the second chug that he noticed the fur-coated woman on the other side of the glass. He pushed open the door and offered her a sip.

"We got problems," Dakota said.

Frankle remembered the broken prophylactic and felt the blood drain from his face. "Problems?"

"Hasn't Terri called you?" She sounded frantic.

"Terri Max?"

"He swore to God to me he called you about the new prints."

Frankle took an unabashed swig from the pint and removed his keys. "You need new prints?"

Dakota referred to her wristwatch. "Do you mind if we talk about it while we're working? I have a job in half an hour."

Frankle followed her up the stairs. The whiskey was working, and when Dakota turned abruptly on the third-floor landing she caught Frankle ogling.

"Here?"

"Here what?" Frankle said.

"Your floor?"

"One more."

Frankle paused before his apartment door to catch his breath. The wall before him was swimming with multicolored lights redolent of a stroboscoped discotheque.

"You shouldn't smoke," Dakota said.

"Nerves."

"What'll cancer do, relax you?"

Frankle held open the door and allowed her to enter first. After tossing his coat on the living room sofa, he offered to take Dakota's fur.

"It's all I got on," she told him.

Frankle uncapped the whiskey for one more shot before gesturing to the staircase. "Shall we?"

"You first," she said.

The studio was chilly, and Frankle turned on two strobes to warm the place.

"So then." Frankle put his hands together in a posture that felt vaguely Oriental. Dakota sat before him on a stool.

"Prints," she said impatiently. "New prints."

"New prints," he repeated. He was drunk.

"Terri said the last ones were completely wrong."

"In what way?"

"I don't know. The moron told me he spoke with you already."

"When?"

"He told me he set up this appointment!" Dakota glanced again at the wristwatch. "I can't believe that moron. I didn't need head shots in the first place. Terri apparently misunderstood what Johnny and his people wanted." She sighed. "Terri tells me you've worked with Johnny?"

"I've done some stills for him."

"What do you think of his films?"

71

"His films? What films?"

"Terri told me Johnny and him make art films. They're casting now. That's why he needs the tits-and-ass prints. Their L.A. people have to make casting call decisions. Terri swore to me he talked to you about this."

"He hasn't."

"Then you'd better talk with him. Because this time they're the ones paying for the prints."

Frankle started downstairs, to telephone privately.

"Incidentally," Dakota said, "if you get this teeny wart on your cock, it came from me. It's just a viral deal. My gynecologist said if you find one to go to a dermatologist and get it burned off."

Frankle slowly wheeled to face her. "Burned off?"

"If you don't, a woman can get cancer from them. Is it true what Terri said? That you did award-winning work for *Concubine*?"

"*Concupiscence.*" And Frankle recommenced his descent of the stairs without disabusing Dakota of the illusion that he'd won anything other than his own sense of anathema for his pornographic photography.

"And get the heat cranked up!" she called. "I don't want goose bumps on my ass."

Frankle dialed Terri Max from the bedroom.

"John Smoke Films."

"Terri Max? Thom Frankle."

"Hey, Thom Frankle. Did I tell you about a dog shoot I've arranged for you?"

"What's with this Dakota?"

"Hey, whatever you do, don't jump her bones. We're trying to impress her with our legitimacy. Did you fuck her already?"

"What the hell are you talking about?"

"Didn't you get my message?"

Frankle looked at the answering machine. No incoming calls were indicated.

"What message?"

"I could've sworn I called you. Who am I thinking of?"

"What's this John Smoke Films thing?"

Terri Max nearly shouted with excitement. "Johnny and I have decided to horizontally expand into the home video field. We're definitely going for it. Basically, Johnny's got friends willing to invest for shelter purposes. It's complicated. Johnny himself couldn't fully explain it over the phone from the Caribbean. He was definitely drunk. But he wants those T-and-A shots of Dakota Pomeroy. Do them on the house for us and I'll nail down this celebrity dog shoot assignment for you at *Trend*. Fair? And incidentally, the magazine gig is possibly merely step one. There are plans for a coffee table spin-off. A book! Or so the *Trend* A.D. insinuated, unless he's full of shit, which isn't impossible. Meanwhile, I could use prints of Dakota yesterday."

Frankle explained that he'd retired from pornographic work because he could no longer justify the consciousness it produced.

"Hey, Thom Frankle," Terri Max said. "I got a zillion things going on here, and they're all going on with zero assistants. Add up the difference yourself. Additionally, try asking yourself who's saying anything about porno. Because these shots aren't for publication."

Frankle breathed deeply. "When did all this . . . happen?"

"Over the weekend. Johnny and a young mover and shaker in publishing, name of—don't laugh!—Busch, were snorkeling or something. They're the notorious Tufts College duo, or some such shit, and they need the prints by tomorrow for another guy, who's unnamed at the moment but apparently well established in porn."

Frankle cleared his throat. "They want color?"

"Why are you being this way? Of course they want color."

"In that case I'll have to pouch the shots to Fairlawn."

"What's wrong with Modern Age?"

"They don't process Kodachrome."

Terri Max called out, "Hey, you! Don't leave the liverwurst and potato salad on the fucking radiator!" Then he told Frankle he didn't care where the prints were processed, so long as they were delivered the following day.

Frankle tried to generate enthusiasm. He cued the nihilistic Talking Heads on the stereo and climbed to the studio affecting effervescence. He'd made a livelihood objectifying women, and to find himself returning to it voluntarily after leaving it involuntarily only exacerbated his pervasive intimation of bad faith.

Dakota lay supine on the sofa in the boots and fur coat. Frankle sat on the stool and loaded film, frowning as if in concentration rather than repentance.

"In case you don't know," Dakota said, " 'venereal' only means genital. If you get a wart, they remove it with an electric cauterizing needle. My ex-boyfriend had them all the time. The dermatologist shoots your shaft with novocaine, and you don't feel a thing when they scorch them. What do you want me to do by way of posing?"

Over the years, Frankle had learned that the least erotic postures were the most orchestrated ones. Moreover, what he usually found sexy in the viewfinder rarely printed sexy. Experience had taught him to encourage the model to use her imagination.

"I'm not here," he said. "It's between you and the camera."

Four rolls of film later, Frankle went downstairs with her. Since they were both heading downtown, Frankle agreed to ride with her to Fifty-ninth Street, where he would disembark to drop the film for pickup.

13

Down in the lobby, Stanley Stark stood reading a poster on a cross-country skiing marathon organized to raise funds to battle an acquired immunological disease contracted through sexual intercourse.

"Gonorrhea," Stark said nostalgically. "Remember that one? A tough, old-fashioned, commensurate-to-the-crime disease compared to these postmodern viruses that eat into your organs and brain and kill you. How remarkable—we are each hazardous-waste sites. Shocking."

He crumpled up the bulletin and pocketed it. Frankle introduced him to Dakota Pomeroy.

"You're awfully young to be bald," she said.

"Born this way, I'm afraid."

"You mean you were bald as a little boy?"

"Utterly. And yet my penis was a fully developed, man-size organ by the age of five."

Dakota turned to Frankle.

"He's a lawyer," Frankle said.

Stark was scrutinizing the model with a lasciviousness Frankle associated with Bernheim, his bald-headed former boss.

"Age five," Stark said. "Bald with a twelve inch—"

Frankle interrupted Stark to ask just what the hell he was doing loitering in the lobby.

"Didn't my secretary confirm our dinner plans?"

"I get it now," Dakota said. "You're Jewish." And she added abruptly, "Don't get the wrong impression. My real name's Deb Stein. Dakota's only my stage and working name."

"I knew," Stark said, "something explained our instant chemistry. Didn't you yourself feel that same chemistry the minute our eyes met? Be honest."

"Chemistry?"

"Have dinner with me," Stark said.

She reached out and massaged his head. "I wouldn't mind, but I booked a previous engagement."

They went outside, and Dakota drifted toward Columbus Avenue to flag a cab. Traffic was backed up as far as Frankle could see.

"Wait a second," Stark said. "What are you saying? You take dates?"

"When I need the money."

"Tonight, for example. This booking?"

"What is it you're asking me? How much I'd charge you?"

"Ballpark figure," Stark said.

"It depends on what you want." She waved for a vacant cab, but a young couple ran through traffic to claim it.

"See me later tonight," Stark pressed.

Dakota dug a card from her wallet, outlined a heart in red ink, and presented it to Stark, who studied the card before slipping it carefully into his wallet.

"The Y," he told Frankle, "has a meat-loaf special tonight. As a resident, I can bring a guest for a ten-percent discount."

"The Y?" Frankle couldn't suppress his incredulity.

"Didn't I tell you last week I was living there?"

"Last week you disappeared in a cab."

"Well, last week I moved into the Sixty-third Street YMCA."

Frankle searched his friend's eyes. "Have you lost your mind, Stanley?"

"What's wrong with the Y?" Stark appealed defensively to Dakota. "Cafeteria, pool, weight room, various adult classes. All for one tenth the cost of my mortgage, which comes complete with my ex-wife's ghost and aborted baby's bloody fingerprints." Stark turned back to Frankle. "I sublet the brownstone for two thousand a month."

Frankle wondered aloud where Susan was supposed to live and practice when she returned from California.

"It's better that Susan relocate. That hit man knows my address. Death threats have spread from my office to the house answering machine. Which reminds me, Thomas. Bought a handgun three days ago from a transient down the hall, name of Oops. Next day he threw an empty pint of gin over the Y roof, then followed after it. Security guard tells me they average two a month."

Stark removed a polished silver pistol with black plastic hand grips.

"Would you mind putting away the gun?" Frankle said.

Stark made a show of restoring the pistol to a pocket beneath his polyester overcoat.

Dakota seemed impressed. "Come with me to Broadway. I need a man to help me catch a cab." She took his arm. "You can wait for me in the lobby while I finish my appointment. Then take me to dinner."

"Fabulous!" Stark escorted her away, without another word or sign to Frankle, who himself proceeded south to the Sixth Avenue lab, whence Dakota's negatives would be pouched to New Jersey for development. From the lab, it was a short walk to St. Patrick's Cathedral.

Because his mother had been Episcopalian and his father Jewish, Frankle was raised without religion. Apparently, great books, faith in human progress, and organized athletics were supposed to fill the void. That they hadn't wasn't only Frankle's problem, but he took it personally.

Because of recent vandalism, the cathedral was locked from midnight till six in the morning. Frankle was the only one left in the place when he was asked to depart.

The internal voice recited:

For every one that doeth evil hateth the light, neither cometh to the light, lest his deeds should be reproved.

Frankle flipped to another page.

Let him drink and forget his poverty, and remember his misery no more.

This Frankle did, at a place uptown, with a green clover leaf on the neon sign.

14

In the morning, Frankle found two roaches drowned in the pot of leftover coffee. While water heated in the kettle, Frankle applied boric acid beneath the kitchen sink. Though he felt less than ecumenical about murdering cockroaches by way of dehydration, he knew that the eight sightings of the previous week (two by clients) would become sixty-four, and that the sixty-four would multiply to 4,096 within the course of one wintry month, requiring a mass chemical slaughter by Armed Forces Day. To avoid this, Frankle entreated That Voice to forgive him the trespass and distributed the poisonous powder. When he had finished, the kettle screamed concurrent with the intercom's signal.

"Yes?"

"Delivery for Thom Frankle."

The telephone rang.

Frankle asked the deliverer to please bring up whatever it was he was delivering.

"Hello?" Frankle said into the telephone.

The operator inquired if anyone would accept charges from Constance Frame.

"I will," Frankle said.

"Go ahead, please."

"I thought," Constance Frame began, "that you'd be in the Caribbean by now."

Frankle cleared his throat. "I lied about that to sound busy." He reached for his cigarettes and lit one. "Why are you calling collect? You out of town?"

"I'm in Boston and didn't have enough change."

"Is anything wrong?"

She told him an explanation was too complicated to go into on his nickel.

"I was wondering about your apartment, Thom. Is it still available?"

He told her, calmly, that it was, then asked, "Why?"

"You remember that guy I mentioned? The actor from Jersey City?"

"Gus somebody?"

"Right. The jerk slapped me, and I moved out."

"He hit you!"

"It was only a slap. But still."

"What are you doing in Boston?"

"I'm staying with my stepparents. They've been taking care of my son."

Frankle slowly settled into a chair.

"Your son?"

"I guess I never told you about Nick, did I?"

"I don't believe you did, no."

"It's why I was calling, actually. To see if you'd be amenable to my moving in with him. He's seven. I thought I'd better give you a chance to think about it."

"I don't have to think about it."

"What does that mean?"

"Just tell me when you think you guys will be here."

"Hold it, hold it! There's one more thing." She told him she'd have to postpone the first month's payment until after the first of the year, by which time her finances would be better organized and she'd reimburse him.

Frankle reiterated that she didn't have to pay him if she was broke.

"It's the only way I'd stay."

"However you want to work it," Frankle said.

Well, she thought it would be a good idea for him to think it over carefully; she would call him in a few days, around Christmas.

"I'll be here," Frankle said.

Constance sounded relieved. "The thought of looking for a new apartment has been giving me bad dreams."

Frankle suggested they select a specific day when she would call to let him know exactly when she'd be coming down.

"I want you to think about us living there, Thom. Because I'll be enrolling Nick in a school downtown."

"The only way to find out," he said, "is to give it a try."

"I'll call you the day before Christmas," she told him. "I'll feel better if you think it over." She sighed. "You ever get the feeling your life's completely out of control?"

"All the time."

"What do you do about it?"

"To be honest, I sit in empty churches and try to find consolation."

"Really?"

He asked for her number in Boston, but she said she didn't know it and was calling from a phone booth outside Nick's school.

"Just make sure, please," Frankle requested, "that you call back."

As he hung up, he remembered the delivery man, who hadn't delivered anything. Grabbing a green plastic bag of garbage, Frankle descended in his bathrobe to the mailboxes. To his consternation, his box was empty.

He tightened his bathrobe in the foyer and then peeked out the door both ways before stealthily dragging the green bag to the sidewalk. It was cold enough now that the city didn't smell of garbage, and Frankle breathed deeply as he closed his eyes and raised his face to the weak wintry sun.

When he opened them again, he noticed an Airedale tied to a parking meter several yards down the block. For sentimental reasons, he started over, holding his robe closed at the neck and knees. Halfway there, he realized the terrier was Jack.

Frankle untethered the excited idiot and watched him bound down the sidewalk to mark the first tree he came upon. Frankle called out, and the terrier raced back, reaching up to lick him while jumping excitedly on his hind legs. Frankle removed an envelope attached to his tags.

I asked Victor's driver to drop Jack with you. Given the vindictive means you used to keep him from me, I hope you enjoy having him back. As it turns out, I'm back myself in Manhattan, finished with Victor and forced by contractual mandate to resume working exclusively on "Still Lives." Since I'll be shooting all day, I figured it would be fairer for Jack to stay with you—so long as I'm allowed visiting privileges.

It was destined to be a day of one surprise after another. Frankle returned from an afternoon run in the park with the Airedale to discover the door to his neighbor's apartment held open by a military duffel bag. Inside the apartment, a suitcase had been emptied all over the living room floor. Frankle stepped over the duffel bag and called to Chambers, whom he subsequently beheld sitting before closed blinds in the dark, smoking a cigarette and still wearing his coat and round, mirror-fronted sunglasses.

"Welcome back."

Chambers nodded expressionlessly and reached into an

open box packed with straw. To Frankle's astonishment, he removed an automatic weapon.

"Thought you'd get a kick out of this." Chambers stood, allowing the weapon to dangle at his side as he extinguished his cigarette. He held the weapon as if he'd carried it before.

"Wonderful weapon, this," he said hoarsely. "Uzi submachine gun. Finest weapon of its type. Manufactured by our Old Testament friends. Thirty-two-round magazine and a feather-light folding stock for convenient carry. Our very own secret service use it."

Chambers held it out for Frankle to examine, but Frankle maintained his distance.

"Don't be afraid," Chambers said. "It's a replica. They all are."

He tossed the weapon onto the sofa and withdrew another from the packing.

"Here's my favorite." He aimed the pistol at Jack, who was sniffing in the kitchen. "U.S. government forty-five automatic. Officer's pistol. Used against Nazis, Japs, and Koreans. Not to mention anything that moved in Vietnam. Incredible knockdown power. She's your classic knock-'em-downer sidearm."

Chambers tossed the gun to Frankle, who caught it while watching Chambers dig out another weapon.

"Now, this one is clearly the worst piece of crap ever constructed for any fighting man in history. M-sixteen assault rifle. When you come under fire and need to bust caps, she's guaranteed to jam on you half the time. Twenty-round magazine and select fire. Should have been sold to Combloc forces, but the Communists know better."

Frankle tossed the pistol onto the sofa. "Put the damn things away."

"I'm showing you facsimiles!" Chambers put his hand to his head as if in pain, then slowly settled back on the sofa.

"These antidepressants make you feel like you're swimming through air. Stand up too fast and your head blacks out and starts to float. Sort of like when you trip a toe popper."

Frankle saluted in farewell and turned away.

"Come back later, and I'll show you the rest of the collection."

Frankle locked and chained his apartment door behind him.

15

With Christmas coming, Frankle volunteered to prepare breakfast three days a week for the homeless at the church across the street. He worked with two elderly women who spoke only Spanish; and worse still, his Cream of Wheat and fried eggs, begun nobly at 6 A.M., were not eaten by the time the cafeteria closed, two hours later. It seemed most of the wrecked men were so ravaged by booze they could manage only instant vegetable broth or black coffee. Frankle suspected he was wasting his time, though he didn't know what else to do with it.

Yet by his third day in the kitchen, Frankle could better accept that he would have to have been a deity to stomach many of the flock he was serving; and he wondered if he was serving them merely to justify photographing the particular disasters present in the faces that warily volunteered to face his camera. Over the weekend, he photographed a dozen homeless men, then ran in the park to keep from considering that while photography was the only living he was trained to make, he wasn't making a living at it—and could well be homeless himself by spring.

In fact, head-shot work fell off so precipitately that after a client canceled her Tuesday two o'clock, Frankle set a tripod holding a telescopic-lensed, time-triggered 35-millimeter on the fire escape outside an open living room window and aimed it at his kitchen table, where he and the terrier sat staring vacantly. Though he had hoped for a Hopperesque twist of a Wegman subject, the derivative results felt so discouraging that Frankle closed the window and opened the whiskey. He was drunk when the telephone rang.

"Pamela Sales," the voice said, "of *Trend* magazine calling for Thom Frankle."

"This is he," Frankle said, slurring slightly.

"Hold for Pamela Sales, please."

Once on the line, Pamela Sales said, "Hi there, Mr. Frankle. Kikki Epstein gave me your phone number. What's new and different?"

"Just trying to beat a thousan' hol-day deadlines!"

"Don't I know!"

Frankle asked Pamela Sales to hold on a second and shouted to Jack, who was mashing a Milk-Bone two feet away, "Tell Elliot Howard I can't worry about the William Morris policy! My last contract requires twice that payment. End of conversation!"

Frankle cleared his throat and lowered his voice to an urbane register. "I'm sorry. You were saying?"

"Terri Max gave me your name." And Pamela Sales proceeded to discuss an April special the magazine was calling "Celebrities' Pets." "Have you worked with animals before?"

Frankle skipped over the neo-expressionist bestiality special he had test-shot for *Concupiscence* the preceding year and referred instead to a free-lance portraiture assignment with a dog he had completed that very afternoon.

Pamela Sales thought that was fine. "Let's understand one thing from the start, Thom. In terms of tone, *Trend* is very different from *Concupiscence*, and I want us to be together on the tone of this shoot. I want something cute. How we doing so far?"

"Time."

"Locationwise, you'll be working with the celebs in their respective homes, which we want incorporated into the shoot as much as possible. The schedule requires two shoots a day for ten days. All the pets will be either cats or dogs or cats *and* dogs. We'll go with the subtitle 'Manhattan's Reigning Cats and Dogs.' We're punning on the old cliché about raining cats and dogs."

"Exciting." Frankle finished his drink.

"We're really excited about it too. We're psyched!"

Frankle was certain other photographers had wanted either too much money or nothing to do with the idiotic concept, and he was determined to demand two hundred a day above expenses—otherwise, no dice.

"We plan to complement your prints with a really cute essay by one of our staff writers, who's volunteered to pretend she's a dog for an entire day and write about it from that dog's point of view. She'll literally crawl around on all fours from nine to five. She's calling the piece 'Dog Daze.' Now, re the fee schedule. We can offer you one hundred a day plus expenses. The kill fee's fifteen percent of that, but let's be optimistic."

Frankle poured more whiskey, momentarily missing the target completely.

"I'll take it," he said, and knocked back the drink.

"One last thing, then, Thom. *Trend*'s list of celebrities is going to remain classified information. We've gone top secret with our free-lance people, due to a disastrous flood of leaks to our competitors. We'll work it this way: one of our people will chauffeur you to each celebrity location on the prearranged day. You won't know where you are going or whom you are shooting, until just before. *There will be no list.* Moreover, we're going to ask you to keep the general assignment strictly confidential. Are we together on this security point?"

Once Frankle had pledged his allegiance, Pamela Sales told

him the contract would be in the mail the following day and that he should expect to hear from her sometime right after the first. She hoped one day to meet him.

That night, Frankle crawled under the covers to listen to a ten o'clock call-in radio program on the Second Coming. Many of the callers feared they had blasphemed the Holy Ghost and would be condemned to hell. Brother Camp assured each that the very fear of blasphemy indicated piety. Then there was a lot of talk of the coming kingdom of Christ's thousand-year reign and the attendant peace and prosperity of the elect.

Be not faithless, That Voice admonished, *but believing*.

With the telephone's fourth ring, Frankle realized the answering machine was off and picked up.

"Hi, Thom. It's me."

Frankle closed his eyes. "I can't talk now."

"You just did!" Monica Webb said.

Frankle clicked off the radio, then moved from bed, walking the telephone to the glass sliding door. "What can I do for you?"

"Guess."

Because he suspected he already had, he said, "I'm very busy in the darkroom."

"Does that mean you miss me and can't sleep?"

"Everything's fine."

"I feel sorry about what happened, Thom."

"We survived."

The blast of a truck's air horn sounded, followed by the scream of brakes.

"Where are you?"

"The sliding door at the terrace."

"Can you see me? I'm still at the studio."

Frankle squinted at the glass ABC complex, two blocks to the south.

"No."

"I can't see you either."

"Is there anything specific you wanted to talk to me about?"

"Our apartment."

"Not tonight, if you don't mind."

"What would you like to do tonight?"

"Monica," he said solemnly, "we've both been through too much to—"

"Skip the lecture! I'm going to need Jack next week for a shoot."

"Okay."

"It's something my agent wants me to do for the publicity. Something about celebrities and their pets."

"For *Trend*?"

"How'd you know? Did they leave word at our apartment?"

"Exactly."

It unnerved him to hear her refer to the place as theirs— not from sentiment so much as from self-protection. Where would he go if she demanded he recognize her legitimate claim on the apartment?

"Let me just say something, Thom. We agreed when we first met that I was allowed my flings, as were you; and we promised to be brave about it."

"I changed."

"No one changes, darling. They just behave differently. I know; I'm an actress. Thom, of all the affairs to take a stand on, why such a minor one? It's really so typical of you, putting your foot down at the wrong time, and after five years of—"

Frankle said good night and hung up.

He opened the burglar gate, stepped onto the terrace, and performed push-ups to calm himself. But the position only generated memories of Monica beneath him, and the ensuing fantasy was vindictive: Monica folded up and whispering submissive words of enthrallment. The buzzer signaled while he was performing jumping jacks.

Inside, he held his breath and pushed the upstairs intercom's Listen button; but he heard only wind whistling under the door of the foyer.

He put on pants beneath his bathrobe and tiptoed down the spiral stairs to make certain the chain lock was in place. In the process, he peeked through the peephole and saw that the hallway was empty.

But when he returned upstairs, he discovered Monica Webb, hands on her hips, wearing a *Still Lives* jacket. Smiling, she collapsed backward on the bed to roughhouse with Jack.

"You should get the lock on the foyer door changed."

"Not tonight, Monica."

"It's freezing in here. Since when do you keep the door wide open? 'Not tonight,' what?"

"*This*," he said.

"So you say. Yet leaving the gate open is something of a giveaway, don't you think?"

"Jack had to take a leak." He closed the door.

"I think a whiskey would make talking about the apartment a whole lot easier for both of us. No ice, please."

"Just one."

"Don't worry, fella. I won't let you get me drunk."

When he returned upstairs with the two drinks, Monica was under the covers with Jack, and her clothes lay in a pile on the floor.

"What do you think you're doing?"

"Getting warm. Which one of those is mine?"

He reached her one.

"Cheers." She sat up, the blankets held to her chest, and drank.

Frankle leaned against the wall and sipped his drink.

"I want to get something straight between us," she said.

"That's high school stuff, Monica."

"You're the guileful one, Thom. For example, *I* didn't hide my infidelities."

"On the other hand," Frankle said angrily, "I wasn't the one who emptied my closet and drawers. Nor was I the one to steal the dog."

"Don't be petulant, Thom. It's embarrassing."

"*You* moved out."

"I did not move out," she said calmly. "I took a vacation with a person you didn't approve of. Get in bed already."

Frankle wanted to glower, but wound up passing his hand over his eyes in exasperation.

"The sublet scares me." She was acting girlish to get her way. "Someone's been phoning late at night."

"Who?"

"I thought maybe it was you."

"It wasn't me."

"Some pervert, then. He knows my name."

The sheet and blanket dropped from one of her breasts; she watched him.

"I'm tired," Frankle said, "of the unkindness."

"The unkindness has been mutual!"

"Admittedly." Frankle polished off the drink. "And it harmed both of us."

"Because life isn't always the nice and easy thing we dream it ought to be."

He turned away to observe her reflection in the glass door; and he wondered about how much of what he had seen in her had been a reflection of aspects of himself he couldn't face.

"Please," he said, "get dressed and go." He turned, to see her smoking a cigarette.

"You opened that gate because you knew it was me."

"Possibly. I'll wait downstairs for you to get dressed."

He lay on the living room sofa. To sleep with her would only start it all over again. Frankle knew the course by heart and didn't need another crash on the rocks to convince him the destination would always end in catastrophe. Yet it frightened him to acknowledge how much a part of him longed for the theater of catastrophe, which, in its distracting theatricality, kept him from getting on with his life.

He could hear her moving around upstairs, and not long afterward she came down, her heels clacking cautiously on the narrow stairs.

He sat up.

"Just remember something," she said quietly. "Remember that you were the one who turned our relationship into something spiteful."

"I'm not being spiteful."

"What then?"

"Self-protective."

She smiled disdainfully. "You've never been anything but self-protective. Though self-involved would be closer. Why do you think I was always looking elsewhere?"

He stood. "I'm sorry."

"So am I. I was trying to make it easy for you."

She went out. Frankle locked the downstairs door and later the upstairs gate.

In bed, he lay as still as possible, his dog's head resting on his chest.

Let not your heart be troubled, whispered That Voice, *neither let it be afraid.*

16

Christmas Eve came, and Frankle hadn't heard from Constance. He felt stupid for having purchased a little spruce tree and decorated it with sparkling slivers of silvery synthetic. At least there was a little present for Jack (a new collar) under the conifer to lend holiday sentiment to the apartment.

The longer Frankle sat in front of the fire, sipping whiskey, the more aggravated he was with himself for not having demanded that Constance give him her stepparents' telephone number in Boston. He had called Information twice, but the list of twenty-seven Frames didn't yield a single clue.

Prokofiev's Piano Concerto No. 2 drove Frankle to drinking directly from the bottle; and he was searching his phone book for someone to call, when his phone rang.

" 'Lo?"

"Thom? Susan Stark speaking."

"Susan! Thom Frankle here!"

"You must be inebriated."

"Merry Christmas, Susan! Hey, how's Stan?"

"Frankly, I was hoping you might tell me. I haven't heard from him."

"Susan, listen. Merry Christmas. Seriously."

"I'm Jewish, Thom."

"So. You shop, don't you!"

Frankle squinted at the booze cabinet to see what was left.

"Thom," Susan said earnestly, "when I returned from California there were strangers living in my brownstone. They showed me an illegal assignment lease, and I was forced to bring in my lawyer and the sheriff to have them evicted. I'm beginning to think Stanley's suffered a psychotic break."

Frankle interposed that he hoped Susan was fully recovered and wanted to wish her the very best for the new year.

"What exactly has Stanley told you?" Susan asked.

Frankle jiggled a cognac bottle and heard a slosh.

"The one time Stan and I spoke, Susan, I was drinking, and you know how dark those blackout drunks can be!" Frankle laughed disconsolately.

"Do you have any interest in knowing what exactly is going on—or are you too drunk again?"

"To be perfectly honest," he said, "the actuality of things so tends to cut the heart out of me that I'm afraid I try to avoid what's going on."

Undeterred, Susan Stark explained that her California gynecologist had supervised a series of blood tests on her. He was looking for causes other than genetic or immunological that might explain the fetal deformity. Her results were nebulous, but he did find lesions in her uterus. Stanley had insisted that as long as he was in California, he, too, should undergo extensive testing; and the test revealed that he was infertile. At this point, Susan conceded, the story got rather too complicated to discuss over the telephone.

"To put it politely," she said, "and to summarize, Stanley reacted hysterically to the news. Speaking as a psychologist, I'm afraid my husband is now on the far side of a nervous breakdown."

Uncorking the cognac, Frankle admitted that so many of his friends seemed broken down or in the process of breaking down that he no longer possessed a basis of comparison.

"Presumably," Susan said, "you're referring to Harry Chambers. How is he?"

"Recovering."

"Where?"

"Where else? Next door."

"Next door?" Susan sounded incredulous. "That man would profit considerably from long-term hospitalization and psychopharmacological treatment."

"Who wouldn't, Susan!" Frankle drank directly from the bottle.

"I've never known you to be so aggressively puerile, Thom. I'm really disappointed." She sounded exasperated and hurt. "Stanley's been under enormous strain of late. The impregnation, or should I say the manner in which I was forced to disclose the impregnation, seems to have exacerbated his predisposition for vindictive reprisal. Yours, too, for that matter. It's bad enough that his messiah complex keeps him up till all hours of the night researching environmental issues he thinks about in the most apocalyptic terms. Add vengefulness to the equation, and you can imagine the level of our aloneness."

"For all we know, Susan"—Frankle paused to pull on the cognac—"the guy's correct in his jeremiads. Did you hear about the Soviet meltdown?"

"Stanley," Susan said imperviously, "has become obsessive about his eating habits. Anorexia is rare in heterosexual males, which gives one pause, especially in light of Stanley's phobia about everyone being systematically poisoned. It's so clearly symptomatic of—"

"Did he mention to you," Frankle interrupted, "that he's received death threats from the Mafia and that he's bought a handgun?"

"No," Susan said meditatively, "but I'm afraid it's not inconsistent. To be perfectly blunt—and I'm telling you this because you're his closest friend—if I haven't located Stanley by tomorrow, I'm going to the police. Is Monica there, by any chance?"

"Monica and I split up for good, Susan."

"She intimated as much months ago. Your choice of words is interesting."

"What choice of words?"

" 'For good.' "

"Susan, if Monica wants to throw her money away on word games with you, that's her business—and yours. I myself don't go in for the stuff."

"That's a complicated statement, Thom. And resistance is an even more complicated phenomenon. But returning to Stan, I'd hate to be required to commit him."

"Can you do something like that?"

"With the assistance of colleagues and my lawyer, absolutely."

"On what grounds would you have him committed?"

Susan exhaled exhaustedly. "It's the holiday season, Thom. His death-threat fantasy is more than likely a projection of suicidal impulses: in this case, the conscious anxiety about death revealing the unconscious wish for immolation."

Frankle stumbled as he bent to ball up some of the evening paper to fuel the burning logs. The blood-red headline announced that due to explosions and fires at a toxic-chemical dump across the river in New Jersey, local authorities recommended area residents to remain indoors. Frankle turned to the window. The foggy firmament appeared weirdly iridescent with ambient light, and scudding clouds, greenish and gigantic, crashed through skyscrapers, obscuring their summits.

But if we hope for what we see not, That Voice intoned, *then we do with patience wait for it.*

"Thom?" Susan Stark said.

"Come to think of it, Susan," Frankle said, "I suddenly

recall Harry Chambers mentioning something about Stanley staying at the Y."

"I learned that much yesterday from the illegal tenants," Susan said.

"Then Chambers did know something?" Frankle didn't know why he was perpetuating this lie.

"What he didn't know was that Stanley moved out of the Y two days ago."

"Have you any idea to where?"

"Isn't that precisely what I'm pestering you about?"

"You'll have to speak up, Susan—we've a bad connection."

"I've been to his office," Susan Stark shouted, bad-temperedly. "His supervising attorney insists Stanley hasn't been there in a week, due to the death threat. The attorney general's office apparently has approved his working and living in an undisclosed location until the Kenway Hauling Company is brought to trial."

"Yes," Frankle said somberly. "Stan claims the mob's after him."

"We've already been through that. Or haven't you been listening?"

"Look, Susan—"

"No, Thom, *you* look. In view of the fact that Stanley's never won a case, and that he's never even gone to trial before this suit and is notorious for settling out of court over long lunches—in view of this, I rather doubt someone is gunning for him. Talk about grandiosity!"

"For all we know, Susan," Frankle countered, "Stan's right about the world ending in environmental catastrophe. The reports on the ozone indicate increases way beyond the worst projections, and there's been a rash of unexplained dolphin deaths all along the East Coast."

"Stop it, Thom! You and Stanley can externalize your anxieties and angers however you wish. To me, Stanley wants not only to unconsciously kill himself but to kill me as well for hiring someone to impregnate me. Once the California specialists insisted Stanley's condition was congenital, how could I possibly deny some kind of subterfuge?"

Frankle claimed a blinding headache, requiring that he continue this conversation at another time.

Susan Stark suggested that they arrange now to meet some other time, for a drink.

"Between your breakup and mine, Thom, I think we each might find a heart-to-heart salutary."

Frankle promised to call her later in the week and hung up, eyes fixed on the disquieting fog.

The doorbell rang.

Frankle opened to Harry Chambers, who stood in the hallway in a military raincoat and aviator glasses.

"Inviting you for a drink with me and Mr. Busch."

Frankle heard Chambers's printer clacking away and smiled drunkenly.

"You're really working away in there!"

"Just a record I play to fool you. Spend all day at my desk, staring out the window with a gun to my head."

Chambers handed Frankle the address of a swank new restaurant on upper Broadway.

"By the way," he said, "I've got to hit you for a loan. I'm totally broke."

"Broke! You just sold a book!"

"For five grand. Which didn't last five minutes. Debts owed, back rent, you name it."

Frankle mustered a dismissive tone of high spirits. "You and I, Harry, we're in the same boat. I'm broke myself!" Frankle proceeded to recommend that Chambers try a roommate to decrease expenses. "It's what I'm doing," he said.

"Couldn't possibly do that," Chambers said. "Privacy's an absolute necessity for a writer."

For an instant, Frankle drunkenly closed his eyes and pictured a woman with cascading hair and a sliding eye. Then there was the image of Harry Chambers, glowering.

"Harry, how can I give you what I don't have? You want fifty bucks, I'll go to the bank machine for you."

Chambers smiled oddly. "I don't know why you're bullshitting me. Because I've got you in my will. Any loan would be guaranteed, if that's what you're worried about."

"Worried?"

Chambers looked down the hallway to the stairwell. "Come by later. Busch is buying."

Frankle reached out for Chambers and patted his shoulder. "I'm not bullshitting you, buddy. If I had it, you know I'd give it to you."

Chambers stepped away. There was a paranoid quality to his withdrawal. "The nice things we would all do for each other, if only we could." The sardonic tone silenced Frankle.

Starting down the steps, Chambers added, "Join us now, Frankle. I'm told by the experts that it's dangerous to drink alone."

17

When she hadn't called by nine, Frankle headed north on Broadway for that drink with Harry Chambers. Though New Year's Eve was still a week away, cliques of pre-Christmas postadolescents, many wearing pointed hats and blowing coiled noisemakers, flaunted their mirth with hoots and shouts.

The crowd at the restaurant revealed a comparable mania, and Frankle chose to believe his own dementia was ennobled by virtue of his restrained comportment. The place was mirrored from floor to ceiling, and though no one else seemed to notice, Frankle counted ten stoical reflections of himself. Even more bizarre, black Formica tables and polyurethaned woodwork reflected in such a way as to bestow a sense of infinity to the sissified setup.

Frankle winnowed his way to an open space at the varnished bar and ordered a whiskey. Failing to find Chambers, he conferred with the headwaiter, who informed him that the Gordon Busch party wasn't expected until eleven.

Frankle was studying the geometry of the ice cubes in his highball when he felt a tapping on his shoulder. The room spun in his eyes as he turned.

Monica Webb smiled, then kissed him.

"I'm with people. Join us."

She pointed to a table of two young men and a middle-aged woman, before pressing against Frankle and sending a shiver of longing through him.

"I'm expected uptown in a minute."

"Come on," she said. "How many demerits can there be for tarrying amidst a harmless temptation?"

"This isn't a soap opera, Monica."

"Isn't it?"

Light glinted in her eyes, which narrowed as her expression took on a quality of mischief and challenge. Frankle felt his arm stray to encircle her waist as he stared at the glinting necklace.

"I bought you this." He touched her jewelry.

"Would you order us some champagne, please."

Their eyes held; and all restraint vanished.

He bought two champagnes and joined her in a quiet corner, darkly recessed to accommodate a cigarette machine.

"What are your friends going to think?" he said.

"Ask me if I could care less."

They touched glasses and drank.

"I like you so much right now," she said. "Are you drunk?"

"No," he told her drunkenly. "Want to come over and watch the fireworks?"

"They're not for another week."

He stepped closer and whispered his answer.

"Gosh." She affected breathlessness. "Let me hurry away and get my coat."

As he watched her return to the table, Frankle noticed Harry Chambers moving through the crowd on the arms of two sleek black women, followed by a young man with startling white hair and faded blue eyes. The music seemed suddenly too loud, and Frankle absconded to the street with the champagne glass concealed beneath his overcoat. He flipped

up the collar and turned his back to the wind as he finished
the drink.

I have a few things against thee, That Voice began, but then
Monica Webb was beside him, yanking him into the street
and calling out for a cab.

As if each wanted something back from the other, perhaps
lost illusions or lost time or lost esteem, they went at it
ravenously on the foldout upstairs. Afterward, Frankle lay
dazed and silent, entwined languorously against Monica's
smoldering body. She felt small and vulnerable in his arms,
and Frankle couldn't decide whether the anguish in his heart
was born of a desire to apologize from love or annihilate her
from hate. And it began to frighten him to consider how
erotically drawn he was to a woman he did not esteem, and
the idea that he had screwed Monica because he was furious
with hurt at someone named Constance Frame made him sit
up and hug his knees. And when she moved her hand along
his back, he understood more vividly than he cared to how
often he had turned away from her like this in the past. How
had he expected her to respond to such detachment? Had
he expected her to solve his ambivalence and then come to
hate her for not making him love her?

"Thom," she whispered.

He turned his head and saw her eyes staring up in the dark.
"Hey."

"Why does it have to be so good?"

"I know." He lit a cigarette and exhaled smoke.

"We should have done this all along," she said dreamily.

"What's that?"

"Just been lovers."

He faced her fully, moving closer, but not close. "Lovers?
In what sense?"

"In the sense that we quit pretending to enjoy the domestic
trappings."

He extinguished the cigarette. "Isn't that pretty much what we did?"

She pulled him to herself.

"We lived such a lie, pretending we wanted to see each other every day, in the stupid belief that if we couldn't be everything to each other we had no business playing together sexually."

The cadence of her speech told Frankle she was acting now, maneuvering him, but he had always too willingly allowed himself to be maneuvered. He lay very still beside her.

She stared into his eyes. "Thom, I like us as lovers. Do I have to give that up because I don't like living with the person I like making love to?"

Frankle stared back, frozen.

"You're no different, Thom. As much as you may want to deny it out of some fancy notion of yourself, you're no different."

He kissed her, then rolled to the clock, which indicated the time to be after two. More than anything, he wanted her to leave.

"Why didn't we make this space the bedroom?"

"You were always cold up here." He spoke with his back to her.

"I'm not now."

He squeezed her hand before standing from the bed and putting on a robe. "I'll be right back."

He went at once to the terrace with the hope of seeing stars. For some reason he imagined stars would calm him; but the sky was still an eerie ceiling of muddy clouds.

A light went on in Chambers's duplex. Then another light, more luminescent, washed across the roof. Frankle raised his eyes in time to see a full moon emerge, then disappear, eclipsed again by clouds.

The lock to Chambers's gate clicked, and the white bars swung open, succeeded by the spectral appearance of Chambers and the three Frankle had seen earlier; and it sounded as if others were congregated inside the study, laughing there.

"Ah!" Chambers said drunkenly, and proceeded to introduce Frankle to Gordon Busch, who stepped forward into another splash of moonlight to shake hands.

"Your neighbor here," Busch said too loudly, "ought better to wear a drinking helmet. Type Mr. William Holden ought better to have been wearing before taking his fatal fall."

A head emerged from the study. "Lines are drawn, gents."

His eyes widening, Busch said to Frankle, "Come celebrate Hanukkah with our Long Island set and their initialed spoons."

Frankle demurred, indicating his own company with a nod of the head, and ducked inside.

"Who's screaming out there?"

"Harry's friends."

Frankle slid under the covers.

"I wish he'd kill himself already." Monica rubbed playfully against him. "I'd love to get his lease and break through."

Frankle pulled her to him.

"He annoys me with his suffering," Monica said. "My father did that for as long as I can remember. He even made a show of his suicide."

Frankle moved her until she was partially impaled. She gasped and pressed closer. He suspected she was talking about her attitude toward him as much as toward her father. Of course, on some level it explained her attraction to him, and her contempt; and it was her contempt that he used to justify his contempt for her.

It didn't take much before she was crumpled beneath him, her ankles on his shoulders, and her eyes stunned and wide-eyed in surrender. She submitted by night, he by day; the exchange left them equally unhappy and alone.

Afterward, when he asked if she'd like to join him in a whiskey, she requested a club soda.

Downstairs, he sipped the booze and stared out the living room window at the empty avenue, in which newsprint swirled in the wind. It was Christmas, which made his vindictive game of Got You Last difficult to stomach.

She was asleep when he returned to the bed. He sat beside her, chasing his whiskey with her club soda, wondering if he had the courage to part with her without the malignant consolation of having been the wronged one.

18

The fierceness of the hangover obliged Frankle to grope blindly, in a hurricane zigzag across the room, for the ringing telephone.

"Hello?"

"Thomas Frankle?"

Frankle cleared his throat and opened his eyes.

"Speaking."

Outside, snow mixed silently with the morning's drizzle.

"In your opinion, Thomas, does one know when one loses one's mind, or does it come on like sleep, so that the transition isn't sensed?"

Frankle turned back to the bed. Monica was gone; a note lay on her pillow.

"It's too early in the morning for this kind of thing, Stan."

"Morning? It's two-thirty in the afternoon."

Frankle slid beneath the comforter, laced with Monica's perfume, and pulled the heavy thing up to his chest before draping an arm over his eyes.

"Susan's been looking for you."

"So's a hit man for Kenway Hauling and Disposal Company. And when the company learns of the testimony I've taken from indicted independent producers, their hired hooligan will be under accelerating pressure to blow away my prosecutorial ass."

Frankle moved cautiously to finish the club soda resting on top of the radio. Jack lay at the foot of the bed, his legs splayed to reveal his weeny nosing pinkly from its sheath.

"I understand you've moved out of the Y."

"For reasons just presented. Cohabiting at present with Deb Stein, whom you know as someone named after a northern plains state. She's working in Westchester this morning, with a couple who pay her to—"

"Did you know," Frankle interrupted, "that Susan had some tenants evicted from your building by her lawyer and a sheriff?"

"Listen, Thomas. It's important we stick to the subject at hand. D.S. won't be back from Westchester until late. I've got midcourt Knick tickets. Would you . . ."

"No interest whatsoever."

"Speaking of sports, I'm afraid I aggravated my hernia the other night schtupping Deb. Handball's absolutely out. When or if I shall ever resume, I can't say. Do you remember the days when Fredrickson would run up the middle between Larsen and Case and how we thought our lives were going to be like that: Giants among men! Stark up the middle for ten, fifteen, twenty yards! Alas, Thomas, now it's always fourth and long, and one is perpetually forced to punt."

"Adulthood, Stan."

"I wouldn't blame biology. It's history. Overpopulation. Too many people seeking personal profit, fighting for a place at the feeding trough. As soon as Susan grants me a divorce, D.S. and I have a strategy regarding survival in the countryside. Which reminds me. Go ahead and guess how many insects per day a brown thrasher consumes."

The hangover demon bashed a pipe behind Frankle's eyes. He folded his hands on his chest but couldn't feel his heart beating.

"I haven't the slightest idea."

"Six thousand, one hundred and eighty! Or the Baltimore oriole, per minute: seventeen hairy caterpillars! This is nature's harmony, Thomas. Pesticides and insecticides have utterly fucked it up. Everything's poisoned now. Agribusiness spraying programs have doubled the quantity of their applications as the insects have grown resistant. So the insects survive as everything higher up the food chain contracts cancer. I needn't remind you that insects have been around for three hundred million years to our fractional four and a half million. They've weathered it all. We're not going to stop them with chlorinated hydrocarbon or organophosphate sprays. Flies shall inherit the earth."

"I can't listen to this anymore, Stan."

"Just a second, please. Let me ask you something. Did you ever hear of a hairy caterpillar developing resistance to a Baltimore oriole? Of course not. But the hairy caterpillar has developed resistance to malathion! Imagine it for a moment, Thomas. Fifty thousand new chemical compounds introduced into the environment since the time Alex Webster ran out of the fullback position for the Giants. Is it any wonder that by the year two thousand twenty percent of today's extant life forms will be driven to extinction? So I ask you, why in God's name am I wasting my time at the utterly ineffectual Environmental Protection Bureau?"

Frankle lit a cigarette and listened to Stark make clucking noises.

"Here's D.S. now, Thomas. Call me. We'll have lunch."

"Lunch? Why bother?"

"Strength to suffer, Thomas. Strength to suffer."

Descending to the living room, Frankle followed the Airedale, who got distracted by a fly. Frankle watched the big
terrier try to work the living room, cutting it in half like a
boxer, but he was having no luck with his faster, winged
opponent.

Frankle read Monica's note:

Thom, let's not give That up. Some people go their whole
life and never even know such intensity exists. Call me and
let me know what night this week's good for you.

She included her phone number.

He played one of her quadriphonic meditation records and
tried to sit quietly with his cup of coffee and hold his mind—
as the record jacket recommended—on a becalming image;
but the sitar music rankled rather than soothed his nerves,
and Frankle was once again in the world of buses and dead
brain cells. He returned upstairs to sleep it off.

Now, That Voice whispered, *the works of the flesh are man-
ifest, which are these: adultery, fornication, uncleanness, lasciviousness, idolatry, hatred, variance, emulations, wrath, strife,
envying, murders, drunkenness, revelings, and such like.* . . .

Laughter began. Frankle sat up, wide-eyed, and peeked
through the bamboo shades. He beheld Gordon Busch and
two black women sitting bundled in coats at a table on the
slushy roof. Busch was holding an umbrella above the two
women as they snorted cocaine from a round face mirror.
And balancing a tray in a parody of chic, Chambers appeared,
distributing Bloody Marys.

The buzzer sounded, startling Frankle. He pushed the intercom's Listen button for a clue to who might be in the
lobby but heard only car horns in the street.

"Yes?"

"Thom?"

"Yes?"

"It's Constance. Could you help me with the suitcases?"

Frankle thought he must be hearing things.

"Constance?"

"Open the door, please," she entreated.

He buzzed her in, then raced downstairs to toss the sheets in the bathroom hamper. Then he stepped into the shower before the water had warmed.

. . . the fruit of the Spirit is love, joy, peace, long suffering, gentleness, faith, meekness, temperance . . .

The doorbell rang.

"One second!"

Frankle rinsed off and wrapped himself in a terry cloth robe. When he opened the door, he saw her standing between two suitcases. Behind her, a little boy with black Buster Brown hair stood balancing a small suitcase on his head.

"Hi, Thom."

"Hi," Frankle said tightly. "Come in."

Her eye was sliding as she stepped inside, holding a little red jacket. The boy sidled close against her, holding her thigh, his head bashfully pressing her hip.

"Is something wrong?" she said weakly.

"Wrong?" He cleared his throat.

"You look so surprised. Didn't you get my phone message?"

He maneuvered around them into the hallway and dragged in the suitcases.

"You called?"

"Last night."

It occurred to Frankle that he hadn't checked for messages after returning with Monica; and he was surprised that in his surprise he wasn't happier to see Constance.

"It's no problem," he said. "The machine screws up all the time."

"This is my son, Nick."

"Hello, Nick. I'm Thom."

The boy glanced at Frankle and then averted his eyes. Tail wagging, Jack sniffed a stuffed rabbit, similar to his own, dangling from Nick's hand.

"He's shy," Constance explained.

Frankle resisted the impulse to rough up the boy's hair with avuncular camp and led them into the living room. There, he apologized for still being in his bathrobe.

"Thom," Constance said, "why don't you put down those heavy suitcases."

He set them down, then abruptly picked them up.

"I'll put them in your bedroom. Would you like to see your bedroom?"

"Are you okay?"

"Fine. And you?"

"Oh, boy," Constance said.

He showed them their room, then the closets and later the bathroom.

"This is your side of the medicine cabinet."

Constance smiled.

"What?"

"You're very . . . organized."

"Would you prefer the other side or something?"

She grabbed his hands. "If you don't calm down you're going to make me nervous too."

Nick wandered back into the bedroom and lay quietly on the bed, staring at the ceiling.

"Little nap, Nicholas?"

The boy nodded to his mother, eyes fixed on the ceiling. Wanting to play, Jack stood on the bed, staring down at the boy. Constance quietly closed the door. Frankle remembered with what fear as a child he watched a door closing in his room. Of all the tormenting things intimacy could be for him, it was a feeling of a closed door in a windowless room that most frequently ruined it for him.

"Does he like the door closed?"

"He'll be fine."

He showed her the upstairs studio, cluttered with head-shot equipment. Then they stepped onto the rooftop terrace and surveyed the surrounding buildings. Frankle could hear Chambers telling a joke in the back garden.

"You're lucky to have such a nice place."

They returned inside. Constance put up a pot of coffee as Frankle dressed. When he joined her, he promptly poured whiskey into his cup, hoping it might ease his regret over the preceding night with Monica.

They were leaning against opposite walls in the kitchenette.

"Is Nick always so quiet?" Frankle asked for the sake of something to say.

Constance explained that since her husband's death, Nick had developed a stammer. "That makes him more tentative than usual around people."

He watched her mix honey in her coffee.

"Before I married Jack," she told him, "I lived with my twin sister. A month after I moved out to get married, Jane got married." She told him that after her parents had died in a car accident when she and Jane were three, they each suffered panic whenever they were left alone.

"I'm one of those people," she said, "who's always with someone, even if it's with a friend crashing at my place for half a year."

Rain began again, and Frankle watched it stream down the window beside Constance.

"Hey," he said. "I almost forgot! Merry Christmas!"

"Merry Christmas to you, too."

Frankle sneezed. "If I'd known you were definitely coming, I'd have made the place merrier."

"The place is just fine, Thom."

"I'll make a fire! Put on some music!"

They sat silently before the burning logs while Tyner played his piano.

Constance wanted to know what time in the morning would be best for her and Nick to use the bathroom.

"Whenever you want."

"What time do you wake up?"

Frankle studied her, as she stared into the fire. "What time do *you* wake up?"

"We're almost always out of the house by eight."

"That's about when I wake up."

"I guess that settles that." The wistfulness of her voice suggested she'd drifted off in thought.

Frankle mused himself, imagining them waking together in the same bed. It would be spring, and outside a window, a bird would be singing.

"I can see the ocean from my house in Venice." Constance stood to gaze out the window. "I just can't get used to these cityscapes."

"Neither can I."

"Why do you live here, then?"

Frankle mentioned his former work and girlfriend. "Now I guess it's just force of habit."

She turned to him. "It's just as well we don't run into each other in the morning. Bad dreams make me pretty terrible first thing."

"I have bad dreams myself."

She sat down on the sofa. "If someone had told me ten years ago that in my thirties the days would be easier to get through than the nights, I wouldn't have known what to make of it. I slept like a log until I was twenty-eight. Why am I telling you my boring little problems?"

"They're not boring." He felt more relaxed and smiled.

"Would you prefer keeping our groceries separate or all mixed up?"

"What's your preference?"

"Mixed up is nice. I'd feel more at home not worrying about whose ketchup I was using."

"Likewise."

"Am I being too willful?"

"We're just going over what's got to be gone over."

He showed her in what cabinets and drawers the silverware and glasses and plates were stored. Owning such artifacts suddenly seemed meaningful with a person who expressed interest in groceries and the refrigerator. Monica had trouble boiling water, and Frankle tended to eat from cans while working in the darkroom.

When Constance asked if he'd like to come downtown with her and Nick to a friend's apartment for Christmas dinner, Frankle, hung over, begged off. While she showered, he lay back on the living room rug and listened to the cascading water. He tried not to picture her, but he couldn't keep his mind from it.

When he woke, the apartment smelled of the charred pine logs, which glowed as embers now, and she and the boy were gone. He found a note, thanking him and saying they'd see him later.

He bundled up and walked down the block to the church. The choir was singing. He sat in the back of the chapel, crowded and brightly lit.

> Amazing Grace! how sweet the sound,
> That saved and set me free!
> I once was lost but now am found,
> Was blind but now I see.

They weren't back by the time he returned, but knowing that they would be gave Frankle a sense of shelter and hopefulness that he hadn't known in a long time; and so instead of begrudging the terrier his tedious late-night walk around the chilly block, Frankle escorted him six blocks up Broadway for ice cream, guessing he'd like the chocolate cone more than the strawberry cone Frankle took for himself.

19

The dishes she and the boy had used at breakfast stood washed in the wooden drying rack. Descending from the studio, Frankle studied them glinting in a shaft of sunlight that fell through a long eastern window. According to the note, she would be buying Nick additional winter clothes and then interviewing for a job.

Frankle thought of her later that morning while frying eggs for the neighborhood's homeless and again while running in the park, and still again that afternoon during his two head-shot sessions. Knowing she'd be back made the fading of the wintry light an invitation to intimacy and calm rather than the usual herald of fearful solitude.

The phone rang while he was preparing for the twilight ritual of walking the day's film to the lab. Dragging his leash, Jack zipped to the phone and knocked the receiver from its cradle.

"Thom Frankle," the woman said. "Pam Sales here. What's new and different?"

"Everything's just about the same, thanks."

"Would you believe I've left my office only twice in ten days! Between me and you and the spider in the corner, rumors are flying that there's a buyout of *Trend*, and nearly everyone's barricaded themselves in their offices. I've never seen so many closed doors. I'm snorting up a storm and circling the wagons. I bet you can hear the stuff frogging my voice? What's the weather like? My radiator's on full blast and totally steamed up my window."

"Typical post-Christmas stillness," Frankle told her. "The rich away. The stores dead."

Pamela Sales sneezed and put him on hold. When she returned, she got down to business, a frantic tone to her voice. "Tomorrow our driver will pick you up at eight sharp. You are responsible for loading all equipment. Our driver will not lift a finger, so be prepared. The shoot calls for an afternoon stop at 70 West 67th Street. Penthouse apartment 4 C. This will be on the itinerary, so don't bother taking notes now."

Frankle listened to papers crumpling.

"Also, Thom, there's no elevator, so be prepared for more lugging. Your client will be Monica Webb of *Still Lives* celebrity and her dog. Now let me get your address."

Frankle reached for a cigarette, his equanimity shot by the unfortuity of the coincidence.

"This is going to amuse you, Pam." And Frankle went on to explain, with a glibness that surprised him, about his recent breakup with the popular soap opera star and that the address Pamela Sales had given him was *his* address but no longer Monica Webb's.

"How incredible!" Shock registered in Pamela Sales's whisper. "Wow, Thom."

"Small world," Frankle offered.

Pamela Sales inhaled deeply. "Tell me something. And you better be honest. Is Monica really as awful as her Clara Ravens role makes you want to believe?"

"Off the record?"

"Absolutely."

Frankle suspected he couldn't trust Pamela Sales, and her sardonic assurance only confirmed his skepticism.

"She's the best. I'm still a big fan."

"This is *great*! We're planning a summer photo special on celebrities' partners, past and present, which we intend to entitle 'Who's Ex, Who's Next!' and we'd love to include you and Monica. You think she'd give it a shot?"

Frankle agreed to ask, though he had no intention of doing so. Pamela Sales was grateful and promised to await eagerly the arrival of the celebrity prints.

Returning from the lab, Frankle telephoned Monica from a Columbus Circle phone booth. He didn't want to bog down in difficulties with her if Constance Frame were in hearing range.

A recording of Monica's voice said, "We're not in. Leave your message, and either Rock or I will get back to you."

Frankle was about to hang up when Monica answered, breathlessly. "Hold on a second!"

Frankle heard muffled words exchanged.

"Hello?"

"It's Thom."

"What can I do for you?"

"I got your note."

"Next week's better for me, actually."

Her fickleness signaled in the darkly furtive tone.

"Listen," Frankle said. "I enjoyed the other night, but it can't happen again."

"I really can't talk about this now, darling."

"*Trend* magazine just called," he said calmly. "You should know that I'm the photographer assigned to shoot you."

"I'm afraid that's not the case, Thom."

"I'm afraid it is the case. Pamela Sales phoned me an hour ago to confirm."

"You're wrong, Thom. My agent received a call half an hour ago, canceling the deal."

Frankle frowned, confounded.

"The magazine canceled or your agent canceled you?"

"*Trend* canceled. Everyone there's been fired."

"You're joking."

"Why would I be joking? I've already rescheduled for a movie go-see. Not that you care, but my new agent's really pushing to test the exclusivity clause of my network contract. He wants me off that soap before I'm irreversibly typecast. Incidentally, the audition is for a triple-X film."

Frankle was alarmed over the loss of the thousand dollars his high hopes had prematurely deposited in the bank.

"I've got to run," he apologized, and told her to break a leg at the audition.

He dialed *Trend*.

"Pamela Sales, please."

"Pamela Sales is away from her desk," the man said. "Perhaps I can help you?"

Frankle introduced himself and explained his "Celebrities' Pets" assignment. He had to shout to be heard over an accelerating bus.

"Mr. Frankle," the man said. "Pamela Sales is no longer with *Trend* magazine. Neither am I, for that matter. And from what I've been told, neither are any of Pam's fresh and innovative concepts. All present assignments have been canceled or frozen until further notice."

"Including mine?"

"That would seem to be the appropriate inference."

Frankle squinted at the sarcastic tone. "When will Pam be back at her desk?"

"I couldn't say. As we speak, they're removing her name from the door. I had to raise my voice to save her plants."

Frankle assumed his most professional tone. "If we're really talking about cancellation, I'm going to need that kill-fee check yesterday."

"I'll notify our legal division about your request."

"Excuse me," Frankle said, "but I spoke with Pam less than two hours ago."

"Admittedly, Mr. Frankle, the timing of the announcement by our West Coast office has given umbrage to nearly everyone on eastern standard time. What else can I say?"

Jack didn't seem upset. The dimwit dragged a branch the ten blocks home, where Frankle mixed a cocktail and lay prostrate on the living room sofa: half a decade of calculated hack work, to end up broke!

The phone rang and the machine intercepted the call. Frankle listened as Chambers's amplified voice announced that he was at their neighborhood watering hole, buying drinks to celebrate a lucrative screenplay deal Gordon Busch had arranged; Frankle should join them.

Frankle nodded off until the doorbell sounded, and a moment later Constance Frame entered with a bag of groceries cradled in one arm. She held Nick's hand with her free hand.

"Is something wrong?"

"Wrong? No."

"Your face is completely flushed, Thom."

Frankle shrugged. "I've been sleeping."

He sat up and polished off his drink. Setting down the heavy bag in the kitchen, she looked tired.

"Would you prefer," she asked, "that I buzz before I come up?"

Frankle said that wasn't necessary and watched her yank a sweater over Nick's head and raised arms. Then Constance opened the refrigerator and poured three glasses of juice in the time it took Frankle to light his cigarette.

"Would you like to join us for spaghetti tonight?"

In gratitude, Frankle began preparing a vinaigrette, as

Constance diced a red pepper and mixed it with sauteeing parsley and mushrooms.

It was during Pharaoh Sanders's elegiac "Love Is Everywhere" saxophone solo, when Constance was quartering tomatoes and adding them to the smoking skillet, that Nick Frame, stricken, dashed into the busy kitchen, his dingaling caught in his fly.

The phone rang, and Frankle turned away from his vinaigrette, reaching the receiver before the answering machine clicked on.

"Would you please hold for Laurie Larsen?"

"Holding," Frankle said, watching Constance free her son's penis and scrutinize it.

"It's just a little scratch."

Laurie Larsen came on the line. "Thom, you rat, how'd you find out so fast?"

Frankle sat down. "Find out what?"

"That *Trend*'s been absorbed under the *Concupiscence* umbrella."

"Oh?"

"We're planning a thoroughly different look, target audience, and marketing attack strategy. We're upscaling with the hope of capturing what we think is still a no-man's-land readership between *People* and *Vanity Fair*."

"*You've* taken over for Pamela Sales?"

"That and a lot more. I'm the new publisher. Bernie bought me the magazine!"

Frankle congratulated her, then explained his thousand-dollar assignment with Pamela Sales.

"Pam Sales is gone, Thom."

"I'm just hoping my assignment isn't."

"What was your assignment?"

When Frankle told her, Laurie Larsen groaned.

"There's the problem with the old *Trend* in a nutshell. Puerility, fluff, and just plain bad taste. I'm going to set a sophisticated pace and just dare the others to try and keep up. *Trend*'s going to create the scene, not merely cover it."

Be that as it may, Frankle explained that he'd been promised a kill fee; and he hoped Laurie understood how much he was counting on that money.

Laurie Larsen understood quite well, but wondered why Thom insisted on working for peanuts.

"A thousand isn't peanuts."

"Yes it is, Thom."

"Laurie, I'd appreciate the kill fee."

She apologized and put him on hold. Across the room, Constance was chopping fresh basil and sprinkling it on the sauce. At her feet, Nick lay recuperatively, staring straight up.

Frankle had counted to ninety-six by fours when Laurie Larsen returned.

"Now, Thom, you worked long enough at *Concupiscence* to know we never wrote in kill fees. As for this *Trend* thing, it's going to take our new contracts department months and months to reorganize. Are you going to sue us over a legitimate delay?"

Frankle discovered Constance's eyes on him and walked down the hallway to whisper, "It's a matter of trying to make ends meet."

"Hey, Thom. Remember what I told you about calculation? At twenty-six, and with my own magazine, I can assure you I didn't get here by trying to make ends meet. Meanwhile, be assured that when my team's ready to take the field, I'll make certain to throw something your way."

Though Frankle was hardly excited about moving along the corporate trough from peanuts to table scraps, he said, "Thanks," and told Laurie Larsen he was certain she would be a great success. But in his unspoken contempt for her, Frankle recognized in his heart the tawdry expectation that she *owed* him something. That he might have surrounded himself with the ungenerous and amoral just so he could blame them took his breath away.

Laurie Larsen said, "Good luck, Thom. And *chin up*. Ciao."

Constance was tossing chives and chunks of blue cheese into a wooden salad bowl.

"Everything okay?"

"Fine." He poured himself three fingers of whiskey and knocked it back. Nick was seated at the kitchenette counter, patting lettuce leaves dry.

"How you doing, Nick?"

"G-good."

Constance bent to check on the burner's blue flame and Frankle stared.

"What can I do?"

"How about more crushed garlic in the vinaigrette?"

Frankle moved to her side, where he reached into the cabinets to bring down the pepper grinder and the garlic press.

"I hope we're not in your way with all this," she said.

"Not at all." Physically, Frankle had never been closer to her. "This is great."

An onion Constance had diced for the salad brought tears to Frankle's eyes as he peeled garlic. She rubbed the last of the onion chunk against her wrist, then held it out and asked if Frankle liked her perfume. He held her wrist to his face and breathed deeply. Against his lips, he could feel her pulse beating.

"Very nice. What's it called?"

"Vidalia."

It was with great reluctance that he released her arm.

A piece of garlic squirted from the press and dropped to the floor. Jack pounced and swallowed it, sniffing for more. Watching the terrier, Nick's eyes opened wide, and after a moment of hesitation, he dropped a piece of lettuce. Frankle didn't know how to deal with the boy's perplexity when the terrier ignored the green leaf. Frankle swooped up the lettuce and ate it himself. Nick's eyes opened wide again; then, smiling, he turned away and began a battle on the table with two plastic dinosaurs.

After dinner, Frankle built a fire and washed the dishes as Constance and Nick ate cookies before the flames and Constance read aloud *The Little Prince.*

Returning from the park after Jack's night walk, Frankle stepped into the bathroom to take a leak and found Nick sliding around in the deep tub, holding two toy ducks who were fighting over the friendship of a frog:

" 'I'll sh-share my b-bread with you!' " " 'I-I'll m-make you a pillow with my feathers!' "

Frankle empathized with the frog's desire for both.

Seated in the living room, listening to Davis's *Seven Steps,* Constance told someone she'd telephone back, hung up, and resumed what Frankle assumed was knitting. The black cables of her own sweater revealed, in its interstices, that she was naked beneath it.

Frankle set about nervously watering plants.

"When I have my sewing machine," she told him, "I make dresses and shirts. After I take my house back, I'll make something for you."

Frankle tossed a dish towel beneath an overflowing asparagus fern.

"I thought you only rented your house?"

No, she told him. After her husband's death, she had rented out the house and gone with Nick to her stepparents' place in Boston, then left Nick and come to New York to stay with her friend Duke.

Frankle said they must have been rich to buy a house by the Pacific, and Constance reported that her ex-husband had made a bundle one year selling cocaine, though at the time she had thought the profits came from his real estate work.

Nick walked into the living room in his pajamas, the top part buttoned crookedly. He kept his head bowed and sat next to his mother, on whose shoulder he now leaned his head.

Frankle knew the feeling.

"Did you brush your teeth and put powder on your rash?"

"Mm-hm."

"Tired?"

The boy nodded and bumped his head against her shoulder.

"You want to say good night to Thom before I tuck you in?"

"Night, T-Thom."

"Sweet dreams, Nick."

The boy took his mother by the hand and led her into the bedroom. When Constance returned, Frankle was standing before the dying embers of the fire. He thanked her for the dinner.

"You're an easy guy to please." At his side, she lifted the poker and jabbed the glowing coals.

"On the contrary," Frankle said.

" 'On the contrary,' what?"

"Nothing."

He wanted to move closer but was afraid; instead, he thrust his hands into the rear pockets of his jeans.

"Mind if I ask you something, Thom?"

"Go ahead."

She put the poker back in its stand. "What is it you like so much about me?"

His eyes held diffidently on his shoetops, and he laughed at her vainglory.

"Your modesty."

"Don't get me wrong," she said. "I like you." Now she was using the little shovel to pile the embers.

"Good." But he answered too quickly, revealing, he feared, his anxiety about her dashing his hopes.

She cleared her throat. "It's because I like you that I want you to know it's nothing personal. Bad timing, probably. Anyway, at the risk of presumption, I wanted to be up-front with you."

"You are being presumptuous," Frankle told her quietly.

She apologized before leaning forward to kiss him quickly. "I'm going to run a bath, so I'll say good night."

"Good night." He watched her go, then climbed to his room.

He lay down on the foldout and listened to her bathwater running.

20

Frankle left for kitchen work at the church before Constance
and Nick had awakened, and by the time he returned they'd
gone. At ten minutes past ten, when his ten o'clock client
canceled, Frankle lugged his gym bag to the Y for a workout.
He jumped rope in full sweatgear until the heavy bag became
available. Then he tightened the straps of his bag gloves and
pretended he possessed a strategy as he pounded the piss out
of the cracked leather bulk. Frankle missed his semimonthly
workouts with the more adroit Johnny Smoke, who he hoped
would return from the Caribbean paunchy from dissolution
and half a second slower with the jab. Frankle would dance
for two rounds, surviving into the third and final round to
close in for the kill, a feat he'd never accomplished in his
three years of sparring with Smoke, who insisted Frankle
would never take a round until he learned to get in range:
*"How will I know when I'm in range?" "You'll get hit." "I don't
want to get hit." "You got to. There's no other way to make your
opponent pay."*

Frankle jabbed and danced in a hot dog ballet around the
heavy bag before stepping in with a right hook to the body
and doubling to the head.

Emboldened and sweating, he loaded up on a crisp right

cross aimed for Smoke's imagined cheek. But the big bag was swinging toward him, and when the punch landed, his thumb jammed; the pain dropped him to his knees.

Helped out of his gloves, he stripped down to a towel and headed for the steam room.

Vaguely outlined in the mist, a man sat in a white bathing cap and black swimmer's goggles, the lenses of which were completely fogged.

"Hi there."

Frankle straightened the aching hand and wrist.

"Sit closer, Sugar," the man said.

Frankle squinted: That Thoreauvian homeliness.

"Stan?"

"Call me Dom, you."

"Knock off that voice."

"Mustn't." But he did, addressing Frankle in a whisper of breathless anxiety. "Witness I subpoenaed in the Kenway case is missing. Sinewy Italian guy name of Sal runs a dry-cleaning plant in Yonkers. Kenway hauls the guy's trichloroethylene used in the cleaning process. We traced the stuff to an illegal waste site used by Kenway. In other words, via Sal, yours truly was closing the evidentiary gap in the case against Kenway. Point is, Sal's missing. Been missing now for three days. Wife says he hasn't taken a vacation in thirty years. I learned of this late yesterday. Day before that, D.S. takes me to a palm reader. A well-known, one-name psychic. Patty. One look at my palm: 'It's a miracle you're with me here tonight, dear.' Portly Southern type with smoldering yellow eyes and a desperate need for electrolysis: sideburns, mustache, ear and nasal matting. Palm reveals to Patty I'm in imminent danger. She sees death, dissipation, a woman named Deb . . .!"

"Sta—"

"Don't call me that!"

Frankle massaged his aching thumb, eyeing his palm.

"Psychic indicated a woman will drastically alter my life. I'll feel like a car wreck at a famous midtown intersection. All for the good, though. Woman's my Guide. Shouldn't judge her by earthly standards. She herself is only dimly conscious of her spiritual function. Now listen to this! Patty says woman is involved in therapy and comes from Idaho or thereabouts."

"I think I broke my thumb."

"There's more. As you know, I'm interested in nature. Patty insists city life is dangerous to my etheric Self's evolution. Must be surrounded by nature—wind, water, weeds; meadows, mountains, mud. Aforementioned female shall shepherd me through this change. We were married in a past life. I was the wife."

"Dom, may I—"

"Let me finish. Sex energy is completely misunderstood. Last night, for example, D.S. stimulated my muladhara chakra by . . . well, of the four well-known ways, she employed the Fourth Way."

"I'm getting some movement in the thumb."

Stark used his fingers to clear the fog from the lens of his goggles. "D.S. is to be in a movie. Something, in fact, your friend John Smoke hopes to produce. Or is it direct? And I thought I heard the name Bernheim mentioned as well. D.S. tried to explain synchronicity to me, but I was too spent from the chakra business to concentrate. Point is, Thomas, everything means something else. And the something else has a logic we cannot fathom by way of the mind."

"Am I fathoming correctly," Frankle put in, "that you'll be relinquishing your bureau chief position before moving to the country?"

Stark nodded in confirmation and played with the chin strap of his latex swim cap.

"Dare I ask what has happened to the tough-minded Camusian I used to know and respect?" Frankle said.

Stark cleared his throat.

"That tough-minded man is now of the opinion that the attorney general's office, for which he broke his ass for a dozen years, has no intention of prosecuting Kenway. Alas, he is now very much of the opinion that threats on his life might well have been initiated by someone *within* the agency!"

"Intraagency?"

"You got it. A conspiracy."

"And so he's decided to quit?"

"Not quite quit yet. He's decided to raise plants. Herbs, shrubs, trees, flowers. Seeds, pots, flats. Sowers, mowers, spreaders. Shit for sale: horse, cow, chicken, pig; bags, piles, bales. Shovel your own and save. House of Father Nature, to be exact. Dom and Deb, proprietors. Responsible gardeners welcome! Parking in rear. Try Deb's herbal hot tub therapy. Individuals and groups welcome. Sign up in the rhododendron garden."

"Shut up, Stan."

Stark stood, naked but for the cap and goggles.

"Get off this island before it's too late, Thomas. Remember Lot's wife!"

The gaunt and begoggled figure disappeared from Frankle's eyes after two steps into the mist. Frankle took the elevator to the fourth-floor pool and dived headfirst from the five-meter board after receiving the required permission from the lifeguard. As he had assumed, the fearful leap and jarring impact cleared his head.

21

Two fat men were lugging a large box up the stairs of the brownstone. Frankle couldn't get around them and so followed patiently in their pungent wake. One or both had a vivid aversion to deodorant.

"Lift the fucking thing, would you!"

"Shut your hole, Wart!"

Bathrobed and smoking a cigar, Chambers waited for the delivery at the doorway of his apartment. He wore mirror-lensed sunglasses enveloped by flaps of pink leather.

"A faggot Martian!"

"Get the fucking thing inside!"

Frankle watched the men set the big square box in Chambers's living room. They seemed impressed by the amount Chambers tipped them; and Chambers himself seemed uncharacteristically effervescent. He gestured for Frankle to come in.

Frankle waited for the fat men to exit before he entered the dark place.

A printer was clacking away upstairs, and light splintered through the two shuttered windows of Chambers's living room. A whip, tied to the spiraling banister, dangled above

Chambers's head, and on the coffee table before the sofa lay tracks of cocaine and a razor blade.

"Beer?" Chambers offered the can he was holding.

Frankle declined, and Chambers sat, promptly snorting two lines through a rolled bill. He rested his head on a sofa cushion and stared at the ceiling.

"Ammo," he sighed. "Couldn't have finished the revisions without ammo."

He sat up and chugged the beer before puffing meditatively on his cigar.

"Ammo tell you this, too. Gordo Busch was there when everyone else had left me for dead. Including you, partner."

"What's in the box?" Frankle asked.

Chambers drained the beer and fired the can toward the kitchen. "Sure feels good when them troops hit the beach!"

He lit a cigarette and left the cigar burning in the ashtray. "The box? The box on the floor before you? The one between me and you? Yeah, more Gordo. It's a TV and a VCR. Sent over so I can bone up on the porno genre." Chambers waved a sheet of paper. "List of cassettes I'm to review before I take a meeting with some of Gordo's script honchos. This is known as support. Support with a capital *S*. I gotta tell ya, Busch is hip. Hip to how my power is his power, and vice versa. You cover my ass, I cover yours. Basic I and Thou of the boonies. You don't believe me, ask anyone happened to survive the slaughter pit."

Frankle nodded. "I've got something in the oven."

"Producer friend of his wants a script by next month. I told Gordo about my next novel, about this wigged-out psycho killer vet, and just like that, Gordo sets up a screenplay deal based on the idea. But go ahead, knock Busch. Knock him all you want."

Chambers leaned forward and snorted another line with the bill.

"Bump up, boogeyman. Bump up! Chambers drummed his knees, then flicked on the stereo. The Talking Heads' "Life During Wartime" blasted from speakers above Frankle. Chambers went on drumming.

"Get with it, boogeyman! No can tell whether you're dead or alive. What are you? You dead or alive?" Chambers stood, moving to the pounding music, the sunglasses bestowing an insane, insectoid quality.

Frankle left him to his psychopathic dance.

A phone message from Constance Frame reported that she would be staying downtown overnight with Nick—something about a late drink with a boutique owner who was interested in buying a line of sweaters and something else about how it would be much easier to get Nick to his special class for dyslexic children the next day. Since she'd quit the dog-grooming job, if Frankle had to reach her, he should try her at Duke's place.

During the endless week she remained downtown, Frankle spoke with her only once, by telephone, and this was half the number of times he shot a client's portrait. But he had befriended a man at the church breakfasts and spent the days following him around town, feeling as homeless as this homeless man, who lived in a sewer passage beneath Grand Central Terminal. Frankle had a hell of a time photographing the dark place. It brought back memories of his days at *Concupiscence* when he was required to use a "pussy light" to detail the magazine's central focus.

Frankle avoided opening his mailbox until after the first of the year. Amid the dreaded bills and the entreaties for donations lay a letter from the law offices of Kappleman, Richardson, and Coch. Incredibly, the letter from Hieronymus Coch III served notice that Coch's client Monica Webb intended to assert her lease rights to the apartment inhabited at present by Thom Frankle on or by April 1. If Frankle wished to contest his client's claim, Coch would see him in court.

Frankle tried to circle his emotional wagons, but panic fired an arrow into his heart and he closed his eyes, hoping it would all go away.

Laughter sounded, and Frankle turned to a knocking on the lobby door. Against the glass pane a white-haired man with startling blue eyes pressed his lips and nose grotesquely. The two black women at his side were nearly a foot taller than he and wore Egyptian-style blond wigs.

"Hey, photog face," Gordon Busch called. "Where's gimpy?"

Frankle opened the door, but the three didn't step inside.

"Schmucko no answer his buzzer," Busch said. "Run up like a good kid and tell Mr. Testicles to quit beatin' his thing and get his butt down here. Rental limo's wasting gas."

Frankle studied the women's curiously large hands.

"Maybe his eye rolled under the bed," Busch told his companions, "and he's having trouble finding his dancing shoes." He then called into the intercom, "Chambers! Shake a leg! Captain Busch here. Do you read? Over."

Gordon Busch winked at Frankle.

Chambers's voice signaled suddenly from the intercom box.

"Yo!" Busch shouted. "Moshe Dayan. Strap your thing on and get with the program. It's rape and plunder time."

"Right down."

"Bring the whip," Busch said. "We'll be in the limo."

Frankle met Chambers on the second-floor landing; he held a beer in one hand and the whip in the other.

"Doing a piece on S and M clubs for *Concupiscence*. Dig this: four grand for two thousand words!"

Frankle heard someone mounting the stairs behind him. He turned to see Monica Webb.

"There's my screenwriter!"

She kissed Chambers on both cheeks before doing the same with Frankle.

In the apartment, the message from Constance Frame indicated that she would be in Connecticut through the weekend.

22

His back to her, he stood in the kitchenette, preparing a transcontinental blend of ground coffee that he knew to be her favorite.

When he finally turned to converse, he discovered her standing directly behind him. She had removed her fur, to reveal a long black cocktail dress and jewelry.

"I thought we might chat until they beep me back to the set."

"What would you like to chat about?"

"Don't be that way, Thom. How was your New Year's Eve?"

"Quiet."

"I miss watching you in the kitchen."

"I bet."

He poured two cups of coffee and offered her one.

"Aren't we going to lace it with whiskey?"

"I'm on the wagon."

She made a scoffing sound. "Since when?"

"Yesterday," Frankle lied.

She pressed playfully into him and stared. "Might your new gal be responsible for this teetotaling?"

"I don't have a new 'gal.' "

Her hands were on his hips. "Give your old one a hug."

He tried to keep it fanciful, hoping, by appearing un-daunted, to defuse the temptation. But the peachy scent of her hair left him inert and disinclined to break the embrace. Still, he managed to step away, patting her ass to make it all seem cavalier.

"Letter came from your attorney today," he told her.

"Did it?"

Frankle fixed on the supercilious light in her eyes.

"What are you going to do in response?" She lifted the cup of coffee and sipped it, watching him with mischief and circumspection.

"I don't know yet."

"What's there to know?"

Frankle hesitated. "What I'm going to do about it."

"Isn't it really pretty simple?" She blew on the coffee to cool it.

"How's that?" He could feel his face furrow with anxiety, and then he was angry with himself for his fear of her.

"As I see it," she said, "we either call it even and stay together, or you have to move out."

"I don't think it's that simple."

She scoffed, her eyes wrinkling in the corners. "Really, Thom, if you want to break up, then you leave. But don't demand we break up and that I leave. You call it quits, you march."

Frankle folded his arms protectively and tucked his hands beneath his armpits. He marveled at how she'd deftly ma-neuvered him into appearing the aggressive and unaccom-modating one.

"Susan Stark," she resumed, "is planning to convert her fourth floor into a rental. You might try her."

"That's a marvelous idea," he said sarcastically. "Clients will just flock to Brooklyn for head shots."

"Then don't go anywhere, darling. You're the one making this thing difficult."

He lit a cigarette and looked out the window.

"Thom," Monica invoked, "the only reason I instructed my attorney to write you the letter is because I know how you have to be pushed to make even the simplest decision."

"We're talking in circles."

She hooked a finger through a belt loop of his jeans. "Everything's going to be okay. Trust me for once. Coch's going to contest that network contract and get me new work. Work that's challenging and won't leave me so bored and cranky." She set down her coffee. "Maybe a movie. No more year in and year out of *Still Lives*. Have you any idea what a schedule like that can do to a person's disposition?"

He disengaged from her. "You can have the apartment," he said quietly.

"Let me tell you about the movie." It was as if she hadn't heard. "What's so funny about it is that Harry Chambers has been hired to do the screenplay. And your former boss is executive producing. Did you know *Concupiscence* has started an independent film division?"

Frankle leaned against the refrigerator. Remarkably, having held his ground with her, for what seemed like the very first time, he saw her as a separate, struggling person.

"I don't want Harry involved, but Coch told me to keep my mouth shut for the moment. He's confident we can muscle him out at the appropriate time. So I'm being nicer than nice."

"Why would you want to muscle him out?"

"Why? Because I'm certain he'll screw my character—artistically speaking."

She lit a cigarette.

"I was at a party last night," she said. "Your friend John Smoke was there. Apparently, Chambers's editor and Smoke were notorious college pals, and this editor has attached him to the project as director. I don't know how they all got together, although rumor reputes drug money."

She exhaled dramatically, her chin lifted in the air.

"Hieronymus tells me the dramatic concept is a conventional thriller with triple-X-rated sex between two established TV stars. I'm one, of course, and the reason I'm so excited about the project is that Dell Jordan has already agreed to co-star."

"That guy who always needs a shave?"

"Yup."

"Would you really do pornography?"

"That's sort of a funny question coming from you."

"Maybe I know enough about it to ask the question."

She smiled. "I'm an actress, darling. I'll do anything to break the network contract and get into film."

A dripping faucet unsettled Frankle; he turned to tighten the sink handles.

"Don't get upset, now." Monica seemed delighted. "I do have my standards, you know. I told them, for example, I wouldn't do onscreen with Dell anything I haven't done voluntarily in my private life."

The beeper sounded on Monica's wrist.

"Ten minutes to Clara Ravens's fifth abortion." She winked. "Walk me to the set?"

He took Jack along. Flurries fell, and the atmosphere was suffused with the kitchen fumes from a Japanese restaurant.

"Why did you stop before?" She was changing into a wig on the street, and people were staring.

"Stop?" he said.

"When I kissed you before?"

Frankle didn't answer.

"I think it's crazy to give up what we have physically." She put her arm around his waist. "It's too rare to give up."

"It's time," he said dispassionately, "to move on to the next thing."

"What's the next thing?"

"I don't know yet." He draped his arm around her shoulders. "I'd appreciate it if you let me stay in the apartment until spring. After that, it's all yours."

They stopped before the studio entrance.

"You're serious, then, about leaving?"

He nodded.

"And you don't want to give the lover thing a try?"

"It can't work."

"It can, darling."

"Not for me."

"I think you're going to be sorry. I really do."

"We can talk about the exact date I leave at a later time."

He took her hand, weirdly emboldened. "I'm sorry for a lot of things."

She frowned. "Are you on tranquilizers, Thom?"

"No."

"You usually are when you make brave pronouncements."

She wheeled and walked away melodramatically. It was a function, Frankle assumed, of years of soap opera work: scenes were scripted to end in envy, revenge, or nervous collapse. Of course, the wounds of actual lives were far more complicated, and the consequent unhappiness far less demonstrative.

For what seemed the first time in his life, Frankle felt the thrilling flush of working without a script.

23

The door to her room was open, and Nick lay in bed, propped
on pillows and eating soup. Constance was holding the spoon
for him, blowing on the puddle to cool it.

"Sick?"

"Overtired."

Frankle leaned against the doorframe. "Hi, Nick."

The boy whispered hello, his eyes held away.

"When you get a second," Frankle told Constance, "I'd like
to talk with you."

"Soon as I'm done."

He went upstairs to the darkroom to reprint shots of the
homeless on harder paper.

He was hanging the pictures to dry when she appeared in
a bathrobe, with her hair pulled back in a ponytail.

"I wanted to ask you out to dinner," Frankle said, "but I
guess you're settling in?"

"I just canceled plans."

"I could order something in for us?"

She told him she was going to bathe and get in bed with
a book. "Come down and talk with me," she said.

"Talk with you?"

"Give me time to get under the bubbles."

By the time Frankle joined Constance in the bathroom, his usual fare of sesame noodles and string beans had been delivered from the Chinese restaurant. He threw a towel on the tiled floor and sat before her, bubbles up to her chin and her feet resting on the bathtub spout.

"There's plenty for you in the kitchen." He nodded to his plate.

"Thank you."

"It's good to see you again, Ms. Frame."

"I have been unusually busy, haven't I."

She slid down, her head disappearing beneath the bubbles as her knees came up, the bath oil leaving them lambent and smooth.

He waited until she surfaced, to ask, "What's new?"

"Business stuff." Her eyes were closed and her hair lay wetly away from her face. Frankle stared at her freckled shoulders. When their eyes met, Frankle diverted his to three beans gathered at the end of his chopsticks.

"I'd tell you more," she said, "but I don't want to jinx things. Those beans look good."

He fed her some.

"God!" Because she was impressed, Frankle reached her the plate, which she rested on her glistening knees.

Frankle returned to the kitchen and prepared another plate for himself before resuming his seat on the towel.

"I wanted to talk to you," she said, "about Jack."

"Your husband?"

"No, our Jack."

It seemed inadvisable to propose to a woman without ever having kissed her—although, if the truth be told, kissing and all the rest had never inspired any urge in Frankle to propose anything more than that she keep on the high heels.

Constance opened her eyes to parody his stare. "What is it?"

He lowered his gaze, embarrassed.

"My friend Paolo," she said, "wants me to design a winter and summer line for his company. In fact, he may take me to Paris with him this spring."

Frankle feared his jealousy was revealed in the deflated congratulations he offered.

She set down her plate on the tub ledge. "I really think he's serious about my work. Though naturally, I'm afraid to say, a man's interest is always just a little suspect."

"That's for sure," Frankle said too quickly.

"Except for you, of course." Her tone was wry but affectionate. She poured shampoo into her hair and scrutinized him a little incredulously.

Frankle watched her naked arms.

"Have you always been so cautious, Thom?"

"Recently."

She smiled. "Me too."

She held her head back to rinse her hair, and Frankle admired her long throat.

"What were we talking about originally?"

"Jack," Frankle said.

"Oh, yeah. Paolo wants to know if you'd consider letting him use Jack as a mascot."

"For what?"

"For my line of sweaters—assuming he takes them."

Frankle used the chopsticks to scratch his head.

"You needn't look so skeptical," Constance said. "He's already written me a check for three grand for six samples and sketches."

"Three grand!" When Frankle rocked forward to offer his hand in congratulations, Constance pulled him close and kissed him quickly.

Frankle then leaned farther forward and kissed her again,

more slowly. Unmindful as he was of the plate he was holding, the noodles and beans slid to the floor.

Their mouths held together for a long time, hers tasting of shampoo.

"Paolo wants to take me to a fashion show tomorrow. You're a good kisser."

"I think you should go, don't you?"

"Why are we whispering?"

"I don't know," he whispered.

"If I asked you to look after Nick while I'm at that show, what would you say?"

"I'd say it would give me an excellent chance to get to know him better." Frankle caught Constance's plate just as it was about to fall into the tub and absently set it down on his own, which now covered its spilled contents. "What do you make of this sudden affection?" he said.

She shrugged. "I'm getting out now. Close your eyes."

"I was hoping you'd ask for help drying off."

"You wash the plates," she said. "And I'll do the drying."

He handed her a towel, then scooped up the food and plates before turning away.

He heard the turbulence of the bathwater as he went to the kitchenette. Down on the avenue, two cabs had bumped fenders. Frankle watched through the window as the polyglot curses changed to punches.

Constance appeared in her bathrobe, her hair dripping.

"Why are you still holding the plates?"

He set them down in the sink and embraced her, drawn to her as inevitably as falling.

"It's time," she whispered, "to say good night until the next exciting episode."

Without looking back, she disappeared into her room.

24

Constance told Nick to be a good kid and listen to Uncle
Thom. Something about the epithet left Frankle feeling more
servile than avuncular, but he waved bye-bye along with the
boy at the corner whence his heartthrob zoomed away in
a cab.

"Hungry?"

"Okay."

At the coffee shop, as Nick ate scrambled eggs and potatoes
while reading about Archie's comic-book travails with Betty
and Veronica, Frankle worked on a Greek salad and fumbled
through Nicholas of Cusa:

*Thou, Lord, does speak in me and say that there is no positive
principle of otherness, and thus it existeth not: for how could
otherness exist without a principle, unless it itself were a principle
of infinity? Now otherness cannot be the principle of being, for
otherness taketh its name from not-being, for because one thing is
not another it is called other. Otherness, therefore, cannot be the
principle of being, because it taketh its name from not-being, nor
hath it the principle of being, since it ariseth from not-being.
Otherness, then, is not anything, but the reason wherefore the sky
is not the earth is because the sky is not infinity's self, which*

*encompasseth all being. Whence, since infinity is absolute infinity,
it resulteth that one thing cannot be another.*

Frankle chewed a carrot slice. "Good lunch?"

"Yes." The boy's black eyes remained on the comic.

"Who's Archie love today?"

"Betty."

"Want anything for dessert?"

"N-no."

They took a bag of peanuts and a loaf of stale bread to the
park. Bundled in his puffy red coat against the January cold,
Nick ministered to a congregation of squirrels and pigeons.
Frankle demonstrated how to hand-feed the squirrels, but
Nick chickened out at the last moment and dropped the
offerings, laughing as the squirrels darted suspiciously away,
their tails snapping while they shelled the nuts and stored
them in their cheeks. Tethered to a tree several yards away,
Jack barked his head off, further exciting Nick, who began
to hurl handfuls of peanuts all over the place while spinning
round manically, until dizziness dropped him. Conscious of
the boy's cold, Frankle picked him up and suggested a hike
to the reservoir to see the ducks. Nick liked the idea and
marched ahead, waving a stick and talking to himself.

They stopped at the rowing pond, the boat slips empty at
the far end of the icy expanse.

"This spring," Frankle proposed, "we'll all go fishing."

"No kill-killing! Fish like to swim."

"Swimming, then."

"Fish swim!"

The boy hurled a stick as if he meant business.

"Animals have r-rights, Thom!"

"I know."

Jack snatched a stick from Nick, and the two raced
away.

"Follow us!"

Frankle followed them north, along the winding path beneath the naked trees of the wooded hill, until they reached the flat expanse of the Great Lawn. Above this muddy field scudded a low ceiling of gray clouds.

Nick stared incredulously at Belvedere Castle, built on a promontory above the frozen pond that bordered the field.

"Kings live in c-castles."

"A long time ago."

"You want to see it?"

"Sure."

They climbed and stood on the stone wall overlooking the pond. Nick stared down the cliff of basaltic rocks that dropped precipitously to the ice. Farther out, on the big muddy field, young men were playing football. Frankle recalled himself and Chambers playing at Prospect Park, in Brooklyn. Frankle had the arm, and Chambers could run a square-and-go that only a land mine could stop.

"Let's climb down."

"Too steep."

The boy's eyes demanded.

"Too steep." Frankle lifted the boy off the wall and set him down at his side.

Jack began barking, and Frankle turned to the approach of three teenagers. They were taunting Jack with whipping sticks, and Frankle whistled for the terrier, who obediently raced to his side and sat down.

One of the teenagers asked Frankle for the time.

"Around noon."

"That dog bite?"

Frankle studied the gang, conscious of the cliff behind him and the boy, and conscious, too, of an ignoble fear and disdain.

"You got five bucks, man? We's hungry."

"So's the dog." And Frankle made a show of restraining the impassive Airedale by the collar.

The spokesman swaggered, staring.

"That dog eat up your black ass!" the smallest in the group told the leader, and they all laughed, walking away and cursing Frankle, who felt ashamed of himself.

When he turned to check on Nick, the boy was gone. Frankle spun fully around, then looked over the cliff. Nick was at the bottom, skating in his shoes on the ice, threading between brown stalks of long grass at the water's edge before shuffling out toward the center.

"Nick!"

The boy turned.

"Get off the ice!"

Frankle motioned with his arm. The boy slipped and fell backward. Frankle waited for him to rise, but Nick lay there, his hands spread out. Frankle wasn't certain what the hell was going on, but he raced around the castle, then down the grassy slope and onto the ice, testing it for several steps before sliding gingerly toward the boy.

Nick's eyes were closed. Frankle knelt, frowning.

"Nick?"

The boy slowly opened his black eyes. "Are y-you the Ab-Abominable Snowman?"

Frankle sat down next to the laughing boy. "What are you doing?"

"Playing."

Frankle watched Nick stare at the sky. "Playing what?"

"A pelican flying upside down!"

Frankle lay beside him. He closed his eyes and listened to the movement of the dry grasses rustling in the wind at the pond's perimeter. His mind moved to a time in the past, and remembering himself in all his boyhood vulnerability, Frankle couldn't determine if his compassion was for himself or for the boy beside him.

"I didn't realize pelicans fly upside down."

We're only pre-tend pelicans."

Frankle remembered the boy's head cold and lifted him up. It felt to him as if Nick was holding more tightly than he had to, as if hugging him. Frankle closed his eyes to remember clinging similarly in ocean surf to his own father, who in death, five years earlier, had moved somehow closer to Frankle than he ever had in thirty-two years of living.

The guard wouldn't permit Frankle to bring Jack into the famous toy store on Fifth Avenue, so Frankle paid him to keep an eye on the Airedale.

The pelican cost more than Frankle had made that week, but Nick kept talking to it, and companionship, Frankle knew, didn't come cheaply—or easily. On another level, one that had more to do with calculation than benevolence, Frankle wanted Constance to be impressed with his generosity.

So Nick carried his new friend on his shoulder back to the apartment, where he walked around the living room, introducing the pelican to all the plants.

"How about a name?" Frankle stealthily poured vodka into one of the two glasses of cranberry juice as Nick studied the stuffed bird.

"Thom!" the boy said, and reached for his juice.

"Thom's my name."

"Thom!"

"Well, cheers."

They touched glasses before Frankle chugged his drink.

Frankle left the boy playing pelican in front of the blazing fireplace and climbed to the terrace for more wood and a half pint's worth of pulls on the vodka stash. Warmed by the stuff, Frankle looked out on the city, wondering what his life might have been like elsewhere—if, say, Monica and he had married and raised those two kids they had paid the gynecologist to scrape into oblivion for two hundred each.

That Voice recited, *Let not your heart be troubled, neither let it be afraid. . . . Hitherto have ye asked nothing in my name: ask, and ye shall receive, that your joy may be full.*

Frankle gathered up wood and returned to the apartment.

25

An hour later, Susan Stark telephoned to announce that she was dining with a friend across the street, and might Frankle like to join them for a drink? Frankle listened to ice tinkling over the line before begging off.

"Well," Susan said, "how would you feel if I dropped in for a drink?"

Beneath the covers of Constance's bed, Nick was asleep, hugging the pelican.

"Another time would really be better, Susan."

"I don't mean to be pushy," Susan said, "but how many times am I going to be right across the street?"

Frankle capitulated, then clicked off the light by which he had been reading *The Little Prince* to the boy and closed the bedroom door.

Susan Stark was drunk. Frankle could tell from the loose, unsteady walk and from the way she greeted him with a kiss, when her normally rigid standards of comportment inclined her to aggressively shake hands. Susan was positively the most humorless person Frankle had ever known.

Beneath the overcoat she asked him to hang up, she wore a mannish baggy black suit with a white shirt and a narrow black tie. Her pretty face was freckled and drawn, sculpted by cropped black hair. He felt her supervise him with her eyes as he hung up the coat.

"I've never seen anything of mine hanging in your place before," she said. "I like the way it makes me feel."

She wobbled into the living room. "I can't decide what I'm in the mood for, drinkwise."

She stared at the bottles racked in Frankle's portable bar, then pointed. "What are those two bottles on top?"

"Unprocessed olive oil and some imported vinegar."

"You drink a lot. What's the difference between gin and vodka?"

Gin, he explained, was something if you got drunk on in adolescence you never drank again.

"Cognac," she said. "That's really what I'm in the mood for. Will you join me in one, please?"

Frankle poured two, and they knocked glasses, still standing.

"You seemed so preoccupied when I phoned."

"I was reading."

"Anything interesting?"

"The Little Prince."

"Aren't we a little old for that?"

When Frankle explained to whom, Susan implored him to let her peek in on the boy.

The hinges needed to be oiled, but the creaking woke only Jack, lying at the foot of the bed, his eyes flashing green in the dark. Frankle could hear Nick breathing raspily.

"May I sit next to him?" She leaned against Frankle as she whispered, her hand on his shoulder.

"You'll wake him."

"Don't be heartless."

"He has a cold, Susan."

Frankle closed the door and escorted Susan back to the living room, where they sat on the sofa. Susan reached into her handbag and took out a package of little cigars. She squinted in concentration, but couldn't get one lit. Frankle helped her.

"I suppose you know about Stanley being in the hospital?"

Frankle assured her that he didn't.

Susan puffed on her cigar. "His lawyer told me testicular cancer. But when my lawyer investigated more carefully, we discovered both Stanley and his lawyer to be liars."

Frankle waited for the truth. Susan laid her head back on the sofa and closed her eyes. The lines in her face indicated that she was indeed seven years older than Stanley Stark.

"Apparently," she said, "your boyhood friend overexerted himself with whatever's-her-name and herniated a water seal he's had since infancy. That's what the lump was all about. Why is it so cold in here?"

Frankle offered her a blanket.

"Couldn't you build up the fire?"

Frankle piled on another log and then handed Susan a blanket. She draped it over her shoulders and shifted closer to Frankle, who was already pressed against the far end of the sofa.

"Has Stanley told you he wants to divorce me so he can marry what's-her-face?"

Frankle agitated his cognac into little waves. "Frankly, Susan, Stan and I only talk sports."

"Really? Is that why he once told me he tells you absolutely everything?"

"You know as well as I that he's an incurable exaggerator." Frankle wondered what was keeping Constance.

"Those weekly handball games, stupid boxing workouts, and dinners," Susan said. "Isn't that when you both tell each other everything? Or were those Wednesday nights out just ploys you and he used to philander?"

"Now, Susan," Frankle said patiently, "Stan and I talked about typical guy stuff: sports and the past, our failed ambitions, lack of money."

"Nothing about failed relationships or lack of love?"

"Not really."

"I find that odd. I really do. Because Stan certainly seemed to know everything about you and Monica. And I have always been under the impression that Stan told you as much about me as Monica told me about you."

Frankle cleared his throat, wondering how best to assuage the analyst.

"Perhaps *I* talk too much, Susan. But Stan's not one for revealing intimate details."

Susan Stark downed her cognac.

"What you are telling me, then, is that Stan never mentioned to you that he has been sterile his entire life and that another man impregnated me. May I have more cognac, please?"

Frankle handed her his glass. "He never discussed anything of the sort with me."

Susan bounced even closer on the sofa. "Two years ago, Thom, my gynecologist told me Stan was sterile. We had tests again and again because, as I've mentioned previously, I was not getting pregnant. Don't ask me why I didn't tell Stanley about the results, because I don't know the answer. I suspect it had taken us so many years to agree to try in the first place that I didn't want to complicate an already all-too-complicated matter. As you can imagine, when he insisted on the California test, the results of which I couldn't doctor, we rather obviously had a number of past and present issues to confront."

"In other words," Frankle said, "he's enraged because you had an affair?"

"An affair's an awfully naive way of putting it."

"Susan, we're being semantical."

"No pun intended?"

"Pardon?"

"I paid someone, Thom. A donor. It goes on all the time, believe me."

Frankle stood and walked to the window to observe litter swirling in the late-January wind.

"*For his semen*, Thom. I advertised and interviewed, then paid for the medical testing and the implantation."

"Artificially?"

"Not technically, no. It took us seven tries. Since then we've remained friends. Are you all right? You're scowling."

"Tired," Frankle whispered.

"It was the only alternative short of adoption."

"And you decided it was best to permit Stan to think it was his child?"

"Let me just say that we did it, the donor and I, in my office, between patients. I wanted to keep it strictly professional. May I have a little more cognac, please?"

Frankle obliged her.

"What can you tell me," Susan Stark slurred slightly, "about this *thing* he's taken up with?"

"Talk to Stan about it, Susan."

"I understand she's a pornographic actress. Which I assume is a fancy way of saying she's a drug addict. Did you introduce them?"

"I hardly know the woman."

"Stan's lawyer insinuated that Stanley implied that you fixed him up with her."

"I took some glamour shots of her for a film company. Stan met her in the lobby by accident."

Susan glowered, dark crescents showing beneath her eyes.

Fearful that she was drunk enough to cross the line into hysteria, Frankle elected to propitiate her. He suggested that though Stan was under tremendous stress, he would surely snap out of it before committing himself to anything foolish.

"That's very stupid of you, Thom. We're all under stress.

It's a central feature of adulthood. I admit that Stanley's upset with my duplicity, but you would think he wouldn't act out his vengeful feelings by taking up with this neurotic tramp."

Frankle nodded politely, wondering how he was ever going to get rid of her. He yawned languidly and rubbed his eyes. "Susan, I hope you won't think I'm rude, but I'm going to take a shower and turn in."

He offered to help her from the sofa. She took his hand, and continued to hold it after she'd risen to her feet.

"You've never allowed yourself to be loved, have you?" Susan stumbled backward, drunkenly, in her high heels.

"Maybe you should sit down, Susan."

"Thom, the real tragedy of remaining the damaged child is its impoverishing influence. I can help you grow up into a marvelous man."

Her eyes seemed vacant and unfocused above the deepening crescents beneath them.

Frankle feigned levity. "I couldn't afford your rates, Stark."

"Thom, I'm going . . . I'm going to be candid."

When he let go of her hand, she began to sway in the windless room.

"I really wish you wouldn't be candid, Susan."

"I'm going to be, Thom." Her eyes closed, as if she were going to fall asleep on her feet, and then they opened abruptly. "Thom, I encouraged Monica to leave you." She found the glass of cognac and finished it. "Now I'm going to say something more. I'm . . . I think I can help you. Let me be blunt. My life's at a standstill. Try to understand. All day long I treat the narcissistically disordered. Spoiled people, Thom, with reprehensible values. I've discussed it with my own analyst. I want to be with a man and I want a man to want to be with me." She began to sag, and Frankle reached for her.

"You're a little drunk," he said. "I'm going to help you into a cab."

He hurried to the closet for her coat and then lifted her to her feet. "You'll feel better outside."

He supported her at the waist as they went downstairs.

On the first-floor landing, she said, "I don't feel at all well."

She began to sag, and Frankle held her to him.

"Are you all right?"

She rested her forehead against his shoulder. "I'm going to be . . . sick."

It came gushing out abruptly, splashing onto his neck and then running down the inside of his shirt. Susan sank to her knees.

Frankle massaged between her shoulder blades, patting gently, as his eyes watered from the vomit. He then removed his shirt and wiped himself off as best he could.

"Put me in a cab," Susan gasped.

He wiped her mouth with the vomitous shirt.

"Help me up!"

His hands left fingerprints on the stairway banister and later on the door handle of the cab.

"Are you going to be all right, Susan?"

"Would you please just close the door!"

Bare-chested, Frankle stepped away from the hateful tone and closed the door. He assumed Susan Stark was livid enough to give the cabdriver not only her address but street directions as well.

26

Frankle showered as Jack carried away the fouled clothing from the steamy bathroom. Eventually, Nick appeared, shielding his eyes from the light.

"Jack smells fun-ny."

"Where is he?"

"Licking your shirt."

"Jack!"

The terrier appeared.

Frankle opened the shower curtain and grabbed the shirt.

"I want to sle-sleep in your room."

Frankle pointed the boy back to his bed. "Before your mom gets home."

"But it stinks in there."

Frankle compromised and let the boy have his way, warning him that it was cold upstairs and that he should make sure to stay under the covers and to be careful going up the spiraling stairs.

"Thanks!"

The boy called excitedly for Jack and raced from the bathroom.

Frankle stealthily followed, dripping water, and watched the boy climb the steps. Then he gathered together his strewn clothing and stuffed it into a plastic garbage bag before racing, shivering, back into the shower, where he cut the lights and sat down, the cataract beating on his back.

In the dark, he studied his hands. Faith: the courage to see that more often than not life is a condition to be accepted rather than a problem to be solved; and in a moment in which he felt a sudden compassion for everyone he knew, Frankle wondered, given the conditions of life, if any of them would ever find consolation.

His mind tried to find something that brought him consolation, and he was about to give up, when *kindness* came to mind. It occurred to him that whenever he had been kind, he hadn't felt alone, and this feeling had provided him with consolation. When he was kind he was outside himself, even if his kindness was only a little thing, like covering his dog with a sweater on a cold night. Perhaps kindness was the proof of faith?

The light flicked on and blinded him. Squinting, he expected to see Nick, but instead he saw Constance, standing in the doorway in her coat and blue beret.

"Hello!"

"Do you know Nick isn't in his bed?" She sounded alarmed.

"He's sleeping upstairs."

"Are you all right?"

The shower spray bounced off the curtain, blurring her image.

"I'm fine."

"I've never seen anyone meditate under a shower."

"I wasn't meditating."

She leaned against the doorframe. "Everything go okay today?"

"Fine. Would you mind getting out of here."

"I'm a little drunk."

He listened to her shoes clack as she went down the hallway

toward the living room; and he imagined her tiptoeing up the staircase to check on Nick. Then Frankle imagined they were a couple and that she had just returned from her sweater store downtown. Would the sense of shelter and solidarity last, or would the everydayness of living together become another kind of loneliness, leading to suspicion, faultfinding, and betrayal?

Frankle realized there was only one way to find out.

He stood, suddenly anxious, and soaped up his hair. His eyes were closed, his face lifted to the showerhead, when he heard the slide of the shower curtain and felt her behind him.

"I'm back," she said, and reached over him for the shelved soap. It felt like electricity going through him.

"Do you mind?" he heard her say.

"No." But he was frozen, his hands stopped in his hair.

"Aren't you going to turn around?"

When he did, he made certain to keep his eyes on her face. Her body was warm as the water, and he pressed against her.

"We should meet like this more often." She was looking up at him.

"I just wish the bus would get here already," he said. "These shelters don't do a thing against the rain."

"Let me get under there." They close-danced in a half circle. Frankle bowed his head to behold her body.

"Does this mean you got the sweater deal?"

She handed him a bar of soap. "Just my shoulders, please." She pirouetted, and Frankle rested his face against her matted hair as he washed her. She wheeled again and put her arms around his waist.

"You're so bashful!"

"You've been drinking gin!"

She had her face against his throat. "The separate flesh of two skinny people."

"Try *sinewy*."

"I like you," she whispered, and quickly kissed his chest.

Frankle massaged the soap in her hair. He hoped that after the longing had been satisfied, there would be a deep tenderness rather than the emptiness and regret with which he was too familiar.

"Listen," he said reluctantly, "I don't know about this."

"Not knowing comes with the territory."

"Maybe we should think about it."

She smiled. "You mean to say you haven't?"

They dried each other and went into her bedroom.

"This door doesn't lock, you know."

"Thom, I can't exactly send Nick to the movies every time we want to be together!"

"I just thought I should mention it."

They slipped under the covers, where his hands and hers imitated each other.

"Don't laugh at what I'm going to ask," he whispered, and he asked her to give him another word for love.

Her eye slid into her nose, and Frankle unconsciously crossed his.

"Hope," she said.

His mouth was on hers.

"What kind of hope?"

"You said *one word*."

"Hope for the future?"

"Hope for now. Hope can't take the pressure of any more than that."

"Day to day," Frankle said.

She leaned away.

"Thom, my melioristic talks are available on cassette and can be listened to at a more propitious time."

"I'll take the set."

"They're all yours."

Later, after time seemed to go away and then come back

in such a way that Frankle could only have taken a wild guess as to where he'd been with her, he said, "I love you."

Her head rested on his chest and her hand moved on his stomach. "I know."

"And just when I thought I had things emotionally in order."

"Emotions don't stay in order."

"Where are we, Constance?"

"Let's start with our names and addresses. You're Thom Frankle and you live on an island off the east coast of the United States. You know my name, and believe it or not, I've got to return to California this week."

Her face rose before his and Frankle studied her. "Seriously?"

"Seriously."

His hand stopped moving.

"Don't drift away, Thom."

He could feel the outline of his body pressed against hers, but he was alone again. Her hand felt small in his hand, and its smallness saddened him.

"My tenants out there just up and left, with all the lights on and the TV and stereo playing. My neighbor left word with my stepparents, who left word with Duke. I've got to go back and take care of it. I can't manage without that rental money."

Frankle let go of her and locked his hands behind his head. "Tell me how I can help, and I will."

"Be patient with me, okay?"

"Haven't I been?"

"Very."

"How long will you be gone?"

"I don't know. I certainly want to get back as soon as I can, to work with Paolo and . . . you know."

"No," he said. "Tell me."

"Be with you."

Afterward, he was dazed and exhausted and didn't want to talk.

"Thom?"

"Thom's in no shape to talk just yet."

"Tell him Constance takes back the part about him being shy."

He tried not to doze off but did; and waking sometime later, he presumed it was Constance who was crawling over him on her way from the bed. When he rolled over, however, he discovered Jack settling between him and Constance; and there was Nick, walking to the futon and sliding beneath the sleeping bag he used as a blanket.

Frankle whispered to Constance, "Guess who's here?"

"I know." She sat up sleepily. "You okay, honey?"

"I woke up."

She climbed from bed, a blanket wrapped around her, and kissed the boy.

"What hap-pened to Thom?"

"He fell asleep with Mommy. Go to sleep now."

When she was under the covers against Frankle, he whispered, "Now what?"

"Go to sleep."

The covers were lifted from their faces, and Nick was standing there, looking.

"What is it, honey?"

The boy stared, and Frankle feigned sleep until he heard the boy move away.

Constance drew the covers over their heads.

"Maybe I should sleep upstairs?" Frankle whispered.

"And convey we've done something wrong?"

He lay there and held her, overwarm with the terrier nestled against him. Then he couldn't sleep from the mystery of it: Two became briefly one but were required to remain two, even though the memory of briefly being one made being two and one concomitantly more difficult than ever before.

That was when the kindness could crumble—when you forgot you were two and demanded to be one. I *and* Thou. It was obvious enough, but try it sometime.

"Hey," she whispered to him. "Stop worrying. You're giving off static electricity."

27

Sunday morning, Frankle woke to the smell of coffee and toast, but by the time he reached the living room, Nick was zipping up his coat and Constance was slinging a bag over her shoulder. The room smelled damply of soil and greenery, and from the appearance of the two watering cans on the counter, Frankle inferred Constance had watered all the plants in the living room.

"There's coffee for you." She whirled past Frankle, who stood barefoot in a bathrobe, skeptically observing the domestic tranquillity of the morning after.

"What's the rush?" Frankle said.

Constance asked Nick if he was ready. The boy raised his hood and grabbed the pelican.

"Yes."

Constance quickly kissed Frankle goodbye, explaining that she had to go downtown to look at a hotel and would explain why later. Then she was going to Orchard Street to buy Nick some warm things.

Frankle proposed that he either make something for dinner or take them out. Constance told him he had a deal. Then Nick, like his mother, went out without looking back.

Had it not been for Johnny Smoke telephoning to set a

time for a run, Frankle feared a Sunday of photographic gallery hopping would have devolved on to whiskey swilling by noon. So in an attempt at kindness toward himself, Frankle resolved to abstain from such sport for the day; and perhaps the following day he would find the conviction to abstain again.

Sufficient unto the day, he heard, *is the evil thereof.*

An hour later, he was performing jumping jacks near the skating rink. Across the park's inner roadway, through the naked trees, the carousel turned in the January cold, circus music piping eerily as wooden animals moved up and down.

Smoke appeared through the trees in a white running suit, which accented his tan. His brown hair, newly marcelled, had been streaked with blond to resemble swirls in trendy ice cream; and an earring bestowed a punkified glitz. Frankle stood in his baggy and torn sweatpants and hooded sweatshirt.

Smoke looked him over with a smirk that suggested amusement. "Some people never change."

"Good to see you, Johnny."

"Actually, it's John now. John Smoke. I'm not kidding you. John Smoke of Smoking Busch Studios, Purveyors of Porn. Have you stretched? Because I stretched in the cab. Let's go for it, before my balls freeze off."

They ambled stiffly north, groaning in the cold.

"You're wondering about the new look," Smoke said. "It's in your eyes."

"Who is she?" Frankle said. "A hairdresser's assistant?"

"That bad?"

"Worse."

"She's a sculptress from Jersey. Nail sculptress."

"Manicurist?"

"Seriously," John Smoke said. "I'm not going to bullshit you. The honest to God truth is I couldn't take it anymore.

The minute Kikki and I got to Barbados, I disappeared for two days in Georgetown. Spent forty-eight hours with a hooker, drinking my brains out. I couldn't take it anymore. The sports videos, the rock videos, this city . . . even combing my hair I couldn't take. Kikki took total charge of the *Trend* gig. I was out of it. Couldn't get it together enough to take a light-meter reading. My total contribution amounted to running up a record three-week bar bill. Thousands. I'm not kidding you. I couldn't function without alcohol. I was blitzed for two straight weeks. I can't imagine what the bar bill came to."

Frankle ignored the puffiness in his friend's face and told him he looked good.

"Even at my drunkest I knew I couldn't survive another minute documenting pituitary ghetto kids executing reverse stuffs. Another high five and I'd totally lose it. My motivation to cover sports hit zero percent. Around this time I got the ear pierced and committed myself to a radical hair change, though the idea to bleach in the streaks didn't occur to me for another week."

They passed the renovated boat house, and the road climbed toward the Metropolitan Museum.

"Let me tell you something, Thom. There aren't enough equatorial islands to accommodate the number of burnouts in the postindustrial world. The hotel people are going to have to find a way of building islands. If I were in construction, that's where I'd pour my R and D money. Someone in Congress should propose a bill: More islands. We don't need a missile defense system. We need more islands. They want an expanding capitalist economy, they'll need something like a federal park system of islands for taxpaying burnouts."

"I'll write my Congressman."

"I'm not shitting you. I caught fire and burned out. A pile of ashes at thirty-seven. This is why I changed my name. The change was proposed by my college chum Gordo Busch, best known for his editing, drugging, sexual heterodoxy, et cetera. Incidentally, with age I realize all wisdom lies in the et cetera. What was I talking about?"

"Gordon Busch." Frankle's breath vaporized as they climbed the hill, the winter sky the no-color of cardboard.

"Gordo came down to cool out as well and catch a few. Also to creatively dialogue with me and your former boss about some filmic concepts. Gordo and I traverse a very common past, from Country Day Prep to Tufts. Once pulled a two on one on some Smithy. Girl turned out to be Kikki's best friend back in the city. You can fill in the rest. But let me tell you something. I look back on those years and marvel at the percentage of usable sex energy the body generated. Where does it go, this sex energy? Seriously, after thirty-five it's like my efficiency percentage dropped off the frigging chart. Could it be taxation? Working forty to seventy percent of the time for Uncle Sam? I'll be honest: unless the country puts money into island construction, there's going to be a revolt."

They passed the reservoir. The playground on the opposite side of the road was iced over, and papers swirled in the winter wind.

"Somehow," Smoke went on, "that was supposed to relate to how I eventually met Kikki one weekend. I think she'd been fucking you around then? Where did you do it, by the way? I don't mean bodily. I mean place. Your place, her place, some other place?"

"What are you on, John? You find some Black Beauties in your yearbook?"

"Gordo does sell Black B's. His principals tend to be writers."

Frankle interjected that Gordon Busch happened to be the editor of Frankle's neighbor, who happened to be a writer.

"I'm getting to that," Smoke said, panting. "Meanwhile, Gordo proposed this film concept to me when he was visiting. We both have very definite ideas about home video pornog-

raphy. Have had for a long time. Our problem has always
been dollars. Gordo tried financing it via drug sales, but it
got too complicated. Tax investigation, et cetera. That
changed when Gordo brought a script idea to Bernheim, who
promised to finance it if we could sign the actors he proposed
for the script. All of which I'm getting to. As I was saying,
Gordo procured script development funds from Bernheim.
Above and beyond that, it's strictly a share-of-the-net-profits
proposition, notwithstanding salaries for the lead actors.
Gordo and I have the lawyer drawing papers now for Smoking
Busch films. Go ahead and guess the lawyer's name. Take
twenty guesses. Take fifty."

"Hieronymus Coch," Frankle said.

Smoke staggered forward, a hand on top of his head in
exgerated incredulity. Harlem was visible through the naked
trees.

"Who the hell told you!"

"He represents Monica."

"Coch represents *our* Monica Webb?" Perspiration vaporized from the top of Smoke's head.

"She hired him," Frankle explained, "to extricate herself
from her network contract."

"Monica Webb?" Smoke repeated. "Your ex?"

"My multiple ex."

"Multiple? Am I to imply you're getting back with her?"

"Infer."

"Infer? What are you implying, Thom?"

"I'm inferring you want Monica for your movie."

Smoke slowed the pace. "Would you let me finish here,
for crying out loud. Gordo and I agree on one evolutionary
aspect of home video. We believe the next ultra-smash picture requires both dramatic suspense and a triple-X-rated
format with two stars. Fuck the kids; we'll get the entire adult
world into the video stores with the right stars. Admittedly,
the concept isn't original. What is original is the willingness

of certain stars to break down the wall of sex taboo in dramatic features. We got the guy we wanted in Dell Jordan."

"Never heard of him."

"You never heard of Dell Jordan!"

"Never."

"Ever hear of something called television?"

Frankle picked up the pace, and Smoke struggled to keep up, sweat dripping steadily from his steaming head.

"Jordan's the actor a triple-X feature has been waiting for. The guy's got an ego imperious as a hard-on. Because you can't tempt an actor of this guy's rep with dollars. It's totally an appeal to ego. Even then you're lucky if you can get past his financial and creative people with a proposal. How we got to him was through Coch."

Smoke reached for Frankle's sopping sweatshirt and yanked it to slow him down.

"Jordie's got a rep as a stick man. He and Bernheim's main squeeze were rumored to be seen getting it on recently in some limo outside a popular Fourteenth Street club. Did he go the distance? I can't answer that. Some question whether he actually exists. I've personally never met him. According to Busch, Bernheim has met him at lunch. It was here the triple-X concept was broached. Dell absolutely wants to be the first star to break down the graphic-sex barrier. Hopefully, the guy's dong's as big as his ego. Because he's definitely in, commitmentwise, and if he's got some four-incher for a dong, we're fucked. Figuratively. Personally, I advocated test shots before any papers were drawn, but the only written stipulation relates to his right to choose the actress he's going to dick on a seventy-millimeter screen. Without hesitation, Thom, the guy's first choice is Clara Ravens of *Still Lives*. He's a major fan. This is why I was blown away to learn *his* rep is *hers*. Because now there's no doubt it's going to happen. It's going to be very big. I'm going to get pushed out creatively, but there's bucks in it for me. And it puts real urgency into whether I dump Kikki before the bucks come in. Because big bucks always make a divorce real inconvenient from a financial angle. Hello?"

"I'm listening, John."

Smoke pulled at the sweatshirt again to slow Frankle's pace.

"You're visual, Thom. Picture the lines at the movie houses for a triple-X dramatic film featuring Dell Jordan and Monica Webb. Picture Dell giving it to your ex on a seventy-millimeter screen with Sound-A-Round stereophonics. On the other hand, who cares about the sound track! We could hire Gary U.S. Bonds or Todd Rundgren to do the sound track, and we'd still need the national guard to control the lines."

They began to climb, the road rising as it twisted west, then south, back downtown. Frankle leaned forward, struggling, as Smoke hung on to the sweatshirt.

"She won't go through with it," Frankle said. "It'll ruin her career."

"Ruin it! She'll make millions."

"The networks will never rehire her. None of the major studios either."

"Are you kidding! They'll bog down in a wage war over her. She'll end up with her own talk show!"

"She won't do it."

Smoke gasped for breath, staggering against the ascent. Frankle slowed when he noticed Smoke's face growing purple. Smoke screamed to keep himself from quitting.

"Celebrity fucking, Thom, is the next big frontier in the home entertainment video revolution. How's it going to be stopped once the stars agree to participate? And once the first two go over the hill, leave the trench, if you will, there'll be no end to it. You'll see celebrities involved from all fields—sports, politics, fashion. Imagine Walter Payton putting it to Jane Fonda in an aerobic bondage scene. Barbara Walters blowing Henry Kissinger. Imagine the private parties featuring these videos! It's the logical next step, given the national voyeurism. Close your eyes. Picture it. 'Here's Molly What's-her-face wearing a Pierre Cardin original and getting fucked by Sly Stallone and the rest of the Stallone stable of brothers and friends!' 'Here's Carly Simon singing her smash new single and getting fucked by Lawrence Taylor, the Super Bowl linebacker!' Thom, you're going to see a *Wide World of Sex* outrating *Wide World of Sports*. They'll outlaw boxing and replace it with fucking. Julie Christie and Joe Montana!"

Smoke practically hung on to Frankle's back for support.

"With these pandemic sex diseases on the rise, Thom, it's a humane alternative. People love *to watch*."

They reached the summit of the hill and slowed to survey the easy descent toward the pond north of the tennis courts.

"Thom, encourage Monica to take the role. If you will—and I confess this is the point of my call—I'll guarantee you in writing five percent of her salary."

"Forget it."

"Let me start over."

"Don't bother."

"One more minute, Thom. People are paying two dollars for a cookie. Five dollars for a beer. They're paying twenty-five bucks for a child-size portion of pasta. Why? Boredom. Despair. Erotic anxiety. All Gordo and I and our people are talking about is upscaling pornography in a similar fashion. Aren't we entitled to creatively exploit boredom, despair, and erotic anxiety like any other entrepreneur? Did you ever hear of freedom of expression? How about free enterprise and the pursuit of happiness? *Thom*, we're targeting fashionable, disease-conscious couples—family types—no longer turned on by overpriced plates of pasta and dull New England weekends in the colonial bed-and-breakfast factories. We're targeting couples who want to stay home in a new version of family night at the hearth after the kids go to bed and the dog's been walked. I want you to talk to her for us. I want you to nail down her commitment."

"Let's change the subject," Frankle said.

"Fine. Kikki's fucking around on me. I sense it. Terri mentioned he saw her and Gordon at a table at Café Luxembourg. It was in your neighborhood, and they were with your neighbor, so I thought maybe your neighbor might have said something."

"Nothing."

"It's not you, is it?"

"How'd you guess?"

"Seriously. She likes guys like you. She goes for weak guys she mistakes as principled. Hamlet-complex guys."

"Kikki's not fucking around on you."

"She is. I'm confident I've finally made her sink to my level of turpitude."

"Johnny, nobody I know is capable of sinking to your—"

"*John*, Thom. Johnny's dead. He couldn't take it anymore."

It started to drizzle, and they ran on, down the final slope, toward the statue of Daniel Webster.

"What's the deal with our screenwriter?" Smoke asked. "How well do you know him? Because the opening sequence Gordo showed me is the sickest thing I've ever read. What's with him—wiggy?"

"Good word."

"Wigged-out vet type?"

"Who shouldn't be encouraged to shovel drugs up his nose by Mr. Busch."

"You want to help your friend? Get Monica to star in his screenplay. All a guy like that needs is the attention of a big payday. This is all Post-Vietnam Syndrome's about: sudden lack of action. Get the guy back into the economic hand-to-hand-combat game, and he'll snap out of it. Drugs don't ruin people, Thom. People who feel ruined blame drugs. Hello?"

They drew even to the pond bordering the Ramble, and Frankle announced he'd be taking the turnoff at Seventy-second Street.

"You don't want to box?"

"Take a urine test first." Frankle veered away.

"Talk to Monica!" Smoke called. "Five percent!"

28

Precisely at two, the Sunday-afternoon client appeared, in jean suit, tortoiseshell sunglasses, and shoulder-length blond hair.

"Whipp Williams?"

The man nodded solemnly and stepped inside, though by the time he had reached the living room, he was doubled over in laughter.

"Don't make me laugh," the man said.

Frankle paused, concentrating on the voice, vaguely familiar; and when the man wheeled back to him, Frankle's suspicions were confirmed.

"Don't make me laugh, Thomas. Stitches are still in the hernia incision, and we don't want to pop them."

Frankle sat down on the sofa and closed his eyes.

"Don't despair, Thomas. Whipp Williams fully intends to pay to have his portrait taken by Frankle of *Concupiscence.* But please, man, refrain from causing him to laugh. The mere weight of his member strains the incision's stitching. But tell me, how do you like the new look? Deb and I worked from composite sketches of the decade's sexiest men."

Frankle opened his eyes and folded his arms protectively against his chest.

"Have you totally lost it, Stan?"

"Lost it! Man, I've finally found it. With Deb Stein's help, I've learned that to lose is to gain, and that to end is to begin. In fact, Deb's decided to drop the Dakota Pomeroy thing and to stay with Deb Stein as both her stage and sex-surrogate sobriquet. Her real name's apparently Louise Goldbaum. What's happening with you? *Qué pasa?*"

"Everything's just about the same."

"Do you dig the wig? I'm having fun with it. I couldn't deal with both a shaved John Thomas and a hairless head. Deb suggested it. Incidentally, she's been approached by John Smoke and Terri Max to do a movie. And did I tell you I've officially resigned from the environmental bureau? Gave notice last week. Came out of the general anesthesia, and the first thought pops into my head is: Quit the environmental job; change your name. Next day Deb and I rented a car and bought a country house. She had to drive. I couldn't move my leg from the incision. Point is, we're really getting out. Soon as the lawyers and bankers arrange the closing, we're upstate. Deb's family left her a small trust."

Frankle ordered Stanley upstairs, where Frankle positioned him on the head-shot stool, then clanged around amid equipment, as if he were considering an artistic strategy. But, in fact, the portrait procedure had become so perfunctory as to require little more than adjustment in the height of lights.

"How will you be paying for this, Stan?"

"Bill Louise Goldbaum. She's the one who wants the shots. Is my wig combed?"

Stark pulled a newspaper clipping from his jean jacket and cleared his throat. "Dig this: 'A new report by the World Watch Institute warned today that the pressures of population and economic expansion are starting to exceed the ability of the earth's natural systems to sustain such activity. . . . Human use of air, water, land, forests, and other systems that support life on earth are pushing those systems over thresholds beyond which they cannot absorb such use without permanent damage.' Article concludes with this: 'No generation has ever faced such a complex set of issues requiring immediate attention. Preceding generations have always been concerned about the future, but we are the first to be faced with decisions that will determine whether the earth our children will inherit will be inhabitable.' "

Stark folded the paper gravely, then searched for Frankle beyond the lights.

"Shall I describe the house Deb and I have bought?"

"Would you first remove the sunglasses, so I can begin shooting?"

"I'm afraid I can't do that. Deb and I have a pact to keep them on for ninety-six hours. It's a symbolic thing, a symbol of our sensitivity to the spiritual light we sense."

Frankle circled to the left and began shooting.

"Both Deb and I want you to know you've got your own room in the country place. We're thinking of going into the health field. Make the house a special spiritual place: yoga, fasting, colonics. I believe I mentioned the plant nursery I'm negotiating to buy?"

Frankle lowered the camera. "Stop talking a minute."

"A café has also come under discussion. A sort of state-of-the-art vegetarian restaurant for the university set. Ithaca boasts both a college and a university. We've looked at a building. There'd be rooms behind the kitchen for after-hour private and group sex counseling. Kids simply don't know what to do with their sex energy, given this new disease dimension. Why are you just standing there?"

"I'm waiting for you to stop talking."

Stark referred to his wristwatch.

"Don't wait too long. Deb's meeting me in midtown in thirty minutes. Wants me to help her evaluate some art films. She's got a screen test upcoming for the part of the girlfriend of a Vietnam-psychopath who keeps her locked away for sexual purposes. It's a submission role, and she wants to familiarize herself with some of the latest domination equipment in the event the producers ask her to extemporize. There's also the possibility that the producers might want to do it personally. Deb knows ways of spiritually separating herself from the body. Why not join us? Afterward, we're doing macrobiotic downtown."

"Too busy." Frankle fired away, moving quickly as Stark stared wistfully into the lights positioned before and above him.

"Try to fathom it, man. The way of possession leading onto dispossession leading, in turn, onto a higher possession. Let's be sincere. How many people do we know who have been bummed out on decade-long bad trips? Remember, we're being sincere."

Frankle rewound the first clip of film. "Let me work, here, Stan."

"Be sincere, man. Go back to a sincere space in your head. I know it's embarrassing. In retrospect, as a spiritually mature Whipp Williams, evaluating my former life as Stanley Stark, I wince at my failure to understand that it profiteth not a man to serve false gods. Money, Mammon, Mammal. Mammal, Man, Manhattan. We're getting out. Of course, first Deb's doing the pornographic film. It takes money to get back to nature."

Frankle finished the second roll, kicked off the lights, and gestured for Stan to take the stairs down to the living room.

"I'll call you when I've got the prints."

"Remember, man. Your own room. Fifty acres of Finger Lake greenery ten miles up a dirt road into the mountains, where everything the eye looks upon is blessed, and where together we shall recite: 'We must dance and we must sing / We are blessed by everything / Everything we look upon is blessed.' "

Frankle escorted Stark to the door downstairs. In the hall-

way, Harry Chambers rose into view at the end of the corridor, breathless from the five-flight ascent. He evinced no
recognition of the costumed Stark, who himself passed in
silence.

Chambers set down three large brown bags. "I buzzed to
get some help. What were you doing, beating your banana?"

The bags were filled with videocassettes.

"Shooting," Frankle said.

"Frankle and his 'beat your banana' photos. I seem to be
slipping into the same." Chambers hoisted a couple of cassettes: *Passage to Ecstasy, Sweet Cheeks*.

"I have to prepare for a client," Frankle said.

"Likewise." Chambers extracted a vial of pills and popped
one. "Interviewing another hooker. This one's twelve. Hope
she ain't Oriental. Wasted a kid about twelve morning of the
afternoon I triggered the toe popper. She was wired and went
up like the fourth of July. Got time for a beer?"

Frankle said he wished, then wished Chambers good luck
and double-locked the door.

29

Bundled in coats against the cold, they walked north on Broadway to the Bahama Mama restaurant. Constance strolled in the middle, holding Nick's right hand with her left and Frankle's left hand with her right. Then Nick dashed to Frankle's side, and Frankle held Nick's left hand with his right and Constance's right hand with his left.

"Is there a purpose to this game, Nicholas?" Constance sounded impatient.

Frankle volunteered that among other things, it kept the mind distracted from the fact that somewhere above the January clouds, flying machines circled the globe awaiting orders to drop nuclear devices.

"Gee, Thom. How do you live with such weighty thoughts?"

"If it weren't for my stoical temperament, I doubt I could."

Constance was quick to remind him that Baudelaire assigned irony to the banality column a hundred years ago.

Fire engines turned onto Broadway and raced south, their sirens loud enough to pull over passenger cars in Jersey City.

Nick covered his ears.

"What's with you tonight?" Frankle asked.

Her sullen shrug convinced him to drop it.

Nick was shooting an imaginary pistol with his free hand. Frankle listened carefully enough to the boy's mumblings to understand he had robbed a bank and the sheriff was giving chase.

"Keep shooting," Frankle said, then returned his attention to Constance, on the other side. She explained that her stepparents would be spending some time in Manhattan so that Nick could remain in school.

"I would have taken care of him," he said.

"I wouldn't have dreamed of asking."

"Why not?"

She shrugged again. "I just wouldn't."

"It's going to cost them a lot of money to stay in a hotel."

"If you want," Constance said churlishly, "you could put them up at your place."

"I'd be happy to."

"I'd love to accept, just to see your face fall."

"It wouldn't fall, Constance." It was their first fight.

They passed the Eighty-fourth Street movie house, with its long lines of teenagers. Stores that had been hallmarks of the neighborhood six months earlier had been replaced by cookie emporia and baby boutiques.

Nick ran ahead, slapping his thigh as if it were his horse.

"How long will you be gone?" Frankle wrapped his arm around Constance's shoulder.

"However long it takes me to rent the house. Unless I decide to sell it. That would probably take a month."

"A month!"

"What can I do?"

Frankle could feel anger building to protect him against his anxiety. Old habits were reasserting themselves, and he petitioned That Voice for instruction; nothing came.

"Are you uncomfortable with me or something?" he asked.

She called to Nick, "Don't you dare cross that street!" and then said to Frankle, "Believe it or not, none of this has anything to do with you."

Nick waited for them to draw even. "There's a b-bank, Thom. Look!"

"Thom and Mommy are talking," Constance said.

Nick appealed to Frankle before skipping across the street.

"I think," Frankle said, "I chose the wrong time to quit drinking."

She stopped and turned to him. "You're just going to have to trust me."

"I trust you," he answered immediately; but he knew the kind of trust in mention was a calculated risk, in which the odds seemed dubious.

"I see no reason to rush into anything," she said.

He lit a cigarette, and then they remained silent for blocks.

"If there's anything I can do for you," he said, finally, "feel free to ask."

"Time's the big test of love's suitability."

"What are you talking about?"

"Skip it. Is this the place?"

Frankle looked straight up, to see the sign of the palm tree. He pictured iced margaritas and daiquiris, and silently rehearsed ordering a club soda with lime.

When he held the door for her, Constance said, "Let's not fight in front of Nick."

"Were we fighting?"

"Very funny."

Three days later, during a cold rain, Constance Frame left for California. According to the calendar, spring was seven weeks away, but the late-January day on which he carried down the suitcases to the street was redolent of November, and Frankle feared it portended a March worse than January.

Nick clutched his pelican and stood beneath the umbrella Constance was holding.

"See y-you soon, Thom!"

Frankle set the suitcases on the wet macadam and bent down to hug the boy. "You'll only be downtown. I'll visit."

Constance and Frankle had slept apart for three nights, and now he feared she had chosen to distance herself irretrievably.

"I'll call you," she said, and kissed him perfunctorily before entering the cab. There was no reassurance in her eyes.

The driver finished loading the bags and slammed down the trunk. Frankle knew that many of her belongings and some of the boy's were still closeted upstairs, so he presumed it was only his paranoia that whispered this was the last time he'd see her.

"I'm gonna miss you guys." The back window was partly open, and he held both hands on its upper rim.

The driver got in behind the wheel, and Constance rolled down the window. She already seemed very far away.

"I hate goodbyes," she said ambiguously.

Frankle squeezed her hand, then stepped away as the cab moved off. Nick waved through the back window and Frankle stood there in the rain, looking down the street.

Inside, he could hear the whir of car tires on the wet macadam and the beeping of a single horn. What was there now but tomorrow and tomorrow and tomorrow?

30

Snow fell throughout the first week of February. Frankle distracted himself from the seasonal zeitgeist through the routines of head-shot work, and he distracted himself from the routines of head-shot work by parodying the garrulous camp of the "shooter." "Come on, Ellen! Give us some mischief with the lips." "Hey, Jim! What's hiding behind those eyes? Give us a clue."

But he felt as far away as the sun in its winter axis, and he hoped that for his clients' sake, the hollowness of his posture would not recapitulate itself in their own. Alas, it did, and instead of capturing particular selves, Frankle merely recorded faces put on to face other faces. Worse, rifling through his shots of "homeless" faces in bus shelters, churches, and breakfast lines, or faces staring out subway car windows, cabs, or coffee shops, Frankle came face to face with clichéd images of urban ennui and solitude. To throw these prints into the fireplace impressed him as comically grandiose; instead, he tossed them into the darkroom wastebasket, numbed with the acceptance that his eyes had nothing new to see.

On Saturday night, as he returned from a black-and-white movie in which he hoped a lighting strategy or a composition might evoke an idea (it didn't), It occurred to him that Constance Frame might have been waiting all week for him to call her, as much as he had been waiting in his insecurity and pride for her to call him.

He tried her twice that night and again on Sunday morning, but the rings went unanswered; and on Sunday evening, when the ringing was at last answered, a computerized voice announced that the number had been disconnected.

The eeriness of a night run in the icy park made the apartment's silence on his return less uncomfortable than before the run, but a hot bath and steaming cup of rose hip tea without whiskey brought forth ghouls who threatened to turn a single Sunday night into a review of several decades of regrets and self-recriminations.

And it didn't help to stand later in the chilly darkroom in a knit cap and bathrobe, watching prints of Constance and Nick develop.

When the telephone rang, Frankle nearly flew to it.

The caller asked to speak with Jack. Frankle couldn't place the accent exactly, though it sounded vaguely French. Frankle explained that Jack was an Airedale and had this thing about taking calls.

"How do you say it?" the man said. "Constance invited me to telephone." He spoke with halting intensity. "I am Paolo Gabriel."

"Oh, yes," Frankle said. "Sweaters. A mascot."

"Right on! Yes." There was a pause. "I am to be in town for interviewing two more days. You could come to see me with your dog? Tomorrow, let us say, to interview with this dog Jack?"

Paolo Gabriel then mentioned that he would be paying five thousand to borrow a dog of his choosing for a week-long shoot.

Frankle calculated that he would have to shoot fifty heads

to gross as much; and if his rate of four clients per week continued, he would not earn in two and a half months what his pet could command for sitting quietly for seven days on a set.

He agreed to meet Paolo Gabriel the next day at the man's Tribeca loft.

31

When the elevator opened in the lobby, a man with three leashed dogs—a dalmatian, a sheep dog, and a Scottish terrier—was yanked from the graffitied space.

"Heel now! Heel now, you bitches!"

Jack appealed to Frankle in evident perplexity, then charged into the elevator, nose down, sniffing.

"Be a good boy," Frankle entreated, though he recognized there was simply no way the terrier could appreciate how much he might help out, if he would only this once not fuck up.

The doors parted on the thirteenth floor, and Frankle entered an empty space that resembled a shiny elementary school gymnasium.

A curtain fluttered at the far end of the room, and a man in baggy red clothing dodged camera equipment in his rush toward Frankle. The clatter of his cowboy boots ricocheted off the walls, and the tropical bird perched on his shoulder appeared to wince from the ringing. The man was short and portly, with long and oily black hair.

"Andrew and Pepper, I bet you!" He offered his hand, smiling. "I am Paolo. Meet me!"

"Thom Frankle and Jack, actually." Frankle shook the guy's hand.

"Of course!" Paolo knelt before Jack. "What a creature we have here! And now if you would unleash him for us to see his articulation."

Frankle instructed Jack to sit, then unleashed him. The terrier immediately shot away, nose to the floor.

"Jack!"

"No, no! Please. We will watch him go hunting, thank you, Thom."

Paolo stood with his arms folded across his chest, studying the hyperactive animal.

"Oh, boy! I am very much impressed with the fabulous coloring. What model is he exactly?"

"Airedale terrier."

"Fabulous! What about you? Something to drink? Scotch, vodka, beer, wine, Perrier, coffee? You would prefer grass?"

Frankle accepted a Perrier.

Paolo hurried from the room, calling playfully to the distracted terrier, and returned with a chilled bottle of ginger ale.

"These terriers," he said gravely, "they are poodles, no?"

"No. *Terriers*. The Airedale's an English breed. They're called king of the terriers because they're the largest of all the terriers."

"Hey, you king-size terrier," Paolo called. "Come over here to me." He waved a dog biscuit.

Frankle whistled. The dog turned to face the two men, then lifted his leg to mark a tripod. Paolo's astonished laugh sounded like a scream.

Jack came racing over and sat by Frankle's side.

"I have not so great rapport with dogs," Paolo said. "But my trainer is an expert and a graduate of dog school." The bird on Paolo's shoulder cocked its green-and-red head and turned in a circle.

Jack jumped up and nearly knocked over the chubby sweater entrepreneur.

"Wow! Big-headed and rugged! Oh, boy!" Paolo cupped his hands and shouted, "Jan! Come out in there, Jan, please!" He turned to Frankle. "You and Jack must try some pickled herring."

Frankle thanked him all the same but said they'd both eaten on the way over.

An anorexic black woman in white sweat clothing peeked out of a doorway at the end of the room.

"What is it now?"

"Darling. Come in to see our latest visitor. Where is Henry?"

Jack jumped again at the parrot, which tried to peck the terrier's head. Frankle grabbed Jack by the collar and commanded him to sit.

"At the shrink's," the woman said.

"Again!"

"*Again!*" she mimicked.

When the door closed, Paolo waved his hand dismissively. "My moody wife." He removed a fully automated 35-millimeter compact, small as a cigarette pack, knelt, and fired. "To present to the trainer as something to show him. Has this big head ever been to Saint Bart's?"

"Not with me."

"You have never been! What a place for so many things, especially for great ass-watching!"

Frankle cleared his throat. "When will you know for certain about Jack?"

"Are you kidding! I love this king's look. All we need now is the trainer's agreement. Because this morning we are all happy with a big shepherd. Even the trainer. But then the shepherd bites! So we have to hope Jack is friendly for the trainer and my models."

Frankle finished a second ginger ale as he waited for the

trainer, who, when he finally showed up, revealed a nose that ticked and a flattop the color of his gray eyes and slacks.

"He don't bite, I hope?"

"He's a big baby," Frankle said.

"He don't run off lead, I hope?"

"I trained him myself," Frankle said.

The trainer asked to be alone with the dog. Frankle didn't like the expression "the dog" but watched from the hallway until the trainer waved him and Paolo back into the big room.

"He don't bite! His leg twitches, but he's not bad." The trainer addressed both Frankle and Paolo. "To me, a wife don't tell you half the story a man's dog does."

Frankle wanted to go home. Paolo said the contract would be simple, guaranteeing Frankle five grand, half before shooting, half upon completion. Paolo and his people would assume all shipping costs.

"Shipping costs?" Frankle said.

"The planes to Saint Bart's. A big one and a puddle jumper."

Frankle didn't get it exactly. "I thought you wanted Jack for Constance's sweater line?"

"Possibly," Paolo explained. "For now, I want him for my new line of dynamite summer tops and shorts."

Two days later, Frankle reluctantly signed a contract, and two days after the signing, Paolo Gabriel and Henry the trainer showed up on a snowy Friday, bundled fashionably in a way that suggested they'd just stepped from a ski slope. Frankle spent ten minutes reviewing feeding instructions and carefully packing Jack's favorite eyeless and dismembered toys.

Paolo told Frankle not to worry. But Frankle was worried and went down to the street to kiss Jack goodbye and help load him in a carrying crate in the van.

Jack pawed the cage forlornly, and Frankle thanked him

in a whisper for helping to keep a roof over their heads until spring.

Shaking Paolo Gabriel's hand, Frankle asked if he had happened to speak with Constance Frame since her return to the West Coast. It so happened Paolo had spoken with her the previous night. He thumbed through his address book, the width of the Bible, and provided Frankle with a number.

"Her sister's place," Paolo said. "A twin sister, married to the baker Steve."

The recorded voice declaimed: "You have reached Jane Frame's Hot Buns Bakery. I'm busy with the cheesecakes right now, so I can't come to the phone. If you have a delivery order, leave your name and number at the tone. All those interested in speaking with my sister should phone this number after eleven P.M."

32

In the darkness, he listened to rain pelting the studio's roof. Each time he closed his eyes in an attempt to return to sleep, he pictured a nightcap of cognac.

He sat up, turned on the bedside lamp, and lit a cigarette.

The forgiveness of sins is perpetual, That Voice intoned, *and righteousness is not required.*

The telephone rang.

"Hello?"

"I bet I can picture what you're doing."

Frankle heard ice tumbling.

"Same here," he told Kikki Epstein.

"What *are* you doing?"

"What's the matter?" Frankle said.

"What isn't the matter. What are you doing?"

"Staring through the dark at the ceiling. What have you been drinking?"

"What haven't I been drinking. What's your schedule look like? What are you doing now, for example?"

"Now?"

"I'm only kidding." She laughed, and Frankle heard ice tumble again. "Let me tell you what I've got on tap at the studio this week. A brassiere shoot to a theme of 'You can depend on a smooth image that shapes and conceals.' Also, a mix-and-match sportswear gig to the tune of 'Slip on a new persona whenever the others haven't done the trick.' Right up your alley, doll."

"Are you asking for help?"

"That's putting it mildly. Terri Max has quit, and Johnny's moved out."

"When?"

"A week now. I had to throw Johnny out. Caught him red-handed in the apartment with that model we once used. Dallas? Anyway, it was a dare. He was daring me to throw him out. I had no choice."

"I know the feeling."

"I bet you do. Why don't we have a drink? You can tell me all about it."

"Lunch would be better."

"Thom! After all the nice shit I've done for you, you're not going to let me come over there and cry on your shoulder?"

"It's two in the morning!"

"So!"

"And you're drunk."

"So!"

"And I'm on the wagon."

"Liar!"

"You're also married and extremely angry at a guy by the name of Johnny Smoke."

"Thom! You talk like we're still twenty years old. We've been around the block a thousand times. My ass has settled half a foot since those days."

Frankle explained that he was living with someone new.

"What!"

"Her name's Constance," Frankle said.

"Put her on the phone a second."

"She's sleeping."

"Is she nice, Thom? Because if she is, I just hope you're not overcompensating. Are you overcompensating? You probably are, after Monica. I find myself looking at boys half my age. Cute little ones I imagine I can boss around like I've been bossed around. My thighs have cellulite I can't get rid of. My teeth need to be capped; the enamel's worn off. Put her on the phone, please. Just wake her up a second."

Frankle closed his eyes, sleepy, finally, with the comfort of a familiar voice.

"Kikki, you're beautiful. Successful, talented, and beautiful."

"Everyone I know is successful, talented, and beautiful!"

"That's not true."

"You sound like an art director."

"Make some coffee."

"Why didn't you say I was giving, supportive, witty, and kind? I'll tell you why. Because I'm bossy and aggressive. I'm doing all the crap hip guys quit doing twenty years ago. I'm a little careerist. I've wasted my youth and my looks on some fucking career!"

"You're just mad at Johnny."

"Mad? I've been fed up with that dirt bag for ten years. You ever try killing yourself?"

"Make that coffee already."

"I'm going to buy myself a pet."

"Good idea."

"I'm going to divorce the dirt bag and buy a nice pet."

"Meanwhile, take two aspirin and drink a lot of water. I'll call you in the morning." Frankle thought he heard her crying. "You okay there?"

"I'm blowing my nose. I'll talk to you later."

He listened to the hang-up *om* and then returned the cradle to its receiver.

He lit another cigarette and stared at the phone; then at the phone number on the scrap of paper from Paolo's address book. He absently extinguished the cigarette as he finished dialing. The phone rang once before being picked up.

"Hello?"

"Constance?"

"Hello?"

"It's Thom."

"Hi!"

"Hi."

"This is funny," she said. "I was just thinking about you."

"I tried you earlier in the week but no luck."

She began to explain, irrelevantly, Frankle thought, that her tenants had run up a four-hundred-dollar phone bill, forcing the company to discontinue service. Frankle didn't understand how this pertained to her not calling him, but he elected not to challenge her.

"I just wish you had told me how to get in touch with you."

"You really couldn't." She asked him to hold while she stepped outside to get her glass of wine.

She seemed to be gone a long time, and a deep weariness went through Frankle. He could hear waves breaking in the background.

"I was just about to phone my folks and Nick," Constance said, breathless now. "But tell me how you are."

He wondered if there were such a thing as a poker voice. If there were, he could use one right about now.

"I'm fine," he said. "How about yourself?"

She sighed. "It's been very strange, Thom. I stand in my house with my hands on my hips, staring vacantly, not knowing what to do. I've tried to pack things but can't seem to. I try to phone a realtor but hang up after dialing. Yesterday I went to the hardware store and bought a For Sale sign and a For Rent sign, then misplaced them somehow on my way home."

"Is the weather nice?"

"You wouldn't believe how nice it's been."

"How's Nick?"

"A little mad at me but okay. My stepparents are having a nice time being in the city."

"Why don't you give me his number?"

"He'd love if you'd call." She gave him the number.

"Anything else?" Frankle feared his disappointed tone would betray him.

"I'm afraid not," Constance said. "I can't tell you how strange it is being back here. I feel so inward. I get flooded with a million emotions and float around in a trance. It's as if the past has a new hold on me and wants me to figure something out before I move on."

Frankle cleared his throat. "Have you any idea when you'll be back?"

"I wish I knew. Did you hear from Paolo?"

"He's the one who gave me this number." And Frankle told her about Jack's journey to the Caribbean.

"I bet you miss him," she said.

"And you."

"I should have called. I'm sorry."

He remembered now the day she left in the cab. He might have known from the way she didn't turn around to wave that she was making a run for it. He couldn't blame her. Why should she have less difficulty with intimacy than he?

"Stay in touch," he said.

"I will."

"So long, then."

"Bye."

He set down the receiver. It could have been worse. She might have thanked him for calling.

When he tried Kikki Epstein, the phone went unanswered.

33

The streetlamps issued a yellow phosphorescence in the dawn's cobalt sky. Cold and anxious, Frankle listened to the icy snowfall ping off parked cars as he stretched for his run. Down the block, the jogger approaching from the park in the black hooded sweatshirt and combat pants revealed himself to be Harry Chambers.

"Best you got a sock over your cock. She making *mucho frío* today." Chambers lit a cigarette. "Up all night finishing the screenplay. What's your excuse?"

"Couldn't sleep."

Chambers looked around. "Where's the dumb dog?"

"Saint Bart's."

"Couldn't talk him into taking you, huh?"

"He wanted some time alone."

Chambers brandished a handgun from his sweatshirt pocket and offered it to Frankle.

"Give your white ass a break. Best to trust old trusty. Bogeymen known to ambush at dawn."

Frankle studied the gun. "Real or one of your facsimiles?"

"Take it. Someone gives you any shit, you'll both find out."

Frankle pushed the gun aside and stuffed a glove in his crotch.

"Which reminds me," Chambers said. "Came across a publication of your work the other day."

"My work's never been published, Harry."

"Bet a corn-beef sandwich at the Carnegie on it?"

"Fine."

"I'll show you on my way downtown with the script."

Frankle wheeled, waving his okay, and set off toward the park, imagining Jack running at his side.

The vagaries of February were such that the sun appeared at noon and the day turned mild as Frankle followed Chambers down to Times Square, where they walked west on Forty-second Street, between crowds loitering beneath the marquees of pornographic movie theaters.

"Uzi's the weapon you'd love to carry in a crowd like this," Chambers said. "Comfortably carried undetected beneath a sports jacket but can wipe out a block of street garbage like this in seconds." He swerved suddenly into a peep show emporium.

"What's this?" Frankle said.

"This is where I did my script research." He patted his carrying bag, containing the screenplay. "Four levels of carnival pornography. Remember not to feed peanuts to the hookers in the one-to-one booths."

Chambers held open the door, and they entered a first-floor section featuring magazines and sexual aids. At the end of the room, a man at a microphone was shouting, "Check it out, check it out, check it out. Live sex, live sex, live sex."

"As opposed to what?" Frankle asked Chambers. "Necrophilia?"

Chambers held open a magazine featuring lesbian bondage. "Know her?"

For health reasons, Frankle didn't want to touch the periodical. "That's what's-her-name?" he said.

"Dakota Pomeroy. She does just this sort of shit in my

screenplay," Chambers flipped the pages to show Frankle the scenario's evolution.

Frankle noticed men wandering furtively in and out of peep show booths in a dark room farther in. A man in a janitor's uniform was mopping the floors of the booths.

"Stanley's been dating her," Frankle said absently, turning back to the magazine.

"Anybody who meets her price dates her," Chambers said. "In fact, John Smoke's got her on some kind of retainer to entertain anybody involved in preproduction. She's a heroin addict."

Chambers closed the page on her, handed Frankle another magazine, entitled *Choice Cuts*, and pointed to a photo copyright credited to Thom Frankle. As it turned out, the entire magazine of photographs had been taken by Frankle. They were cribbed test shots taken years ago for *Concupiscence*.

"Didn't I tell you? Surprised?" There was an acerbic and condescending quality to Chambers's tone. "Busch and I came across them last week. He admired the detail of the work. Thinks you should work for a science magazine."

Frankle frowned in mortification. "These things must be six years old."

Chambers patted him on the back. "I thought you might enjoy seeing them. In the event you're tempted to pull moral rank on me for writing a porno script, I wanted you to see your own rarefied contribution to culture. Shall I have them gift-wrapped, or will a plain brown bag do?"

Frankle returned the magazine to the table.

"What kind of way is that to treat your one and only publication?"

"Save it, Harry."

"Come upstairs," Chambers said. "They got a 'Chicks with Dicks' sex show I'd like to check out before I order my corn-beef sandwich with a side of potato salad."

Frankle told him he'd wait outside.

Chambers popped his glass eye from its socket and stared at Frankle. "Ten minutes."

Frankle watched Chambers hobble upstairs. A video screen adjacent to the stairway was flashing highlights of the sex show.

"Don't you think of anything but sex?" a man said, and Frankle turned to behold a smiling Terri Max. He was wearing a baseball cap and a leather bomber jacket. "Guess who's with me here?" he said.

Frankle thrust his hands in his pockets and shrugged. "Johnny Smoke?"

"Try Monica Webb."

Frankle's eyes searched the place.

"Check it out," Max said. "Booth eleven. Boning up on domination material. Our screenwriter's come up with some scenarios I've never before seen choreographed. He's got ideas make you want to quadruple-lock your door at night."

A blue-suited older man came over, holding a plastic sex aid the size of a child's leg. When he pushed a button, the thing sounded like a blender. "Who's this for, I wonder? The pet elephant?"

"You'd be surprised," Terri Max said.

"Undoubtedly," the man said.

"Booth twenty-three," Terri Max told him. "Upstairs in the back. Check it out."

"I've seen quite enough, thank you."

"Squeamish type, Hieronymus?"

Coch turned to Frankle and passed a hand through his silver hair before offering to shake. "Hieronymus Coch. You wouldn't be the wardrobe guy?"

Frankle explained he was a photographer.

"You're supposed to say your name now," Terri Max rebuked, before introducing the two men. Then he pointed to something behind Coch, who turned and laughed briefly.

"Red light goes on again in booth eleven!" Terri Max shook his head, amused.

"Dedication," Coch said sardonically.

"No shit," Terri Max said. "Did you know this guy used to be our Miss Webb's ex?"

"For God's sake," Hieronymus Coch said. "You wouldn't be the Thom Frankle to whom I just dictated a certified letter?"

Frankle nodded.

"Well, I'm the Hieronymus Coch who is Monica's lawyer and agent."

"Did Monica tell you," Terri Max asked Frankle, "that the network's trying to sue to keep her from doing our film?"

"Let them," Coch said. "That exclusivity clause is about as binding as papier-mâché handcuffs."

They fell silent, watching the light go off and on again in booth eleven.

Terri Max referred to his watch. "Long time no see," he said to Frankle.

"I've been away," Frankle said. "Shooting in Saint Bart's."

"Really! What'd it do, rain?"

"Sun block," Frankle said.

"Sun block!" Terri Max said. "Let me tell you of my ideal sun block. Can you imagine the covering I'm talking about between, say, the hours of eleven to two?"

"Incidentally, Mr. Frankle." Hieronymus Coch shifted into a casual stance. "You and Ms. Webb really gotta get together on this apartment issue. I'm confident neither one of you wants to waste my time and your money in court. As I told Monica, I recommend you guys double the rent and sublet it to some assholic yuppie until you can get your post-relationship act together. Think about it, will you?"

"Hey," Terri Max said, pushing Frankle on the shoulder. "Dakota tells me you and Stanley Stark are old buddies. How frigging small is the world anyway?"

Frankle watched the light in booth eleven flick off, then go on again.

"Tell me," Terri Max said, "is the guy dangerous or something?"

"Who?" Frankle said.

"Stark. He called me the other night and warned me not to hang out with Dakota. Said she was his fiancée. What is he, nuts?"

Monica Webb emerged from the booth and approached them; she appeared shocked.

"That sound track is so out of sync it's disgusting."

"Forget the dialogue, for Christ's sake," Terri Max said.

"Seriously," Monica said, "I can't say lines like that."

"Don't worry about the lines!"

She turned to Coch. "Dell and I need latitude. I'm serious. I want the right of improv in the contract."

"We'll talk to John."

"John!" Monica scoffed. "Gordon's making all the creative decisions, and you know it."

"Look who's here." Terri Max pushed Frankle into her.

Monica flushed. "What is this, Thom? Are you following me around?"

"Of course not."

"No? Then what are you doing here?"

"I'm waiting for Chambers to finish up some research, so I can buy him a sandwich."

"Would you both kindly cut the crap!" Coch smiled, thrusting the sex aid between them.

"Tell Chambers I had to leave, would you?" Frankle turned from Max and headed for the door.

"Quit following me around," Monica Webb called.

Frankle bought Chambers a corn-beef sandwich and half a pound of potato salad and left it in a brown paper bag before his neighbor's apartment door.

34

No martyrdom in the world was worth Frankle's stepping into the jockstrap that dangled from the hook in his locker at the Y. He used his shoe to push the frayed thing to the floor, then kicked it beneath a water fountain. Changing into trunks and high-tops, he draped a jumping rope round his neck.

In the crowded gymnasium, a basketball game proceeded at a furious pace. John Smoke took an outlet pass off a rebound and raced downcourt to drive in for a lay-up. He missed.

"Pass the ball, motherfucker!"

Frankle went to the corner and set the floor clock for five minutes and jumped till the bell rang. Then he reset the clock for three minutes and shuffled around the heavy bag, his shoulders rocking as he slowly punched from a crouched, flat-footed posture. He imagined that his sticklike figure looked ridiculous, but he concentrated on the bag. Jab, jab. Hook to the body, double to the head, move away. He leaped back in with a Pattersonesque right cross to the chin, following with a left hook to the body. The bag was hurt, and Frankle threw a flurry to its head, bobbing and weaving and ducking to avoid the counterpunches. The referee halted the fight on a TKO at two minutes, fifty-three seconds into the round. Frankle raised his arms in victory, his lungs about to burst.

He plopped down on a canvas mat and watched the basketball game. John Smoke put one up from twenty feet: Air ball.

"Pass it!"

Smoke told the dude to kiss his ass and stepped off the court. "Whip your butt in two rounds!"

"You wouldn't go one," Frankle promised.

Smoke smiled wryly. "What's with the tone? You think I twisted her arm or something? Coch is the one instrumental in this. I'm just a former hack director of professional sports videos taking advantage—"

"Skip it." Frankle stood and flicked a jab. Smoke slipped it easily and kept dancing.

"I gotta say it, Thom. No offense, but I've got to tell you. I'm impressed. Monica is definitely impressive. She's unbelievable in the raw. I've got to say that much. Because for the first time since I've known you, I can understand why you put up with so much shit over so many years. Just incredible. This was also the sentiment of my test-shot people. Not in so many words, but they were spilling things and tripping over their own jaws. Laurie Larsen was there. She can't understand why you ever wanted to be with her, Laurie, I mean."

Frankle turned away to shadowbox.

"I gotta tell you, Thom. You should have seen Dell Jordan's face when he met Monica. First thing he tells her is, he's her biggest fan. Of course, as you know, Monica's undauntable. She's an *actress*. But no fooling. Dell's beard stubble impressed even her. It's fascinating in its subtlety: brown blond, brown red, brown brown, blond brown, blond red . . ."

Frankle turned to face Smoke and led with a right hand, which missed as Smoke bobbed away reflexively.

"The guy's a character," Smoke said. "I called him last night. This is after midnight. Some of us wanted to invite him out for a drink. We were in the neighborhood of the hotel. I lost the flip to Busch and had to. So who answers the phone but your ex."

Frankle flicked a jab. Smoke countered and slapped him twice in the face with two blinding jabs. They were both feinting and sliding now.

"She tells me they're rehearsing, and Dell can't come to the phone! I loved it. *Rehearsing!* Can you believe it?"

Frankle shuffled in with two jabs and threw another wild overhead right. Smoke countered with a lead right cross and hit Frankle, palm open, in the left ear.

Frankle's head began to float with the ringing, and he faked a right jab, then threw a wild left hook that found Smoke's ear. Smoke shook it off.

"Nothing, Thom. Nothing behind it." Smoke danced around wildly. "Everyone's having the time of their life. The entire cast has taken blood tests. Totally free of viral infections. This means bodily fluids can be exchanged on the set."

Frankle stopped. "That head shot didn't hurt you?"

"Nothing."

Frankle pulled off his gloves. "I feel like I broke my hand!"

"I got rocks in my head, Thom. You know why I can say that? Because you've been with Kikki, and I didn't even know it."

Frankle gazed up from his hand. "What?"

"Don't 'what' me. She told me."

"She's trying to get you mad."

"You calling her a liar?"

"I'm calling you an idiot. For taking the bait."

"You're really not fucking her?"

Frankle threw his gloves at Smoke and started toward the shower room.

35

Jack's safe return from the Caribbean coincided with the unseasonable appearance of a pair of robins, one of whom threnodied at dawn and dusk from the top of a water tower across the street from Frankle's terrace. This went on through the middle two weeks of February, which passed more slowly than the preceding two years.

But then, all at once, it seemed, spring impended. The angle of light changed sharply, striking sections of buildings hidden all winter in shadows; and by month's end, as the temperature swung suddenly into the fifties, the robins elected to build their nest in the budding dogwood tree on Frankle's terrace.

In the five years since its planting in a whiskey barrel, the tree had grown as high as the roof of the duplex. Frankle climbed up there with his camera and tripod and discovered a convenient location for chronicling what he assumed would be the laying and hatching of blue eggs. He spent hour after hour behind a blind of burlap, photographing the laboring birds, and during the second week of March he found two eggs.

On the very night of his discovery, he received a message from Constance Frame, requesting that he call her back as soon as he could. Though he'd written her off every time he'd gone across the street to the church to pray for perspective, he returned the call immediately. But he got no closer to her than her brother-in-law, Steve Lucas, who informed Frankle that Constance had left for a week with her sister, somewhere in the Yucatán. This was less interesting to Frankle than Steve Lucas's disclosure that Constance had decided to put her house in Venice up for sale. She had made that decision, Steve said, as impulsively as she had decided to fly off with Jane.

Initially, Frankle felt fed up with Constance's continuous evasions; she seemed to contact him exclusively to communicate that Frankle wouldn't be able to contact her. But during his dinner of rice and beans, he recognized that he was in some sense grateful for her disappearances: Even though he would have preferred her to be more emotionally predictable, he knew full well that had she been too enthusiastically decided about him, he would have run the other way. What her unpredictability had demonstrated to him (about himself) was that he was much happier with her than without her; but more than that, whenever they had managed to be together, she had been kind without demanding assurances or guarantees.

To Frankle's amazement, by the time he stopped staring at his plate of cold food, he realized that next time he saw Constance Frame he intended to ask her to marry him. And at the moment of his impetuous resolution, astounded at how a life can turn irreversibly in an instant, he heard the scream-like call of blue jays.

But it was only after he returned to the roof to cover his camera equipment and noticed the two blue eggs missing from the nest that he understood the meaning of the jays' call. The sudden absence of the eggs made Frankle's heart sink.

Sorrow drove him to lace his nightcap of hot lemonade

with enough honey to drown a blue jay, and he climbed into bed with the Bible open to the Book of Job. He had underlined *Why is light given to a man whose way is hid, and whom God hath hedged in?* when the telephone rang.

Hieronymus Coch apologized for telephoning after ten. "I take it," Coch said, "that I'm not disturbing you?"

Frankle asked what he could do for Mr. Coch.

The lawyer explained that to his way of thinking, the right to renew the original lease to the apartment cohabited by Thom Frankle and Monica Webb clearly belonged to both lessees, and upon Monica's exercising of the lease renewal in 1985, she implicitly served as an agent for both previous signators. Of course, had Frankle been away for significant periods of time or had the lease checks not been paid equitably, the matter might arguably be of a different status. But Coch could assure Frankle, as he had assured his client Monica Webb, that the court's method of resolving these matters was almost always unsatisfactory to both parties, who were, generally speaking, pissed off sufficiently to begin with not to need the trauma of a court ruling, which inevitably only exacerbated that pissed-off feeling.

"Consequently," Hieronymus Coch said, "if you are not, at present, in a financial position to compensate Monica Webb for purposes of relocation, I recommend that you accept her extraordinary settlement offer of twenty thousand dollars for you to sign over the residence to her." Coch fell into a fit of coughing before affirming that since the only alternative was cohabitation, an arrangement both parties contended was no longer acceptable, and since it was clear that the court would rule in favor of a financial settlement, Coch strongly felt that Frankle should accept Monica's offer, which, Coch had been led to believe, Frankle would be unable to match. "And may I remind you, Mr. Frankle," Coch concluded, "that the aforementioned will permit circumvention not only of painful and

protracted legal procedures but of astronomical legal expenses as well." Coch took a deep breath. "Now then. May
I tell Monica Webb that you accept her offer?"

Frankle closed the book he had been reading. "You may
tell her I'll take it under advisement."

"May I tell her, sir, when we might expect your answer?"

"Sooner than later."

"Would it be suitable to your purposes if I told her sometime later this week?"

"You may tell her 'sooner than later.' Good night now."

Jack, who had his ways of heralding an evacuation, was
beginning to circle in the far corner of the bedroom. Frankle
needed to walk off a number of quandaries anyway and
dressed faster than a fireman.

The sultry weather kept the streets crowded with cars and
late-night strollers. Jack veered down the sidewalk, sniffing.
Frankle closed his eyes and pictured Constance Frame standing on a beach facing breaking waves before a sudden com-
motion restored him, and he discovered Jack squatting
unpropitiously in the middle of the crowded sidewalk.

Bagging the business, Frankle straightened abashedly when
a voice called out, "Thom and Jack!"

Frankle turned to behold Monica Webb, waving from the
corner of Broadway, a man at her side. With an underhand
release, Frankle lofted the bag in a bull's-eye parabola into a
nearby bin. Then he followed the untethered Airedale to the
corner.

"I just tried to call you!" Monica ruffled the terrier's head.
"We were having drinks around the corner at the Café Luxembourg. Did you know your machine's not on?"

She wore tight jeans and a scalloped sweater beneath an
open leather jacket.

"Didn't Dominique answer?" Frankle said perversely.

"Dominique?"

"She must have been taking her bath."

Monica turned to the man on whose arm she now leaned affectionately.

"Thom is a free-lance photographer. He earns poverty level shooting aspiring actresses who work tables to earn poverty level. They're usually—what, Thommie?—nineteen and from Nebraska?"

The man winked at Frankle and offered his hand. "Dell Jordan."

Frankle accepted the big shot's hand the way he'd been taught in the Cub Scouts: looking him in the eyes.

"Did my attorney call you?" Monica said.

"You don't want to talk about that now," Frankle suggested.

"I wouldn't talk about it now, darling, but Dell and I are going out of town tomorrow." In parodying his hauteur, she was warning him not to even try matching her pretension for pretension.

"Did Coch mention the party?" she asked.

"Not a word."

"Are you serious?"

"Completely." Frankle whistled for Jack, who was following a couple with dripping ice cream cones up Broadway.

"I'm going to throw a party on the roof to celebrate the casting of the movie. The weather's turning, and I thought it would be much more fun than at some stupid VIP room at a disco."

Frankle said that would be fine with him, but he would rather talk about it some other time.

"I've told a caterer and a florist they can drop in to look at the layout of the roof garden. I thought you should know that."

"Call him!" Dell Jordan said emphatically, and winked again at Frankle.

"I'll call you from Dell's place in Key West."

"Call him from the plane."

"I'll call you from Dell's plane on our way to Key West."
Jack had returned, and Frankle leashed him.

"Thom, you and Jack are looking more and more like father
and son."

Frankle said goodbye pleasantly and turned away. He
counted to twenty before turning around again. They had
their arms around each other's waists. Window shopping, they
exuded the kind of confidence you'd expect from two idols
of an idolatrous culture.

Once in bed, Frankle lay like a piece of beach wreckage, the
terrier's woolly face resting lovingly on his chest. He listened
to the breeze blowing leftover leaves on the roof garden
beyond the open windows as the humid smell of the river
wafted in; and then he lit a candle before opening the leath-
erbound book.

*Two are better than one; because they have a good reward for
their labor. For if they fall, the one will lift up his fellow: but
woe to him that is alone when he falleth; for he hath not another
to help him up. Again, if two lie together, then they have heat:
but how can one be warm alone?*

The Airedale rolled onto his back, groaning and rubbing
his head with his paws. Frankle took comfort in imitating the
groan. Then he heard footsteps in the roof garden. Drunken
laughter was followed by someone stumbling; then something
fell over.

"What are you so mad about?" a woman's voice said.

"Gordon's been told to ease me off the script."

"Really? I think it's great."

"There's too much talk. Webb's unhappy. What makes her
unhappy makes Dell unhappy."

"I bet the same thing will happen to me."

"John told you not to worry, didn't he?"

"Like I really trust John."

"I'll talk to him."

"If you're gonna be canned, what good'll that do?"

"Hey, don't worry so much."

Frankle heard throaty laughter, then moaning.

"What do you think you're doing?"

"What's it look like?"

"Not like that, you're not!"

"I told you, I had the test."

"The test's meaningless. You screw anything that moves."

"Look who's talking!"

A silence ensued. Frankle found himself holding his breath.

"Put this on."

"What for? They always break."

"Leave room at the tip."

"At least help me with the dumb thing!" A car passed below, its horn blaring.

"Did you call the realtor yet, Harry?"

"Not since the last time you asked me this afternoon, no."

"Good. Because I did. There's a place right on the beach, starting Memorial weekend."

"They'll be shooting the movie then."

"So! I have less than a week on the set. What am I going to do for the rest of the summer?"

"I can't get this fucking thing on!"

"You don't unroll it first! Give me the box." Then the woman said, "Try it now."

Their breathing took on an urgency, which evolved into moans fraught with implications.

Later, the man said, "Stay after they leave."

"Where are they going?"

"Lay off some lines."

Frankle went downstairs and made himself a snack. An argument was taking place on the other side of the living room wall. He couldn't make out the words until he heard Gordon shout, "Betrayed! You've already got fifty thou, and they're kicking in another twenty-five. Betrayed? Fuck you, Chambers!"

The door to his neighbor's apartment opened, and Frankle listened to footsteps disappearing down the hall.

Standing at the window with his peanut butter and jelly sandwich, Frankle watched the corner until Gordon Busch and John Smoke appeared. They were laughing about something as they stepped into a cab.

36

In what he knew to be his last days as a lessee, Frankle peacefully sipped his morning coffee in the sunshine of the terrace. Musing eastward, he didn't turn when he heard the gate to Chambers's studio opening behind him.

"I wonder when the hell this happened," Chambers said.

"What's 'this' mean?" Dakota Pomeroy said irritably.

"Daylight."

"Let's see. I bet the daylight began sometime after the sun came up. What's your guess?"

"Shut up."

"You shut up!"

Chambers groaned. "What the fuck was in that stuff anyway?"

Dakota Pomeroy laughed unpleasantly. "Now you know the difference between solid and liquid hits."

Frankle heard chairs being moved.

"How long have we been talking? When did Gordon leave?"

"Nine hours ago. Quit pulling at your face."

Frankle turned in the chair. They appeared oily and exhausted. Chambers picked up a beer from the terrace's ledge and drained what was left in it.

"I hate this time of year," he said. "I'm allergic to every

fucking thing that grows. If I were mayor, I'd cut down all the trees in the park and pave it over."

"Exactly why we need to rent that house at the beach. Ocean breezes cure allergies. If we don't rent a place soon, we're going to get stuck off the beach. You'll scratch your eyes out by June!"

A garbage truck's compactor started in the street below, and the smell of diesel fuel rose in a black cloud to the roof. Dakota and Chambers moved indoors, coughing.

By noon it was sixty degrees, and Frankle went strolling with his Leica in the crowded park. He wanted to capture the faces of couples to juxtapose to his shots of faces in prayer. Would there be a difference?

He was shooting a man and a woman propped on a tandem bicycle against a water fountain and bickering about something, when a man in baggy pants and a pink sweatshirt moved across the frame of the viewfinder on roller skates. Frankle lowered the camera and followed the man, whose arms flailed as if he were struggling for balance on a rolling log, until, sunglasses and wig flying, he fell backward.

The man turned and waved to Frankle. "It's all right. I can get up myself."

Stanley Stark stood tentatively on the skates and rearranged the wig and sunglasses before stumbling over. He collapsed on the bench beside Frankle with a great sigh of relief.

"Trying to teach myself before Deb returns from Florida."

Frankle let it pass. "Teach yourself what?"

"To engage with impunity in fashionable leisure activities. How'd I look?"

Stark's eyes glistened small and sad as Frankle took the picture.

"Ungainly."

"It's the declines. I'm hoping to get good enough to negotiate country dirt roads by autumn."

Frankle looked into the maple trees, the buds swelling into red flowers. "You have to drag a toe, Stan."

"You should see the trees at the country place. Deb and I want to give them names: Tony, Pepper, Ellen. The generic labels of maple, oak, hickory seem so coldly scientific. I just got back from the place last night. I've got the toilet working on the second floor and the electricity wired in the kitchen. Right before I left, I put a hundred bucks down on a Labrador puppy that isn't born yet. Deb's in Florida doing a swimsuit shoot. How's you?"

"Fine."

"Deb wants me to try transplanting hair from my chest. She's in Florida for something. She was very vague. What's your reaction to the transplant? Be honest."

"I'm used to you bald."

"The wig makes people smirk."

"Understandably."

"My baldness makes them smirk too."

Frankle shrugged. "Perhaps the trick is to inure yourself to smirks."

"Absolutely. But with the wig or without it?"

Frankle was stumped and lit a cigarette.

"Photosynthesis!" Stark declared. "It does something to the blood. Chlorophyll and so forth. You look awful, Thomas."

"Tired."

"You smoke too much. The vitamin loss is obvious in the rings under your eyes."

"I quit drinking."

"Which reminds me. Deb's working to procure an organic hallucinogenic for the wedding punch. The floral arrangement is going to be built around the motif of hay. The dress will be very informal: work boots, overalls, T-shirts. You'll be the best man, of course."

"Okay."

"She's dropping 'Dakota Pomeroy' and 'Louise Goldbaum' and is going to officially register as Deborah Stein. Incidentally, you don't have to wear overalls if you don't want."

A couple passed, pushing a baby stroller. The man seemed to linger behind, sullen and withdrawn. Frankle gave up on the shot when a horse and carriage, carrying a couple, eclipsed them.

He lowered the camera. "When will you be moving north?"

"Not permanently until Deb finishes the film. Apparently, they're incorporating a safe-sex gang-bang sequence she's written. Reportedly, mouth and vaginal plates and retainers are seeing a major sales upswing. If I'd only put my money in Trojans. Incidentally, Deb's thinking maybe midwifery would better suit our back-to-nature lifestyle than the sex-surrogacy therapy. Personally, the birthing process horrifies me: blood, eyes, mucus, cords."

Frankle pushed Stark in the shoulder and stood. "I have to go downtown."

Stark cautiously stood too. "And I must head home to keep my black bean soup from overcooking. Deb and I, incidentally, are committed to the vegetarian way. We're opposed to eating our fellow mammals: blood, bones, eyes, muscles." Stark rolled away from the bench onto a collision course with a stop sign.

"Drag your toe, Stan!"

Trying to, Stark pirouetted wildly, losing his wig and sunglasses before crashing into a green metal stop sign. Somehow, he avoided falling.

"It worked, Thomas!"

37

Frankle walked south on Ninth Avenue, toward a plant nursery in the midtown butchershop section. The fixed eyes of three women, pacing in swimsuits beneath a Lincoln Tunnel entrance sign, became the central focus in his viewfinder. The irony was cheap but irresistible—just the kind of kitsch a gallery might go for. Unbidden, the one in the red bikini and fake-fur shoulder wrap offered to do it for fifteen with a bag, twenty-five without one. Frankle stepped up his pace, until he noticed three dead lambs hanging upside down from black metal hooks in a windowfront; and in the next window, two white rabbits hung similarly, their undersides ripped open in a long purplish gash from throat to hind legs. At his owner's side, Jack stared too; but unlike Frankle, he didn't appear disquieted by the dead.

At the nursery, Frankle bought a flat of flowers and balanced it on his head on his return uptown.

The sun was hot on the roof, and he removed his worn sweater and T-shirt while gardening. The four coffin-size cedar troughs that outlined the garden still supported last season's dried stalks and needed to be prepared for the new season's flowers; and the four Japanese cherry trees in the ivy-covered whiskey barrels had to be pruned. Frankle worked as if the garden were contiguous with the earth, rather than five flights above a sushi den. Once the clippings were bagged, he swept and washed down the turf, so that for a moment, sparkling in the afternoon sunlight, the synthetic surface appeared as green and living as a lawn. Finally, Frankle cultivated the soil in the troughs and added fertilizer, before removing a fold-up chair from its tarpaulin cover and resting with his eyes closed and his face lifted to the fading sun. He pictured again the Pacific. Blue waves were breaking, and Constance was swimming beyond them, waving for him to come in.

Frankle opened his eyes and sat up. Then, as he stood to survey the cityscape, he could hear in his mind That Voice as clearly as if the thought were his very own: *It is finished*. Indeed, he accepted at last that whatever it was he had tried to create for himself after a decade in the city was finished now.

He leaned against the waist-high wall surrounding the roof. The sensation of seeing the city as if for the first time was suddenly strange and terrible. He beheld the famous skyline in the middle distance and the overarching dirty sky, and nothing his eyes appropriated made him want to stay and struggle on there. The Big Apple had cored him, and now he was getting out.

He was superstitious enough to believe that in finishing things properly with Monica Webb he would advance the possibility for himself of a propitious beginning, although what in this ending that new beginning might be, he had no definite idea.

Ye ask and receive not, That Voice whispered, *because ye ask amiss, that ye may consume it upon your lusts*.

Frankle arranged the flat of flowers in the coffins of soil, then watered the little annuals with water from a rusty bucket.

For a crazy moment, struck into quiet by the blossoms' beauty, he imagined that he envied Stanley Stark his plans for a plant nursery.

A shadow appeared on the green carpet beyond his shoes. Frankle lifted up his eyes to behold a bathrobed Harry Chambers, who dangled on crutches, his prosthetic foot and glass eye missing.

"How in fuck's name am I supposed to sleep with you clanging around out here?" Chambers used his fingers to open the cavity of his eyeless socket before surveying the roof as if through a telescope. "Who you talking to anyway, the flowers? Because I hope to hell it isn't to bird shit."

Frankle calmly promised to keep it down.

Chambers bobbed his head contemptuously in rhythm with Frankle's words, then lowered himself into Frankle's vacated chair. Something in the blue of the late-March sky and the moist odor of the soil made Frankle want to hurl his Marlboros from the rooftop.

"My script's been fucked." Chambers lit a cigarette and bowed his forehead into his open hand. "Jerk-offs galore are getting involved now. Faggots from Hollywood. You know, the fussy types with no sense of narrative strategy, who like to talk about how the film will *look*." Chambers snorted. "They got themselves a new writer, and I'm out. I've been terminated. Private Chambers all over again. They give me a Purple Heart and think—what?—I won't come back to haunt them?"

Frankle maintained his silence. Not only did he feel no sympathy for Chambers; secretly he hoped the entire vulgar project would meet with doom.

Chambers flicked away his cigarette, and Frankle watched it smoke in one of the flower troughs. "I got that old and very bad feeling again. It doesn't ever go away. How can it? The studio people had me fucked from the get go. They know the jungle they're operating in better than any sorry-assed writer. Ship you in completely green, and as soon as you've learned the rules of the jungle, they fire your ass and start with the next sucker who doesn't know shit. Same as in Vietnam. Everywhere you go in this world the power brokers fuck you."

Frankle had heard the complaining a thousand times and didn't want to hear it again.

"The scummy little fucks," Chambers said. "I've eaten a lifetime of their shit. It's no wonder I can't get the taste out of my mouth."

Chambers aimed a crutch at Frankle and fired. "I can see now how I've been set up. How easily one can be set up when one seeks acceptance. Of course, I suspect I can tell you who is going to laugh last in this case. But listen to me: don't tell anybody I'm telling you this. It's top secret, you read me?" Chambers laughed. "Isn't it remarkable how people get killed over the dumbest shit? Of course, these entertainment types, they're addicted to showdowns. They can't pass up an opportunity for dramatic climax. Maybe they think they don't bleed real blood." Chambers removed his glass eye from his pocket and stared at it. "Theoretically speaking, I'm in favor of peace. But wouldn't I be less than honest if I told you I thought peace could be achieved without superior firepower?"

Chambers inserted his eye and stood to swing on his crutches. "Why do you plant all this shit? Don't you even care that I'm allergic?"

"I've got a call to make, Harry."

Frankle tossed his planting tools into a bucket and silently passed Chambers. In the open area of sky between the duplexes's roofs, he spotted a robin perched across the street on top of a shingled water tower. It occurred to Frankle that the bird was as high as any wingless creature could go.

"Myself," Chambers said to Frankle's back, "I was willing to die for my country. Similarly I'm willing to die, you know, for my career. Why not? But you, Frankle? You never were willing to die for anything. Would you happen to know why? It's because you *never lived for anything!*"

Frankle didn't bother to turn around to address Chambers at the end of the alley. The robin trilled softly, and Frankle paused on the terrace. He hoped the bird understood that Frankle had intended no harm in photographing the nest of eggs.

"You know what you are?" Chambers called. "You're nothing, Frankle. You can't do shit—beyond cash a corporate check and put frozen food in a microwave! You're like millions. You're nothing."

Frankle turned, looked through Chambers, then went inside, locking the gate behind him.

38

To the Airedale's consternation, Frankle spent the night emptying closets, separating his recordings from Monica Webb's, and carefully packing his favorite photographs. The process evoked memories that rendered Frankle catatonic with reveries.

Sometime after dawn, as he was working toward a twenty-fifth push-up, Kikki Epstein telephoned to invite him to breakfast.

"Breakfast?" Frankle said.

"Is this a bad time, Thom? It sounds like I'm interrupting something."

"Push-ups."

"Please. I hate when guys put it that way."

"Literally. What's the matter?"

"I'm down the block having tea. I want to talk with you."

Frankle glanced past Jack to the clock radio.

"What are you doing down the block at seven-thirty in the morning?"

"Drinking tea. Hurry up already."

The weather was so eerily sultry that Frankle needed nothing heavier than his frayed denim jacket.

Kikki sat slumped in a baggy batik getup, her hair piled

haphazardly. She was cleaning a fingernail with a toothpick when Frankle slid into the booth across from her and ordered coffee.

Kikki folded her hands on the table, and Frankle reached to hold them.

"What?" he asked.

"I wish I knew."

"Tell me."

Kikki raised her eyes to him. "You ever want to kill someone?"

"Only the people I've loved."

The coffee came. Frankle added cream until the cup overflowed, then slurped it, his body bent forward.

"I told him I want a divorce, and he said fine. I couldn't believe it. Ten years together, and all he can say is fine. The resentment in such a remark overwhelms me."

Frankle understood he was supposed to sit and listen supportively.

"I haven't seen him in three days," Kikki said. "I don't know whether I want him back or whether I just don't want him fucking around. Did you ever wish someone would just die? I wish a brick or an air conditioner would fall from a building and hit him right on the head. He wouldn't know what hit him, and I'd be free of the jerk."

The floor rumbled with the passing of a subway train.

"Is a pet good company, Thom?"

"Sometimes."

Kikki pressed her lips together and squinted, looking away in concentration. "Why couldn't one of those giant cranes topple over and crush him? Why do I miss someone who's not nice to me?"

Frankle studied her, then shrugged.

"Tell me," she said.

What was he supposed to tell her—that their hope and love and faith was and probably always had been, for the wrong things? "It seems," he said, "that we need to be braver than we know how to be."

She looked at him as if in expectation of something more, then said, "You know what I hate? I hate loneliness."

"If you get a dog," Frankle said, "get one smaller than an Airedale."

"I don't want to stay with Johnny, but I'm afraid to be alone. It's amazing. Just being angry at him keeps me company. Sometimes, when he snores, I think I'll put a pillow over his head and suffocate him. But then I worry I'll be lonely."

Frankle looked straight up and discovered a trapped fly buzzing inside a light fixture. What could he do for Kikki Epstein when he couldn't even help a fly? What could you ever do?

"Do you remember," she asked, "my former apartment on Jane Street? No counter space, but I cooked all the time. We made lasagna one time." She set her chin against her fist. "Now I have a kitchen out of *Architectural Digest*, and I never cook. Maybe I could poison him."

She swung the sodden tea bag, staring.

"Did you ever wonder what it would be like if we'd kept seeing each other?" she asked. "Do you think our lives would have been better if we'd gotten married? Maybe we should get married now. You've already got a dog. All we need is a cat and a house a million miles from here. Let's really do it."

Frankle lit a cigarette, and Kikki swiped it from his mouth

"This is excellent, Thom. I think we'll be very happy together. Now, how do we kill Johnny?"

"We hire someone."

"Perfect. We should have had this talk years ago." She buried her face in her hands. "God, I'm so depressed I can't stand it."

Kikki spread her fingers and peeked at Frankle. "Last night I couldn't sleep. All at once it came rushing out—this longing for children. For two boys. It's all I could think of. Two sons. I'd name them something nice and warm, something Middle Western, like Spud and Doc. I lay awake for hours, picturing the house I'd live in and the nice lawn and trees in the yard. I was standing at the foot of the stairs holding a ball glove and was calling out, 'Spud, whose glove is this? Yours or Doc's?' I miss a home something god-awful, Thom. Why didn't I create one? Why didn't I make two handsome sons and name them Skipper and Mike? Or Cap and Harvey?"

"It's not too late, Kikki."

"I've never been pregnant. I know women who've had five abortions because of accidental pregnancies, but I've never been pregnant. Something must be wrong, but I've never looked into it. I've never wanted to be a mother until last night. What have I done with my life anyway? Created a successful photography studio. That's it."

"This is winter talking," Frankle said. "Spring's coming. It's just days away."

Kikki frowned at her wristwatch. "I've got a roller-skate shoot in the park in half an hour. You should meet this A.D. All he talks about is *dappled* light." Kikki gulped down her tea, then bit into the lemon wedge. "I have a serious proposal for you, Thom. I want you to be my partner. Regardless of what happens with Johnny and me. I need someone in the studio. I can guarantee you a salary of thirty a year, plus a percentage of the net. Don't say anything now. Sleep on it."

Frankle looked at her.

"Seriously," she said. "You'd be doing me a favor." She reached across the table and took his hand. "It's really why I asked to see you. It's why I called the other night. I really think it will work for both of us. I've given it a lot of thought."

"I can't," Frankle said simply.

"Don't say that."

"I can't."

"Why can't you?"

"Because the photography we do is a desecration."

"Oh, come on," Kikki said. "Call it a big fucking lie, if you want. But 'desecration' makes you sound unstable."

Frankle leaned forward as if afraid to be overheard. "I'm getting out of here. I have to leave."

"And go where?"

Frankle shrugged.

"Thommie," Kikki said earnestly, "I want you to listen to me. I'll cut you in for two percent of the gross. You'll make a lot. Everyone who makes a lot of money enjoys Manhattan. Look at me, for example."

"I'm finished."

She scrutinized him with sorrowful eyes. "What will you do?"

"I don't know."

"Sure you do."

"I have no idea."

"Come *on*."

"Maybe I'll teach kids."

"Teach them what?"

"What else? Photography."

"Spud and Mike? Cap and Harvey?"

"Why not?" he said hopefully.

"Why not? Because all kids want to do is photograph their pets. You'll stand in a darkroom all day overseeing the development of ten million prints of Spot and Rover."

"I want to teach them how to see."

She shook her head skeptically. "I liked your chances a lot better when you said you had no idea." She held out her hand and examined her nails. "Teach children how to see! Really, take the thirty grand plus the two percent."

"I've already started packing. I want to be out as soon as possible."

Kikki exhaled cigarette smoke. "Now I get it," she said. "It just occurred to me. Your girlfriend. You're leaving town to be with her, and you're only pretending you don't know what you're doing. Be honest: is she pregnant?"

"She already has a kid."

"Je-sus!" Kikki Epstein blanched as she extinguished her cigarette.

"And she's not my girlfriend. And she's in Mexico."

"Now I see it perfectly, Thom. She's the one from California. She has a house there, and you're fantasizing about moving in."

"She's selling the house."

"So what are you going to do? Meet in Kansas after clicking your respective heels three times?"

Frankle picked up the check and stood. "I'll walk you to the park."

"Listen to me," Kikki resumed outside. "You're going to think about my offer. You're going to sleep on it." She yanked his jacket at the elbow. "Look into my eyes, Thommie. Look into my eyes and go into a deep trance. Stay in the deep trance until tomorrow morning. At which time you'll call me and accept my offer. Do you understand? Are you in a trance yet?"

Frankle took her in his arms and hugged her.

39

Frankle introduced himself over the phone to Constance's stepmother and arranged to visit Nick after the boy returned from school. The Gilberts had moved from the hotel into a friend's Chelsea apartment on Eighteenth Street, and Frankle drank tea with the gray-haired Mrs. Gilbert in a book-lined room while waiting for Nick. Frankle feigned an enthusiasm for a career as a free-lance photographer rather than elaborating on the specifics of a mid-life letdown characteristic, he imagined, of millions of ambitious young men whose earlier dreams had been reduced to a struggle to pay the rent.

Mrs. Gilbert observed Frankle, or so Frankle imagined, with a polite skepticism when he described his relationship to Constance as a good friendship.

Somberly, she offered him a plate of cookies. "Her former husband was a very foolish young man."

Frankle frowned, munching a cookie. "I hope," he said politely, "you don't think I'm a foolish young man."

Mrs. Gilbert helped herself to a cookie. "My impression is that you are a very fine young man."

Frankle thanked her and looked away. He was surprised at how much comfort he derived from sitting in a pleasant room talking to a sensible gray-haired woman. He supposed he would spend his entire life wondering why his own mother and he could not engage in such simple and sincere dialogue without recriminations surfacing or something being thrown. Perhaps their antipathy explained Frankle's fascination with a theology that provided a compassionate cosmic family featuring an omnipotent father, virginal mother, and peace-keeping Holy Ghost. But no member of this trinity ever showed up for dinner or made cloudy days any less endless; at least not in the palpable sense required by Frankle's eyes.

Nick returned from school with a crayon portrait of a pelican on which the name TOM was printed at the bottom of the yellow construction paper. Though Frankle was touched by the drawing, when "Grandma" invited him to stay for dinner, he declined, fearful an acceptance might resurrect the many family ghosts he was just as happy to keep interred.

Instead, he took Nick for a walk to the Hudson. It didn't seem like much of an idea, but the late-afternoon sky was clear and sunny, and going to a river seemed an appropriate rite of spring. Dressed in overalls and his red coat, Nick bounced a tennis ball the four blocks to the West Side highway. There, Frankle took the boy by the hand until they had crossed safely to the wooden wharfs. Once the main portage for transatlantic passenger ships, the disrepaired docks were now used for drinking, jogging, and sexual arcana.

The wind from the river was unexpectedly cold on the deserted pier; and across the brown expanse of the Hudson, the continent, which seemed part of another universe, began in the detritus of Jersey City.

"Where's Calif-fornia?" Nick stood at Frankle's side, staring across the river.

"Far away."

"I'm from there."

"I know."

"I don't like it here."

"You want to go back to California?"

"Mom s-said we are."

"Soon?"

"After school."

Nick tossed his tennis ball up and down, then bounced it on the wooden planks. Backing away, Frankle clapped his hands, and Nick threw him the ball. The boy had a good arm, which surprised Frankle, since he didn't seem the athletic type. Frankle threw it back in a gentle arch.

"Chuck it!" Nick fired the ball through the wind to Frankle.

Frankle threw it more directly. The wind caused it to curve, but Nick adroitly snagged it.

"You play baseball?" Frankle called.

"My dad-dad did."

Nick threw Frankle a pop. "M-maybe outta here!"

Frankle pedaled back, the wind carrying the ball so that Frankle stood close to the pier's edge when he grabbed it.

Nick clapped his hands in approval, and Frankle marveled, seeing an entirely different side of the boy.

"He's tag-tagging up!"

Nick squatted in a catcher's stance, and Frankle felt twenty-five years disappear as he pegged it home. But he released the ball too high, and it sailed over Nick's reach, bounced off a rotting post, and ricocheted down into the swirling water.

They trotted to the wharf's side to watch it.

"Sorry," Frankle said.

"Get it!"

"Hey," Frankle said. "Easy."

"Get it!" Nick's faced filled with blood as he stared at the ball beginning to drift away.

"How am I supposed to get it? There's no way down."

"There!" Nick pointed to a rotting ladder as he wiped his eyes.

"Come on," Frankle said. "I'll buy you a new can of tennis balls."

"No. It's my dad's." The boy turned away and stood as still as a stone, his hair flapping.

Frankle remembered how his own father's insensitivity had driven Frankle deeper and deeper into himself and how his adolescence had been a series of retreats from a sense of esteem. Returning to the surface of things and trying to hold to it had demanded more courage than any of Frankle's photographs could ever adequately convey.

Perhaps, then, Frankle decided to retrieve the ball merely to prove to himself that he was at least a better man than his own dead and buried father.

He undressed to his underpants and cautiously descended the rotting ladder. With his toe, he tested the freezing water before launching himself toward the ball with a cry of shock. And though he remained submerged no more than a minute, his muscles knotted so abruptly that he could barely manage the seven-rung ascent of the rotting ladder.

Restored to the pier, he felt his teeth clicking as he dried himself with his T-shirt. Removing the soaked underpants, he put on his jeans and sweater.

Nick mumbled a thanks but kept his eyes away as he bounced the wet ball against the wooden planks. Frankle embraced himself and jumped up and down to get his blood moving.

"My fault," he told the boy.

"Thank you," Nick repeated.

They walked to a café on Hudson Street and ordered hot chocolates. A moody silence set in between them, and Frankle couldn't find a way of breaking it until he told Nick that Jack missed him and said hello.

The boy smiled and raised his bashful eyes, held away until he finished a cup of hot chocolate.

"Are we going-going to live together again?"

"I hope so."

"Does Jack like cats?"

"I think."

"I have two cats. Are you m-mad at me?"

"Of course not." Then Frankle asked him why he missed California.

"My cats."

"What are their names?"

"Lucy and Mike. They had kittens once."

"Those are nice names." Frankle felt blood returning to his toes and ordered two more hot chocolates.

"Some people drown kittens. I gave them all n-names. They live in the backyard now."

"I've never had a cat. Only dogs."

"My d-dad died."

"I know."

"Mom cried."

"My dad," Frankle said, "died five years ago."

"Did you cry?"

"Sure. Didn't you?"

"No."

The hot chocolates came, and Nick blew the bubbles around the rim of the cup.

"Are you married, Thom?"

"No."

"Are you going to marry my mom?"

"I'm going to ask her to marry me. Is that okay with you?"

"I saw saw you in Mom's bed."

Frankle felt his face coloring. "Yes?"

"Are you going to sleep over tonight?"

"I can't." Frankle flipped over the check and lit a cigarette.

"Thom?"

"Is the smoke bothering you?"

"Do you like the ocean?"

"Very much."

"Our house is right next-next to it. We watch sunsets."

Frankle looked at a wall clock and realized he was late in

getting the boy home. They finished the hot chocolate and went out to the street.

"Thanks," Nick said.

"You don't have to thank me."

"Grandma said."

When they reached the apartment, Frankle hugged Nick goodbye, but the boy remained at Frankle's side, bouncing the ball up and down.

"You want to k-keep the ball till n-next time?"

He reached up the ball to Frankle with an expression of entreaty. Frankle understood and accepted it.

"You want to play catch tom-morrow?"

"Not tomorrow," Frankle said. "But soon. Okay?"

Nick nodded and went up the stairs of the brownstone.

"Bye-bye."

Frankle held up his hand. "God bless, Nick."

The boy disappeared into the building.

Frankle waited. With his eyes closed, he could picture his room of thirty years ago so vividly that it surprised him he couldn't hear them shouting at each other downstairs.

When he opened his eyes, Nick was at the window with his grandmother. Frankle waved before turning away.

40

He was about to hail a cab at the corner of Eighth and Eighteenth when he heard his name called. Turning, he saw Susan Stark signaling from the doorway of a café. He joined her at a corner table within a glass enclosure facing the sidewalk. He ordered a hot tea with lemon.

"Why's your hair wet?"

"I fell into a river."

"You *fell* into a river? How did you happen to fall into a river?"

Frankle explained that it had been a long and traumatic winter and he had leapt impulsively.

"Very funny, Thom."

"What are you doing in this neck of the woods, Susan?"

"A women's group. Our weekly meeting. Did you receive my apology on your phone machine?"

Frankle couldn't remember such a message but said he had, and insisted no apology had been necessary.

"I thought you would have called me back," Susan Stark said.

"I've been incredibly busy."

"Jumping into rivers." She studied him with a psychother-

apist's impassive gravity. "Thom, someone told me they saw
you going into a church."

"Probably."

"Something *is* troubling you, isn't it?"

"Isn't something always troubling everyone?"

Susan Stark nodded watchfully. "Let me see if I understand
the feeling," she said. "The road feels wholly lost and gone,
but there's no turning back. You attempt to pray in a place
like a church for a miracle before accepting the reality that
passive fantasies of intervention aren't going to get it done.
Prayer is the final resistance to the truth that whoever you
are, you proceed one step at a time through whatever mess
you must confront."

Frankle sipped his steaming tea. "Sometimes prayer gives
you the courage to take the steps, Susan."

"Admittedly. But aren't we simply praying to a deeper part
of ourself—namely, our subconscious?"

"No."

"You look disdainful, Thom."

"Forgive me. I just pulled myself from a river."

Susan folded her hands. "I think it's unfair of you to blame
me for Monica's decision to leave you. Never mind that you
two were entirely inappropriate for each other. What matters
is that she was my patient, and I had my first responsibility
to help her work through what she felt was vitally important
to her own growth and individuation."

"Susan . . ."

"I was drunk and fantasizing that night, Thom. It was a
psychotic episode."

"You needn't explain."

"I'm all right now. I'm seeing my patients again and not as
depressed as that night I spoke with you. I've even negotiated
an adoption with a young Catholic couple. The fee's ten thousand plus medical and legal costs, which might more than
double the expense, and I've even included a free rental for

them in the top floor of the brownstone. Admittedly, it is somewhat unusual to have the biological parents literally living on top of you, but the competition for the rights to this pregnancy was so acute that I needed a little icing on the cake. Six months from now, I'll be a mother."

Frankle nodded, then turned to the clock reflected in a mirror above the bar. He apologized for having to run off for a head-shot appointment, then stood up.

"Why do I feel so uncomfortable about having told you all this?"

Susan's expression soured when Frankle shrugged. "Get yourself a therapist, Thom. You're just rancid with resentment."

Frankle didn't say it, but he suspected that a nap and a hot bath would work just as well as a therapist.

A cab was pulling onto Eighth Avenue. Frankle whistled and waved, but was abruptly stopped by a chest pain. The cigarette dropped from his mouth as he went directly to his knees. For the longest moment, he couldn't breathe and reflexively bowed his head. When the dizziness commenced, he sat back and closed his eyes. And it was from a sitting position, many minutes later, that he signaled to the next passing cab.

41

Confident after his hot bath that the momentary attack had been more a reaction to the freezing Hudson than an intimation of heart failure, Frankle stood atop a stepladder in his bathrobe, watering a thorny asparagus fern. When the potted plant's chain, bolted to the living room ceiling, began to vibrate, Frankle deduced that someone was walking around in the roof garden; he went upstairs to investigate.

Outside the window, Monica Webb was conversing with a man wearing a safari shirt and baggy shorts and scribbling on a clipboarded pad of paper.

Frankle joined them. "I thought you were going out of town."

"Creative people decided to fly in and dialogue with Dell and me."

"Anyhow," the man said, "if, as I presume, you want the round tables with the cloths and umbrellas, then there's no possibility of arranging more than four. And even though the guest list is small, I still recommend we stay with the buffet concept."

He and Monica referred to a page on the clipboard, then the man gestured to Chambers's side of the roof.

"We'll put the buffet table and the canopy there. On your side, we'll just have to move these horrible coffiny things."

"Thom will do that."

"We'll coordinate the canopy color scheme with the umbrellas and the bar. Ultimately, everything will coalesce with the daffodil motif."

"Monica," Frankle interrupted, "may I speak with you?"

"Thom, we are not going to argue about this. It's one afternoon and evening. If it makes you unhappy, go out of town."

"I only want to advise you," Frankle said, "to get Chambers's permission before you use his space."

"He's invited, for God's sake!"

"He's also angry about being taken off the script and thinks you're responsible."

"Thom." Monica's tone betrayed impatience. "Gordon spoke with Harry last night, and Harry has very graciously given me, via Gordon, permission to use the entire roof space. And no one's had him taken off the script; it's been bought from him for a lot of money."

"One big decision," the man interjected, "is do we hire a quartet or do we go with the taping system?"

"Dell loves the idea of the quartet. But do we have room?"

Frankle told Monica he'd be downstairs.

"Good," she answered.

"The sarcasm isn't necessary."

"Our five years together weren't necessary. But what's that got to do with anything?"

Frankle held his eyes closed, then turned away.

"Don't give me *that*, Thom. Hieronymus offered you twenty grand to get out of here."

"That wasn't necessary either."

She came downstairs while Frankle was finishing with the plants.

"Why," she asked, "are you being so unfriendly?"

He set the copper watering can her parents had given them on the mantel. "I think I'm being friendly."

She sat down on the sofa and tucked her legs beneath her. "I need to have this party. To perform the stuff I'm required to, I need to feel a special closeness with the cast. I'm going to you-know-what in front of them."

Frankle massaged the back of his neck. "Why are you doing this movie? Because of Dell Jordan?"

"I happen to be in love with Dell Jordan, if that's what you mean."

"Love? How can you love someone in two weeks?"

"I loved him in two seconds. I loved you in one second."

Frankle was disarmed by her words, which defused his anger and left him silent.

"You gave me confidence in myself as a woman, Thom. I was just a girl when we met. I'll always love you for that. But now we're both moving on—changed. Don't you see, it's the kind of happy ending people dream about."

"Sounds more like a sitcom wrap-up to me, frankly."

Monica's expression hardened. "I came down here to ask if you'd accept a check for relocating. Because I think we should be practical. I'll eventually get it. I can afford it, and you can't."

"I already told you I'm leaving."

"Oh? When?"

"I'll be out before Memorial weekend."

Their eyes held and then she smiled. "I'll send you the check next week."

"I don't want the money."

"You're entitled to it."

"No, I'm not."

"Have it your way." She secured her handbag strap on her shoulder. "The party's in two weeks. I'll send you an invitation."

She went to the door and turned to him.

"Be happy, Thom."

He could imagine her imagining the camera cutting to him for his reaction; and he was tempted to smile with rueful appreciation as he watched her open the door and go out. Instead, at least as best as he could tell, he stood vacantly, without the consolation of a conclusive emotion.

42

Toward the end of the week, a postcard arrived from Mexico.

Dear Thom,
    You really are a favorite of the family. I phoned Nick
the other day and he talked of little else but you. Where's
Thom? Thom's handsome. Thom's nice. He is obsessed
with you! And he has a new word: Painful. It's *painful* I'm
away; school's *painful*; not seeing his cats is *painful*. As for
myself, I didn't want it to be so, but it's painful being separated from you. I miss you.   Constance

Frankle raced upstairs to telephone Mrs. Gilbert and ask
if she had Constance's number in Mexico.

When the long-distance call finally went through, a man
answered and told Frankle in broken English that the sisters
had signed out of the hotel the day before.

That evening, Frankle tried Constance several times at the
number her brother-in-law had provided earlier in the month.
One time, he let the phone ring ninety-nine times before
accepting the fact that he'd have to raise anchor on a decade
of customs and habits without knowing precisely when and
to where he'd be setting sail. Such a predicament could only
exacerbate the confusions of a man who didn't know how to

navigate the stars and who harbored a primitive fear that the earth might indeed be flat.

The next morning, Frankle set out to collect boxes at the supermarket. Backing into the brownstone with a pile of them, he stumbled on a step, and the empty containers tumbled to the foyer floor. Amid them, Stanley Stark stood, propped against a wall, reading the *Times*. He wore a brown polyester suit over a shirt and tie, and his customary toupee was taped crookedly to his head.

"Here's something of citizen interest." Stanley folded the sheet of print to read it more conveniently. " 'The nuclear disaster at Chernobyl emitted as much long-term radiation into the world's air, topsoil, and water as all the nuclear tests and bombs ever exploded.' "

Frankle tossed Stark his keys and rearranged the boxes in his arms. Stark opened the foyer door, then resumed reading. " 'The Soviet reactor may even have emitted fifty percent more radioactive cesium, the primary long-term component in fallout, than have the total of hundreds of atmospheric tests and the two nuclear bombs dropped on Japan at the end of World War Two.' "

They ascended the stairway in single file, Stark leading the way as Frankle balanced the boxes and climbed the stairs from memory.

"How remarkable, indeed," Stark declaimed, "that the world should end just the way the physicists who've created the means for its destruction hypothesize it began: with a big bang."

Also from memory, Frankle recited to himself, "*Thou shall be visited of the Lord of hosts with thunder, and with earthquake, and great noise, with storm and tempest, and the flame of the devouring fire. Ye shall conceive chaff, ye shall bring forth stubble: your breath, as fire, shall devour you. And the people shall be as the burnings of lime: as thorns cut up shall they be burned in the fire.*"

"Frankly, Thomas, my biggest fear is what we shall do with ourselves if the bombs don't bang big."

They entered the apartment, and Frankle dropped the boxes in the living room. There, the windows were open in celebration of spring, and though the sun slanted in broad beams, the room was filled with the furious noise of commuter traffic and the droning of garbage trucks.

"Why don't you just tell me what's really on your mind, Stan?"

Stark stood in a dusty shaft of light, his eyes closed to the sun. "To make a long story short, Thomas, Dakota Pomeroy and Stanley Stark have decided to go their separate ways. I came to my half of the decision when I was told she'd call the police if I didn't have my belongings out by yesterday."

Frankle had to raise his voice to be heard above a sudden blare of horns. "Don't you think the Deb Stein affair has been designed to distract you from more profound issues?"

"Such as?" Stark turned from the sun and frowned at Frankle.

"Such as the dissolution of your marriage and the family you had hoped to create."

"Frankly, Thomas, I don't see what the hell that has to do with the far more profound fact that Dakota Pomeroy is the only woman with whom I've ever enjoyed sexual relations."

"There's nothing profound," Frankle began, "about isolating sex with an inapprop—"

"Curious," Stark interrupted, "that you sound so much like Susan. She phoned me last night at the Y in a panic. These Catholic kids living upstairs are supposed to hand over their baby to her. Suddenly, however, Susan's not feeling so hot about the arrangement and wanted to talk to me about it. Suddenly she wants to help these Catholic kids marry and keep the infant. She's offered to let them live upstairs, rent free, for as long they want. What do you make of it?"

Frankle opened kitchenette cabinets to bring down plates for packing.

"I guess decency no longer makes sense to you, Stan."

"Decency? The woman was adulterously impregnated, and you call her decent? Incidentally, last night, lying awake at the Y, I resolved to work with peasants in a left-wing Central American country. Then this morning I noticed the headline about the American engineer executed by a right-wing death squad. At heart, Thomas, I decided I don't want to have my brains blown out. As a consequence, though I've rejoined the Environmental Bureau after my medical leave of absence, I've announced plans to settle the Kenway case out of court, to avoid assassination."

Frankle gathered glasses and inquired about the country house.

"Interesting that you should bring up the country house. Closing's scheduled for this weekend. Two days ago, the county inspector called to tell me the crumbling mess is sitting on a natural radon vault. Radon levels in the basement stagger the educated imagination. Just to ventilate the place properly would cost me half the raise I've been offered by the Bureau. But what's that matter in light of the fact that I've probably contracted something fatal by committing popular unnatural acts with a hooker all these months? Do you think I latched onto her to contract something fatal?"

"You latched onto her," Frankle said, "to distract yourself from the fatality of your baby."

"It wasn't mine!" Stark turned at the slamming of garbage cans down below and closed the window behind him. "Inasmuch as I've told the Bureau people I'd return to the office, and inasmuch as my fiancée has broken our engagement and withdrawn her financial share from the country venture, I'm wondering if you would be interested in purchasing a house in the country."

Frankle studied Stanley as he nervously adjusted his toupee. "Why not take a drive with Susan and show her the place?"

Stark sat on the window ledge and reached into the tendrils of a spider plant. "Tell me something, Thomas. Tell me how the same person and circumstances we once blamed for being the source of our despair can later become our only prospect for hope and survival. And then tell me why I have never found comfort or strength in love."

With Frankle's silence, Stark set his hands on his knees and slowly stood. "Well, I'm grateful you don't pretend to understand. Is there anything more deceitful than pretending to understand?"

"Don't laugh," Frankle said, "but I wonder if obedience isn't more important than understanding."

"Obedience?" Stark said derisively. "To what? Teachers, coaches, and honored guests? Wife, mother, and country?"

"I don't know what to call it," Frankle said. "Something that whispers in the silence."

"Conscience?" Stark said. "Obedience to our conscience! That voice our parents and the nation's advertisers plant in our head so that we eventually don't need any external authority telling us not to run in the halls or lift up Mary Ellen's dress and rip away her underpants? Have you completely lost your mind, Thomas?"

Stark picked up his briefcase. "Deb wants me to escort her to Monica's cast party. Even though we're finished, she wants me there. Producers have been forcing themselves on her, apparently. Two at once sometimes. I told her I had to think about it. You've no idea how much I underestimated the irrational and self-destructive ramifications inherent in simultaneous orgasm."

Stark removed a handgun from his sports jacket pocket and stared at it admiringly.

"Thirty eight snub nose. Been practicing with it at a pistol range in Queens. Just in case."

"Just in case what, Stan?"

"Any number of things. The Kenway people, obviously. Also, if I'm going to effect a rapprochement with Susan, you don't expect me to show up unarmed."

"Leave the dumb thing here."

"Susan tells me Monica's invited her to the cast party. I can't remember if it's Susan who wants to meet Dell Jordan or Monica who wants to introduce Susan to him. Why all the boxes?"

Frankle cleared his throat. "Photographic idea."

"As in the way we're all boxed in by cultural ideology?"

"Not exactly."

Stark looked around the room. "We spend our entire lives in one kind of box or another. Get out of one box, find yourself in a bigger box. In hell, you know, the boxes we'll be forced to inhabit won't have windows. Whenever I'm inclined to feel sorry for myself, I remember that at least the boxes we inhabit on earth have windows."

Stark headed for the door. "Keep the faith, Thomas."

43

By twilight, Frankle had his belongings boxed and piled in the living room. If necessary, he could be gone in the time it took to fill a suitcase, phone a moving company, and lug a dozen boxes down the stairs. All that was left was for Constance to say "yes"; though "maybe" would do.

It surprised him how ordinary the apartment looked minus a few personal touches, and without the plants, it might just as well have been a motel suite situated in an extraterrestrial city of iron and cement, where the citizenry spoke in polyglot and worshiped celluloid images.

That night, he burned the last of the winter's supply of logs. Though it was almost April, the fireplace spread the smell of autumn through the apartment. Frankle sat down on the floor before the flickering light, reading about the upcoming baseball season and eating cold baked beans from a can. The phone rang as he prepared to jump shoot the empty tin into the kitchen wastebasket, but when he picked up, the line went dead.

A moment later, the buzzer signaled. He pushed the Listen button and could hear a key opening the lobby door, followed by footsteps in the hallway and the door clicking shut.

He slid the chain lock on the door and hurried upstairs to make sure the burglar gate to the roof was locked.

The doorbell signaled as he stood staring through the bars into the springlike night; he returned cautiously downstairs to peek into the hallway through the peephole. Someone had put a finger on the opening.

"Who is it?"

"Open up!"

It was a made-up voice, a woman trying to sound villainous. Frankle paused to picture Monica's gloating expression when she noticed the boxes and the bare walls.

He opened the door as far as the chain lock would allow and beheld a blue duffel bag slung over the shoulder of a very tanned Constance Frame.

"Surprise! . . . I hope."

Frankle was all thumbs unlocking the door; and when he wrapped his arms around her and the duffel bag, he breathed in the stale smell of an airplane's interior.

"Come in! Come in!"

Jack went a little ape himself.

"Who's this!" Frankle inquired. "Who's this, Jack!"

"Hi, Jack! Hi, Thom!"

"What are you doing here? Where's Nick? Let me help you with that duffel!"

"I'd sure love some of that coffee it looks like you've been drinking."

She dragged the duffel bag into the living room, halting to frown at the boxes.

"Moving out?"

"Let me get our coffee!"

"What happened to the tapestries of the ducks and hens?"

Jack was sniffing her knees, his tail wagging. Frankle knew the feeling and stared at her long blue dress and handmade sweater.

"You certainly are a sight for sore eyes!" He searched his pockets frantically. "Where are my cigarettes?"

"Hey," she said, "one more hug."

They held each other a long time, their cheeks together. It felt so good to Frankle that he closed his eyes.

"I quit drinking," he whispered.

"That's the one problem I didn't think you had," she whispered back.

Frankle held her at arms' length.

"Why the hell didn't you call me?"

"I know, I know. It won't happen again. Promise."

They shook hands on it. Then his happiness transmuted to suspicion.

"You're not back because of an emergency or something?"

"Everything's fine. How about that coffee?"

He prepared the stuff as Constance lay down on the sofa. When he brought her a cup, she lifted her legs, then resettled her feet in his lap once he'd sat.

"What's with the boxes?"

"Spring cleaning."

He stared at her face, tanned and more aged than he remembered it.

"How was Mexico?"

She sat up momentarily to sip the coffee.

"Restful. Until, that is—confession, confession!—I realized my heart belonged to you. My sister helped me see that. Afterward, I couldn't sit still for five minutes."

Frankle turned to Jack while lighting a cigarette. "You're a witness to that statement." Then he turned back to Constance. "I wish you sounded happier about it."

"You ever know anyone past the age of thirty who falls happily in love?"

"Shut up," he said kindly.

"Remember your first roller coaster ride? That's the feeling."

Frankle didn't want to think about paradoxes, ambivalences, or vicissitudes.

"Does Nick know you're in town?"

"He will tomorrow morning." She glanced around the living room. "What are you doing in here, repainting?"

He extinguished his cigarette and cleared his throat. "I would have discussed my decision to give this place back to Monica, but you weren't exactly reachable."

She sat up and scrutinized him. Then she sipped her coffee and looked away.

"What?" he said.

"It's kind of uncanny, that's all."

"What is?"

"Your decision and mine."

"Those being?"

"Yours to move, mine to stay."

"Stay?"

"In my house."

"In Venice."

Constance stared into her cup. "The longer I stayed, the less inclined I was to give it up." She seemed to drift off in thought.

"And us?" he said. "Is there a point in talking about staying together?"

"Assuming we can define what we mean by 'together.' "

"Shall I unpack the dictionary?"

"Hey, because of Nick, things are a little more thorny than they might be."

"Agreed."

"And I think to promise anything at this point is a little reckless."

"Be that as it may, will you do me a big favor and marry me?"

Constance laughed affectionately and set down her coffee on the floor. "*Thom*, we hardly know each other."

"We know enough."

"On the other hand," she conceded, "to say we'll just see how it goes seems unfair to Nick. Or do I just feel safe using Nick as an excuse?"

"The point is," he told her, "people have to make promises in order to get to know each other."

She smiled. "How wonderfully old-fashioned of you." Then she stood up. "I'm going to have an anxiety attack."

"I'll join you."

He stood beside her, touching her shoulder, fearful of presuming further.

"What are you thinking?"

She put her arm around his waist and exhaled deeply. Then she said, "I was thinking you could come out to California. Maybe rent a little place in Venice. It would let you see what you thought of the town and what kind of work you could find."

"A place of my own," Frankle said.

"To remove some of the pressure of living together."

They looked at each other.

"A place of my own in Venice," Frankle said.

"It doesn't *have* to be Venice."

"I'd like it to be right next door to you or across the road. No point in being too far away."

She put her face in his neck. "What is it with you, Thom? Sometimes I think you're more of an Airedale than Jack."

"In fairness to Jack, my dependency is more complex and less appealing."

"I bet you're the sort who barks and scratches at the door if you get closed out for the night."

"I'm a lot happier curled up on the bed."

Constance whispered, "I like to read poetry before I go to sleep."

"I don't mind."

"Aloud."

"I'll pretend I'm listening."

She held him tight. "There are lots of actors out there who need head shots."

"What kind of work will you do?"

"I can be more specific about that after meeting with Paolo tomorrow."

Frankle separated from her and nervously picked up the poker to rearrange the burning logs. Constance moved to his side; for the longest time, they stared at burning logs and ashes.

"How's about a shower?" she said finally.

"What's this thing with you and showers?"

"They seem to be an important dimension of our relationship."

"I see."

"But bear in mind that most romances have a very limited number of showers."

"Good point."

Later, they fell asleep upstairs with the windows open behind them. The night breeze blew the bamboo shades back and forth.

Frankle woke with his face buried in Constance's cascading hair and listened to her breathing. Even loving her, or because he loved her, he had no illusions about them ever being one. Life was a long time, and no one could save you. Yet neither did he have any illusion about going it all alone anymore, and he could think of nothing as important to him as Constance Frame—not even his dog, which meant, he imagined, that somehow, during a single miserable winter, he had traversed irrevocably into so-called adulthood. For the life of him, he couldn't remember of what he'd been so afraid.

44

Frankle rose first and went to the terrace to smoke a cigarette in the sun. Afterward, he wandered into the back garden to stare sleepily at the planted flowers, and it was there that he noticed a cardinal rise in a flash of red from a rhododendron and disappear down into the street's stunted trees.

I have yet many things to say unto you, intoned That Voice, *but ye cannot hear them now.*

Footsteps sounded, and Frankle turned. Constance appeared, wearing his robe and carrying two cups of steaming coffee. He watched her move through the darkened corridor and emerge into the garden's sunlight.

"Light," she said, reaching him the cup. "No sugar."

She lifted her face to the sun and closed her eyes. Frankle watched her, sipping his coffee. High above them, geese were migrating north in a series of chevrons. Frankle could faintly hear their honking.

"You know," Constance said raspily, "for a bashful guy, you're just full of surprises when the lights go out." She opened one eye. "Where did you learn that stuff?"

"It's you."

"Me?" She closed her eyes again, sighing. "Who would have thought."

Frankle pulled chairs into the sun, and they sat to drink their coffee in silence. He wondered if they would spend the rest of their lives together.

An hour later, Constance left for a nine o'clock appointment with Paolo Gabriel. Holding her hand, Frankle walked with her and Jack to the subway. He had never been so happy. But what could you do to protect happiness? The more you tried to protect it, the more unprotectable it became. Perhaps the courage to surrender to a greater protection was the hallmark of an enduring happiness.

"Bye, Thom." Constance kissed him quickly.

"Good luck." He slowly released her hand.

"Listen," she said to Jack, "when Thom comes back from wherever he is, tell him I love him, okay?"

As she left, he released part of himself to go with her, keeping another part to remain within himself so that he might stand on his own two feet.

"See you for dinner."

"With Nick," she called back, and then disappeared into the descending crowd.

Frankle had an idea for photographs on "Work." He was trying to get a light-meter reading on a patrol of black carpenter ants on the wall encircling the roof, when the telephone interrupted him. Laurie Larsen's secretary was calling from *Trend* and instructed a breathless Frankle to hold.

"I think," Laurie Larsen said a moment later, "that I might have something for your piggy bank."

It was the first time the metaphor had ever made sense, and Frankle thanked her prodigiously before explaining he had retired from magazine work.

Laurie Larsen couldn't blame him. "It never got you very far, did it?"

"No," Frankle said, "not at all."

"I think the real reason I'm calling, Thom, is to tell you

Bernie and I are getting married. I'm pregnant and wanted to tell you personally before you read it somewhere. Can you imagine yours truly with a baby!"

"I can," Frankle said, a little too forlornly, he thought, adding, "Congratulations," to protect himself.

"Did you hear I finally met Monica? I did an interview with her and Dell. We're featuring them in the August *Trend* to hype the film project. Bernie thinks it's better suited for *Concupiscence*, since there's to be a suggestive photo essay in addition to the party shots. But I had my lawyers beat his lawyers to the deal. Ergo, Thom, if you could use a quick thousand you can shoot the party for us. Monica tells me it's to be held at you guys' place."

Frankle repeated his gratitude before declining again.

"Does that mean you won't be at the party to notice how pregnancy has bestowed on me an otherworldly quality?"

Frankle laughed furtively along with Laurie Larsen; fearfully, he wondered if each was not more cynical than the other.

"Tell me the truth," she said. "Doesn't last fall seem like a million years ago?"

"At least a million," he told her, though in fact it seemed like yesterday; and Frankle understood you didn't distance yourself from the choices of your past so much as look at them each day of your life with less and less comprehension.

"Listen," he said cheerfully, "it really was more than lust."

Laurie Larsen made a kissing sound and told him to stay in touch.

As it turned out, that evening Constance returned without Nick, who had elected, instead, to go to the movies with his grandparents. Sitting on her bed beside Frankle, Constance confessed she was very happy to be alone again with him. For his part, Frankle was superstitious about expressing his own happiness and responded by taking Constance's hand as

he listened to her recount Paolo Gabriel's offer to buy six
styles of her sweaters at a dozen pieces per style for his fall
line. He would pay her three thousand as a flat fee, and if
they caught on, she would be asked to do others exclusively
for Paolo Gabriel. In the meantime, since there were questions about color and one or two neckline designs, and since
Paolo wanted her to be happy with any changes they might
make, he had invited her to Paris to meet with his manufacturing people. The sweaters themselves would be produced
in Italy by women who would receive twenty-five dollars per
sweater. Constance didn't think that was very fair, but she
figured all she could do about the way money made the world
go round was stay as far on the periphery as possible. Frankle's
feeling exactly, though he wasn't sure he was as secure in his
peripheralness as Ms. Frame.

"When will you go to Paris?" he asked.

"You'll come with me, I hope?" Her eyes remained earnestly on him.

"Will we have the money?"

"I'll have enough for us," she said. "Wouldn't you like a
little vacation before we go back to a summer in California?"

Frankle nodded, thrilled and afraid simultaneously, and lay
back on the bed. He closed his eyes to picture the Pacific.

Live joyfully, That Voice kicked in, *with the wife whom thou
lovest all the days of the life of vanity, which he hath given thee
under the sun, all the days of thy vanity: for that is thy portion
in this life. . . .*

"Thom?"

He opened his eyes. "I'm here."

She must have seen it in his eyes, for she plopped down
beside him and whispered, "Neurasthenic Thom."

"You overwhelm me," he told her.

She put her hands around his throat as if to strangle him.

"Couldn't we give a try to very calmly loving each other?"

They shifted their sides, embracing.

Frankle reached over her to click off the light, then slid above her.

"Not just yet," he answered.

Much later, Frankle woke frightened from a nightmare, not knowing where he was, his heart pounding. He lit a cigarette and used an empty tin of stir-fried rice as an ashtray. The bedside clock indicated 3:13.

By her breathing, Frankle knew she was sleeping. He placed the side of his face to the blanket covering her chest and listened to her heart. With his eyes closed, the beating seemed an infinity away. This was the obvious and inevitable sadness inherent to the ways of the flesh.

He felt a hand move on his shoulder.

"I thought you were sleeping," he whispered.

"No."

"Me neither."

"I'm so sleepy."

"So sleep." He extinguished his cigarette as Constance curled into him.

Gradually, her breathing slowed and deepened. For what seemed a long time, he remained awake, listening.

45

The next morning, a sunny Saturday, the moving van arrived a day behind schedule, to ship Frankle's possessions west. With Constance and Nick walking Jack in the park, Frankle phoned Monica Webb at the Westbury Hotel to ask about a sofa and a library table.

Dell Jordan picked up.

"She's meditating."

"I'm moving out and need to ask a question. Emphasize moving out."

Monica came immediately to the phone. "Did you get the invitation?"

"For what?"

"Tomorrow's do."

Frankle told her he hadn't and that he'd be at Yankee Stadium.

"Surely you'll stop in to say goodbye?"

He didn't think that would be possible and inquired about the furniture.

"I don't want any of it, Thom. Not a single spoon. Take it all. Or trash it."

"You don't want the sofas or bed?"

"Throw them out the window for all I care, honey. Just

259

save yourself and your girlfriend and come to the party. You've got to let me *warn* her at least!" Monica laughed. "Did my check arrive?"

Frankle insisted that all he wanted from her now was the Airedale's papers.

Monica agreed to turn the documents over only if Frankle introduced her to his "new squeeze."

"Her name's Constance."

"And for your information," Monica said, "I think Mr. Chambers and I will be able to live peacefully as neighbors. Dell and I have contributed a chunk of advertising money for the jerk's forthcoming novel. He's very pleased."

"I bet," Frankle said.

"Writers are so obvious. Give them a little pat on the head, and they'll absolutely sit and roll over."

Frankle could only imagine what she had to say about photographers. He said he'd see her the following day.

"And I want to hear all about your new apartment. I bet Dell a pizza with everything on it that you're moving to Hoboken."

Frankle stepped aside and let the remark sail harmlessly out the window. He'd learned something after all.

Nick returned with his mother and Jack and helped Frankle carry two boxes of discarded clothes to the church. After piling the boxes in the basement, Frankle considered saying goodbye to the woman who ran the breakfast program, then decided he didn't like her enough to bother. Instead, he took Nick into the empty chapel, where they sat in the back, near the votive candles.

"Mom says God's a fairy-fairy tale."

Frankle placed his arm around the boy's bony shoulders. The empty eyes of a concrete Christ seemed to fix themselves inward, and Frankle confessed that he didn't know anything about God. God was something you experienced, or thought you experienced, but never knew. As with Love or Beauty or Truth, the more you tried to talk about God, the stupider you sounded.

Nick said the chapel was too dark, and they went outside into the cool spring morning. Down the block, beneath the line of budding sycamore trees, Frankle's old oak bureau dropped from the moving van. One of the movers had a good laugh.

"Can we go to the roof party tomorrow before flying away?"

"Maybe."

"Mommy told me your first wife was a m-movie star."

"She did?"

"I want to get her autograph."

"If we have time," Frankle said.

"Are we still going to the baseball game tomorrow?"

"Absolutely."

"I want to get autographs there, too."

With the movers gone and the apartment empty, Frankle spent the afternoon with Constance and Nick at the movies, a double bill of Laurel and Hardy. Suddenly nervous about leaving next day, Frankle missed most of the gags, musing instead at the paint peeling from the theater's ceiling.

And after dinner with the Gilberts, when he was invited to stay overnight with them and Nick and Constance rather than remain alone in his apartment, he used needing to walk and feed Jack as an excuse to be alone.

Constance walked him to the subway entrance on Fourteenth Street. It was raining gently. Standing at the summit of the steps, Frankle remembered the night in autumn when he first met her and asked her to move in with him.

"Are you okay?" Constance asked.

"I'm fine," he said, distracted.

"You're not having second thoughts, I hope."

"Of course I'm not."

"You have the right to change your mind, you know."

"So do you, for that matter," he said suspiciously.

"I won't."

"Neither will I."

They embraced, pressing together for a long time.

"I'd be nervous, too, if I were leaving," she told him.

"That's not what I was thinking."

"What then?"

He cleared his throat.

"I was thinking how much more sense my life makes since I met you."

When Constance said she hoped he would always feel that way, Frankle got nervous about her walking four blocks home alone, and instead of taking the subway uptown, escorted her back to the apartment on Eighteenth Street before hailing a cab uptown.

46

At dawn Frankle heard rainwater purling in the roof's down-spout, and outside the window Harry Chambers was standing in the garden in a poncho, staring straight up, his arms out-stretched and his mouth open to catch the rain. But by late morning the rain had ceased, and by the time the sun emerged, big potted plants had been distributed around the perimeter of the roof and two men were setting up tables, canopies, and chairs.

Downstairs, as Frankle shaved, two caterers, weighted down with trays and pans of food, let themselves into the apartment. Frankle had no idea how the women had acquired keys and didn't bother to ask. The older one seemed espe-cially annoyed and astonished at the absence of a kitchen table, and when Frankle asked her to make sure his dog remained closed in the back bedroom with his water and his biscuits, she assured Frankle the last thing they needed was a big hungry dog nosing around their exotic dishes.

Nick sat entranced as the Red Sox trashed the Bronx Bomb-ers, 13–0. Abstaining from beer, Frankle feared the game would become an eternal exercise in futile pitching changes. Happily, however, their seats were in the sun, and with the addition of peanuts and iced soda, it felt like a summer day from a long gone past.

After the final out, Frankle bought Nick a souvenir baseball, featuring the autographs of all his Red Sox heroes.

They were expected at Constance's stepparents' for a farewell drink at six. Frankle would pick up his suitcase and Jack at the apartment, let Nick get Dell Jordan's autograph, then get out. In eleven hours they would be on the other side of the continent.

They rode back to Manhattan on the Lexington Avenue express, and when at last they emerged from underground, Frankle was hopeful he had survived his very last subway ride.

He heard the racket on the roof as soon as they reached the second floor. The fire door at the stairway's summit was open, and music and mirthful conversation issued downward. Frankle climbed toward the door's oblong of light, with Constance and Nick trailing; but on the fifth floor, he detoured into the apartment to check on Jack.

A man in a bartender's uniform was emptying bags of ice, and beyond him, at the southern end of the apartment, the sun struck the windows in such a way that they were made opaque with dust. Frankle felt a surge of entrapment and turned to the bedroom. The door there was open, and Frankle's voice betrayed his anxiety about the whereabouts of his dog. The younger caterer told him, in an accent redolent of Frankle's long deceased great-aunt Pauline, that the mistress had brought the dog upstairs.

Frankle proposed to Constance that he go up alone, then meet them in an hour at her family's place.

Constance smiled wryly. "I'd like to meet all the skeletons."

They went up the winding staircase to the empty studio. What was once his darkroom was now filled with coats hanging from a portable rack; and through the windows Frankle

could see a small crowd milling in the roof garden. For an
instant, he feared he might encounter his former self out
there, spectral and inebriated, glad-handing the guests and
chain-smoking.

He let Constance and Nick go out first onto the terrace,
lined with pots of daffodils. The sun had fallen to the west,
and Frankle had to shield his eyes to see as far as the open
gate on Chambers's side of the roof. A woman stood there,
laughing, in a backless dress. From the shoulder blades, Frankle thought he recognized Dakota Pomeroy. He took Constance's hand and led the way down the darkened alley toward
the back garden, cast now in a golden hue from the sun's low
angle and its fiery reflection off the vertical line of windows
in the high white wall of an adjacent building.

Despite the loud music, Frankle could hear his heart
pounding in his chest as he scanned the crowd. People were
dancing to a disco recording, wildly as poltergeists, in the
suffusion of sun; and on Chambers's side of the garden, protected festively with a yellow-and-white canopy, and divided
from Monica's side by a long buffet table, people crowded
the bar, talking. And behind them, too, the white wall and
blazing windows rose straight into the sky.

Frankle heard his name called, and turned. Monica Webb
waved from a table, where she was seated with Dell Jordan
and Laurie Larsen. Begging, Jack was seated nearby, taking
food from John Smoke and Bernard Bernheim. Frankle
turned through a burst of sunlight to ask Constance if he
could get her something from the bar and found that she was
already there, in the far corner of Chambers's roof space,
handing Nick a glass of juice. Beside her, Stanley Stark was
standing at the bar with Terri Max and Hieronymus Coch.
Frankle urgently wished to distill, into the simplest chore-
ography, the acts of grabbing Jack, acquiring the autograph
for Nick, and getting away.

Pigeons flew overhead, and their shadows splashed against

the high white wall. Then another kind of shadow appeared, and Frankle raised his eyes to the roof of Harry Chambers's duplex. Gordon Busch came into view, with Chambers on his shoulders. Chambers clawed the air in what Frankle construed to be a parody of menace. The two seemed surpassingly drunk, and for reasons Frankle couldn't understand, their acrobatics evoked applause from several onlookers.

Then Monica Webb said into his ear, "The Abbott and Costello of cocaine!" and pinched him in a familiar way. "You even swept Jack's hair from the floor," she added. "Aren't you saintly."

"I'm going to have to say hi and run," Frankle said, and he looked around, unable to meet her eyes for fear of finding his own ambivalence reflected there.

"Stay," she said. "Kikki's coming later. So's Susan. She's got a new guy. Her former shrink."

"I can't stay."

She said something about wanting his new telephone number and then held up her left hand. Frankle saw a ring glittering there.

"I still can't believe it!" She laughed and hugged him.

He returned the hug and whispered, "Congratulations."

"Will you come to the wedding if I invite you?"

"Of course not." Still holding her hand, he glanced over her shoulder to Jack, who was eating something from Dell Jordan's hand. Laurie Larsen waved, and Frankle waved back.

"Guess the name of the film," she said.

When he couldn't, she told him, "*The Spirit of Flesh*. It's Harry's, and we all love it."

"Why's the music so loud?" He leaned forward to keep from shouting.

"It's a party, Thom. People would just run away from a party if there weren't music."

"Do you have Jack's papers?"

"I'll mail them to you." She pulled him toward the shadow of the canopy. "Come on. Introduce me to her."

The two women greeted each other politely, and then Monica knelt to converse with Nick. It surprised Frankle to see how comfortable Monica appeared with the boy; and leaning against Constance to order a club soda, Frankle told her that he loved her. Still, he could not remember ever wanting a shot of whiskey so desperately, and from this thirst he understood it was time to go. And at once.

The music changed to what Frankle and his boyhood friends once called a slow dance, and Frankle noticed John Smoke and Dakota Pomeroy grinding drunkenly, their arms around each other. Beyond them, Gordon Busch and Harry Chambers were staring out the window of Chambers's study, pinching their noses. Frankle wondered when they had come down from the roof. Then his shoulder was tapped, and Stanley Stark, smelling strongly of Scotch, was shouting something about garbage.

"Fourteen thousand *tons* per day in New York City alone. The world's largest source of garbage, Thomas! *Chazerai* capital of the world."

He was wearing a black baseball cap with the words *Smoking Busch Productions* etched in silver letters across the crown.

"Now, what's this I hear about you leaving town?" Stark hung his arm around Frankle's shoulder and then grabbed Frankle in a headlock.

"Stop it, Stan." Frankle had to fight him off.

Nick passed, led by Monica Webb, who escorted him to where Dell Jordan was sitting. Frankle watched the celebrity shake the boy's hand, then lean forward to listen. A moment later, Jordan was searching his linen jacket for a pen, though it was Bernheim who finally came up with one.

Frankle thought he heard a robin's threnody, until he realized it was, rather, some new age electronic recording. Still, from memory, he turned and looked down the alleyway between the duplexes to the water tower that crested the apartment building to the south. From the silhouette at the summit of the tower, Frankle knew the bird was a dove. He squinted into the penumbra of light encompassing the shingled tower, and the bird took flight in the slow, predictable pattern that made it so popular with hunters.

The music segued suddenly into something slower and more seductive, and a woman was dancing alone and swinging a scarf. People moved away, and as Frankle leaned forward to identify the dancer, a backfire sounded from the street. Abruptly, the crowd parted as if panicked, and Frankle noticed that the dancer had been knocked backward and down, and lay prostrate now by the downspout of Chambers's duplex.

The music stopped. Frankle recognized the woman as Dakota Pomeroy. Blood was spreading down her white dress. Her look of astonishment was directed over Frankle's left shoulder, and he turned to behold Stanley Stark, still pointing a revolver. He stood in a path of dusty sunlight, and his slack mouth was twitching, as if he were suppressing laughter or tears.

"Stan?"

Stark held a hand up to shield his eyes from the sun and stared vacantly. Frankle noticed that his friend's leg had begun to tremble and that he couldn't hold the pistol steady in his hand.

"You're scaring everyone, Stan." Frankle tried to find Nick and Constance in the blur of the crowd. "Put the gun down now."

Stark aimed the gun at Frankle with both hands. "Is she dead, Thomas? She looks dead."

"Please . . . the gun, Stan."

"Check if she's dead!"

Frankle raised his hands in a gesture to calm Stark and took a step forward, hoping to cover the exposure of people be-hind him. Cautiously, he reached out his hand for the silver pistol.

"Come on now, Stan. Hand it over."

Stark's eyes seemed to clear and to focus on Frankle.

"The gun, Stan."

Frankle thought he saw Stark's eyes submit, when footsteps sounded. Harry Chambers drew to Frankle's side, brandishing an automatic weapon; he glanced from Dakota Pomeroy to Stanley Stark.

"What the fuck is this!"

Stark smiled oddly. "You can't fool me, Harry Chambers. That's just a facsimile of what you used on the women and children."

"What if it is?"

Something passed before the sun, a bird or a plane. A shadow darted at Frankle's feet, before dread rendered the moment so strangely silent that all he could hear was the regimental beating of his heart.

"Stan. Please give me the gun."

Squinting, Stark tried to shield his eyes from the blinding sunlight.

"Don't be their hero, Thomas. Let Harry Chambers." Stark moved his eyes. "Come on, Harry Chambers. Be their hero."

Frankle was about to step protectively in front of Chambers, when Gordon Busch came charging through the fire door behind Stark. Concurrently, Chambers himself charged forward, crying out as he started on the bad leg that would, a step later, collapse beneath the weight of his sudden surge for Stark, thereby preventing Chambers from ever reaching the handgun. Still, more than likely, this fall spared Chambers his life, for when Busch slammed into Stark's back, the gun discharged, tracing a line that would have found its mark in Chambers's brain. In that sense, Chambers's fall was most fortunate; and so instead of him, the target became an astonished Thom Frankle, who discovered himself lying supine, seared into unconsciousness by a vision of purgatorial flames.

And then it seemed to Frankle that he had begun a journey, ascending into a luminescent haze, which he assumed must be the sky; but when this incalculable volume began to contract darkly, Frankle, fearing he was dying, yielded to a crushing breathlessness.

However incredible this bad luck, it spared him the horrible witness of an enraged Harry Chambers smashing in Stanley Stark's skull with one home-run swing of a facsimile M-16.

It all happened so suddenly that, in retrospect, nearly no one could agree on what exactly had transpired. One thing was certain, however: by the time the photographer for the homicide division had completed his shots of the dead, the party had ended, and Frankle was long gone from the scene.

47

During the seven days the city's morbid tabloids chose to focus their headline attention on Harry Chambers, making him their hero, Thomas Frankle lay in a windowless hospital room, protected from the press. And when Frankle was willing, finally, to talk about the incident, reporters considered him and the entire episode old news and moved on to yet another of the city's endless incidents of mayhem and catastrophic melodrama. Secretly, Frankle bemoaned the missed opportunity for some gritty, citywide exposure, believing it would have done far more for his moribund photographic career than the genius God hadn't granted him or a well-reviewed gallery opening that a decade of work had deservedly never received.

On the other hand, some—like Constance Frame, who came to visit—said he was a fortunate man and marveled at how a handgun's bullet had torn through the right side of his upper chest without puncturing a lung or breaking a single bone.

Constance was wearing a light-blue dress the first day she visited. The dress matched the flowers she brought him.

"Forget-me-nots," she said, taking Frankle's hand.

Nick stood close to his mother, his eyes bashfully averted to the pelican that dangled from his hand.

"How do you f-feel, Thom?"

Frankle stared at them. "Lucky," he whispered.

Prayers, it seemed, had the most mysterious ways of being answered. Harry Chambers, for example, subsequent to a grand jury's dismissal of murder charges, achieved the momentary heroics about which he had dreamed since the day he volunteered for Vietnam. In a single month of spring he became the brilliant screenwriter of an audacious new film as well as the author of a soon-to-be-reissued trilogy of riveting war novels.

As for Frankle, time compelled him to understand that he had prayed for a very different kind of heroism, one in which he might be granted the courage to live compassionately from one ordinary day to the next. And no matter what others might think of Frankle's new life, everyone concurred that it had to be happier than the fate of Stanley Stark, who was buried during a thunderstorm in a Brooklyn cemetery, at his father's right side.

In marrying Constance Frame on a distant shore on a sunny winter's day the following year, Frankle experienced an indelible sense of appreciation for his unexpected second life. Whether such appreciation anticipated a kind of faith that would bring him spiritual peace, or merely the stoicism required to abide the paradoxes of circumstance to which all flesh is heir, this would remain—by virtue of one's life in time—to be seen.